MW01596632

DO YOU BELIEVE?

TOM SANTULLI

DO YOU BELIEVE?

DID I NOT TELL YOU THAT IF YOU BELIEVE,
YOU WILL SEE THE GLORY OF GOD?
JOHN 11:40

TATE PUBLISHING
AND ENTERPRISES, LLC

Published by Tate Publishing & Enterprises, LLC
127 E. Trade Center Terrace | Mustang, Oklahoma 73064 USA
1.888.361.9473 | www.tatepublishing.com

Tate Publishing is committed to excellence in the publishing industry. The company reflects the philosophy established by the founders, based on Psalm 68:11,
"The Lord gave the word and great was the company of those who published it."

Book design copyright © 2015 by Tate Publishing, LLC. All rights reserved.
Cover design by Nikolai Purpura
Interior design by Honeylette Pino

Published in the United States of America

ISBN: 978-1-63268-570-4
Fiction / Thrillers / Technological
15.06.18

To My Wife and My Daughter
I Love You

CONTENTS

Stay Away from Her! 9

Jesus versus Satan 15

The Cliché King 33

This Is Not Gambling 45

Mind Reading Mayhem 55

The Bank Robber 73

Hypothetical Free-For-All 85

The Principal's Office 97

The Five-Dollar Bill 115

Eating Like a Pig 129

Terrifying Prediction 145

The Last Shall Be First 163

Trouble at Home 187

Who Is This Man? 197

An Impossible Situation 207

Get Here Immediately! 221

Do You Believe?..233

Words to Live By...239

Testament of Faith.......................................249

A True Hero 255

Epilogue 259

STAY AWAY FROM HER!

Golf is just like the real world in that, in both, we can learn more from our failures than from our triumphs. At the Rock Creek Golf Course, I played my best round in quite a while, mostly because of the fantastic score I had on the last nine holes. The back nine is like getting a second chance as far as I'm concerned. Fortunately, golf is such a relaxing game. I was actually able to fall asleep quickly that night, for a change. Sadly, I woke up at about 2 AM in a hazy mixture of panic and confusion combined with the vague memory of a bizarre dream about a laptop computer gone rogue. I've had some weird dreams lately, but none as unpleasant as this. My computer somehow took on humanistic traits and had a nasty disposition, but it could tell me the truth about anything I wanted to know. I pleaded for it to reveal the meaning of life, the nature of God, how life originated, and the Super Bowl winner for the next three years. Unfortunately, when I woke up, all I did remember was holding that blasted computer above my head at the top of the Washington Monument while I threatened to drop it 555 feet to its destruction if it didn't comply with all my requests for information.

I stayed in bed for quite a while after I woke up and stared at the ceiling. My mind raced in many different directions until my thoughts drifted back to when I taught high school math years ago. I sometimes missed my role as a professional educator, and since I couldn't sleep anyway, I reflected back to this tumultuous yet rewarding time in my life. I vividly remembered many of the remarkable details since there certainly were many joys… and sorrows.

When I began teaching, I knew that I could make a difference in the lives of my students, and many of them did seem to relate to me very well. I was glad because I wanted to be a positive influence and a role model. I helped coach the freshman boys' basketball team, and I worked with a boy named Jake Lyle. I stayed with him after practice on numerous occasions, and I helped him perfect his three-point shooting. We also played plenty of one-on-one games, and I even let him beat me a few times to help build up his confidence. By the end of the season, I usually didn't have to *let* him beat me, if you know what I mean. We talked a lot. I often drove him home after practice, and I got him a job at a nearby deli after the season so he could help his parents who were barely making ends meet. I could see that Jake needed someone to talk to and to take an interest in him, so I did.

In addition, Susan Taylor was a junior in my computer science class. She was quite gifted and wanted to study engineering in college. She needed a tutor for her college entrance exams. Her family didn't have a lot of money, so I volunteered to work with her on Saturdays for free. Sue and her family were most appreciative, and I was delighted that I could help them out.

There was another student whom I really wanted to help during my first year of teaching, and I was very proud that I was able to make a huge difference in her life. Heather Thompson was a senior in my calculus class who was getting grades of Cs and Ds when I knew that she was capable of getting As. This girl was having serious family problems, trouble with her boyfriend, and self-esteem issues that were taking their toll on her. Since the very beginning of the school year, she developed a rapport with me and I encouraged her to come to me for extra help as often as she could. I worked with her after school and sometimes during lunch. I not only helped her with math and physics, but I also tried to help her put everything in perspective. She seemed to respond positively to my extra help, encouragement, and advice. As the school year continued, her grades improved remarkably, and she broke up with her boyfriend who was taking advantage of her and taking her for granted. The problem was that many people within the school including other teachers and administrators thought that I acted improperly, and some even thought that I was somehow taking advantage of the situation. Nothing could be further from the truth. I knew that since I was only a few years older, some people were very suspicious, but I decided that it was a chance I had to take. A few teachers even told me that I was using my position as a role model for my own personal gain, and that I was exploiting her vulnerability. Sorry, but I thought that helping people was what teachers were supposed to do. I had to reassure everyone within the school that I took my role as a professional educator very seriously, and I would never act inappropriately or jeopardize the welfare of a student in any way. At the end of the day, I simply would not turn my back on a student who looked up to me and who clearly benefitted from my compassion and help.

I ended up in the office of the district's superintendent of schools, Dr. Andrew Morgan. He had the audacity to imply that I had ulterior motives in befriending a student who needed my assistance with not only math but also with some serious life issues. Dr. Morgan was direct and blunt. "Tom, some people have told me that they have seen you outside of school with her in various places in town. Is that true?"

I was not willing to share *everything* with him at that point, so I offered a token response that was only partially true. "Yes, sir, that is true. I bumped into her at a coffee shop in town once, and we talked for a few minutes. I didn't see that as problematic, do you?"

"Not really, but unfortunately, I was recently made aware of some information that requires me to look into this matter further."

I gulped. I knew there was nothing inappropriate going on, so I retold the whole story about the extra help in math and physics, usually during my lunch period. I told him that I was trying to steer Heather in the right direction, and that I unequivocally would never do anything improper. At first, he seemed to believe me; but then suddenly, he changed his tune.

"Tom, she's pregnant! She probably won't even be able to finish out the school year and graduate."

No kidding, I thought. I was already aware of all that, and in fact, I had been talking to Heather about it. Instead of admitting everything to him right then and there, I acted surprised, "Oh no! What a shame. I had no idea!"

He probably couldn't believe my naivety, but at least his tone softened. "Tom, stay away from her from now on. You thought you acted with her best interest in mind, and you tried to help her. There's nothing wrong with that. It is very commendable. But it's over now. Stay away from her, no matter what!"

Now I interrupted him as I couldn't stand it any longer. "Okay, I hear you, and I understand where you're coming from." I felt compelled to get out of his office as quickly as possible. I couldn't discuss anything else with him, and I am sure that Dr. Morgan would not have liked hearing the entire truth, that there was much more to our relationship than I ever revealed to anyone. "I have a class now." I pretended to look at my watch. Just then, I noticed that my hands were sweaty, and my knees were trembling. I couldn't even shake his hand; my palms were so wet. I waved when I left his office, and I simply thanked him with a perfunctory, "Thank you, Dr. Morgan." But for what? For telling me what I already knew? I drifted through my next two classes, understandably since I definitely had some serious thinking and soul searching to do.

I was still determined that this would not force me to give up my role as someone who could make a difference in this girl's life. I was proud to be able to be of assistance to a student who obviously needed someone; however, I knew that I might be in way over my head. I also knew that Heather was eighteen years old, and she could make decisions for herself. I was not a guidance counselor or a social worker. I knew that my career was involved since I actually had known that Heather was pregnant for some time. I had been talking to her about having the baby while she was preparing to have an abortion and terminate the pregnancy. I got her through the first three months when no one else even knew that she was having a baby. I tried to convince her to at least have her baby, and then give him or her up for adoption. Time was running out, and she was on the verge of going ahead with the abortion. I knew I had some work to do, but Dr. Morgan was clear when he said to "Stay away from her!"

Clearly, it would have been a huge risk to continue talking to Heather, let alone meet with her and counsel her. On the other hand, I desperately wanted to see this through and not give up so easily. Lives were at stake, especially an innocent, precious, unborn life.

Regrettably, it did not work out the way I hoped; and after a couple of weeks, Heather dropped out of school in late March while she was a little over four months pregnant. Heather was able to bring her grade up from a C minus to an A in calculus. Then again, that was so trivial compared to what was really going on. The last time I spoke to her, I found out the disheartening truth—she was ready to have that abortion and still drop out of school. Heather and her parents were so ashamed and devastated that they all moved out of the state.

I now anxiously wished that I would have agreed to meet up with Heather one last time. At least then, I would have had a chance to save her baby. Unfortunately, I let fear overcome my better judgment. Heather indeed asked me to continue to see her outside of school on several occasions. We could have met on a weekend at a place far from the school where there was no chance for us to be seen by anyone. Yet I was reluctant. The warning from Dr. Morgan instilled a panic so deep within me that I shook with trepidation every time I thought about it, even now. Regrettably, my decision to avoid any further contact with her was also a burden that I have carried with me to this day.

My last words to Heather on the phone were, "Heather, you are better than that. I hope that you understand why I can't meet with you anymore. Please don't give up on yourself or your baby. You will never forgive yourself for the rest of your life. Just trust in God."

Unfortunately, I remembered that her last words to *me* were, "I'm having the abortion. Nothing you can say or do will stop me." I heard the click of the phone after I heard her voice for the last time. At first, I believed that I did the right thing by helping a student in need who trusted me and who looked to me for help. I tried to emphasize that she had to believe in herself and trust herself and that faith in God goes a long, long way. Needless to say, I evidently failed. I thought it was ironic that Dr. Morgan said that my work with Heather was commendable. Clearly, he didn't know the entire truth including the fact that I had seen and spoken to Heather many times outside of school and that I was in fact very fond of her. When I decided to never contact Heather again, I knew that it would be a decision that I would ultimately regret. In addition, I have always been burdened with feelings of guilt and even shame for everything that took place between us. It is a good thing that the mind has a way of blocking out painful thoughts from the past, and I seldom think about any part of my relationship with Heather.

JESUS VERSUS SATAN

I felt wide awake at that point, so I went down to my computer in the basement, and I decided to update my resume, which gave me a good chance to reflect on my career and my life. My very first official title at the Agency was "Data Scientist," and I still have a copy of the ad that I answered fifteen years ago:

> Do you have a passion for solving problems? Can you help find solutions to the most challenging dilemmas in the United States and around the world? We need individuals adept in technology, computers, and critical thinking. The CIA is seeking candidates with a master's degree in data analysis, computer science, or statistics.

Two out of three? Not too bad, I thought. As I updated my resume, I decided to keep the information that outlined my first two years of working as a high school teacher. After all, that time was instrumental in forming who I am today. The past ten years that I worked as a CIA "computer analyst" and team leader was also a sensational time for me. I have explored the magnificent underwater caves off the South American coast, studied the atmosphere and unreachable terrain of Mars, and analyzed the devastating effects of the shrinking polar ice caps of the Arctic Circle. All of this, of course, was supposedly in the interest of national security. Although I was not literally present in any of those places, I lived vicariously through a team of experts. I used some of the most advanced computer simulation programs that I helped to develop over the past fifteen years. I loved the fact that the scientists and researchers did the leg work and "heavy lifting" while my team and I analyzed the results using statistical analysis and state-of-the-art computer resources. I did much of the work from my office at Langley or from the comfort of my three-bedroom Cape in Vienna, Virginia. My team usually consisted of anywhere from six to ten highly qualified professionals including leading scientists and researchers. Nevertheless, I was the one who was ultimately responsible for compiling the final report. We often used computer modeling to examine how the situation would likely play out and determine how our national security was ultimately affected. At one time, I even worked with the Science and Technology analysts to determine if the US computer systems could withstand any type of terroristic infiltration.

I decided to go to the CIA home page and peruse the jobs currently posted. I was usually content with my role as analyst because I seemed to be making a difference, and I was held in high regard by my colleagues. On the other hand, it never hurts to see what's out there and to keep my options open.

I noticed an e-mail that my daughter, April, must have sent me before she went to bed last night. It had an attached photo, and I recognized that it was from last summer when I took April and her mom Sally to Myrtle Beach over the weekend of the Fourth of July for some sun, sand, and surf. In the photo, April was riding a wave nicely; and she added the caption, "I can do all things through Christ who strengthens me." I was so proud of her. I drifted back to last summer and vividly recalled it as one of the most memorable times of my life. April began surfing the previous summer after she was inspired by the Bethany Hamilton story. Two winters ago, April read the story about Bethany, a gifted and courageous surfer from Hawaii who was attacked by a shark at the age of thirteen. Bethany lost her arm in the attack, but she miraculously survived, and she believed in God wholeheartedly and trusted that God would allow her to surf again. Not only did Bethany Hamilton surf competitively again, but her faith in God served as an inspiration to so many people throughout the world, including April. April was inspired by Bethany Hamilton's trust in God, faith, and perseverance. Last fall, when Bethany made an appearance and gave an inspirational speech at Georgetown, we all went to see her, and April spoke to her for a few minutes in person.

On our second day at Myrtle Beach, the waves were particularly rough, but Sally was adamant about giving surfing a try even though she had never done it before. We hooked up with a young man originally from Australia named Albert who was an awesome surfing instructor.

"Sally, the surf looks rough today. You should be careful with this sort of thing," I suggested.

"It looks easy," she retorted right back.

I turned to Albert to plead my case. "Albert, you look like a reasonable man. Do you think she'll be able to handle it?" I asked with noticeable nervousness.

"No worries, mate," Albert answered with only the slightest apprehension.

"Please take it easy on her," I pleaded. "She's my wife, and she's the only one I got."

"Oh, stay out of it," Sally enjoined. "This doesn't concern you!"

At that point, I knew it was best for me to step back. Fortunately, when I reached into the beach bag, I found that someone packed the video camera. Somehow I knew that we would be in for a treat of some sort. When April still had some time remaining on her lesson with Albert, he gladly agreed to let Sally give it a try. In fact, Sally was actually able to catch a wave a few times, stand up on the board, and keep her balance for a few seconds.

"Okay, hon, that was great. I got it all on the video camera!"

"Yeah, Mom, that was nice," April chimed in. "Can *I* take over now?"

Albert even added his words of encouragement, "That was great for someone…"

He probably meant to say, "For someone of your age," but he caught himself, hoping to live long enough to make it back to Australia someday.

"Are you kidding? I can do better than *nice*. I want to try to do even better than April," Sally replied. *Here we go again*, I thought. Sally was showing her competitive side. How unusual. After a few brief, uneventful tumbles into the water, Sally stayed under a wave and the surfboard for an inordinate amount of time. When she finally got up and on her feet, she stumbled out of the water looking like a drowned rat—a beautiful, well-proportioned drowned rat, mind you, but a drowned rodent of some type nevertheless.

"I wrecked my knee," she quivered. "I need ice. Badly. I couldn't get up for a few seconds. I almost drowned!" I had to admit, she did look more than a little shaken up. "That really hurt!" she painfully admitted directly to me. "Did you ever fall down and find out that you couldn't get up, no matter how hard you tried?"

I sympathized with her, but I quipped, "Yes, just once. But that was at a New Year's Eve Party!"

"No, I'm serious. Please get me some ice!" Sally exclaimed as she dried off, clearly in pain.

Albert then tried to explain what went wrong with Sally's ride, so at least April would learn from it. "Your mom had her feet much too close together, so when she shifted her weight, she didn't have good balance, and she went right in the drink."

Well, we said good-bye to Albert. And even though he felt horribly, it wasn't nearly as bad as what Sally was feeling. For the next six weeks, she needed physical therapy to rehabilitate her right knee, and I had to train my brain to avoid the whole "I told you so" routine with Sally. Not only that, but our triathlon on August 25 was in jeopardy.

I snapped back to focus my attention to the computer screen, and I spotted an attractive position for a "research scientist" that human resources must have recently posted. The pay was certainly appealing, but I probably would have to work toward a PhD. I enjoyed being the leader of my small dedicated staff, and I liked working under Jack Russell, the deputy director of Science and Technology for the agency. Jack will be retiring within a year. I knew I could decide then if I wanted to pursue something in another area of the CIA because whenever Jack *does* retire, I would hate to have to break in another boss. All kidding aside, Jack is indisputably an extraordinary administrator. He almost retired two years ago when he was passed over for the elite position of executive director. I was delighted when he agreed to stay with science and technology for a few more years and appreciated it when he backed me when I was at my all-time lowest about seven years ago. I cracked under the pressure of losing my sister, and I would have lost everything if it were not for his support. In fact, his tutelage as my direct supervisor the past ten years has been instrumental to any success I have had.

My mind wandered once again as I looked over to the wall where I displayed a case with a special bat that I used when I played high school baseball. I was the team's MVP my senior year, and I set the school record for home runs. Sometimes, I wish I could include some of my high school accomplishments on my resume, but I knew that was unrealistic. On the other hand, there were times when I wanted to forget everything that happened to me in high school.

I printed out a copy of my updated resume and glanced at it for a few seconds. I wanted to make a difference, but I already had my chance working as a teacher. I then crumpled up my two-page resume and shot it into the wastepaper basket across the room, banking it successfully against the wall. *Not now*, I thought. Jack had to deliver an important speech next Saturday night, and I tried to help him not look like a real hack by supplying him with a few good lines along with some jokes to keep it light. Jack was brilliant, and he was an extraordinary administrator; but sometimes he was a little, how shall I say, "clumsy" in public. I learned a long time ago that one of the most important responsibilities of an employee is to make his superiors look good, so I tried to help Jack come up with a high-quality speech. The problem is that Jack is how we say in Italian, a real *testa dura* or hard head. Needless to say, some of the top leaders in the CIA would be at this function. Each branch of the CIA had its own director and deputy director and therefore some representatives from Intelligence, the National Clandestine Service, as well as our own Science and Technology would be there. I was surprised to find out that Jack would be the keynote speaker, but fortunately, the protocol for these events was to keep the speeches brief. On the other hand, Jack's own philosophy was to "tell the audience *what* you are going to tell them, *tell* them, then tell them what you *told* them." Jack came to me a few weeks ago asking for help, writing his words of wisdom for the dinner ceremony officially announcing a major CIA initiative pertaining to big data analysis. I insisted that he speak for less than fifteen minutes, interject a joke and a few funny lines, and then let the people enjoy their dinner.

"Jack," I pleaded, "why not take the George Burns approach?"

"What might that be, Tom?" he reluctantly inquired.

"Have a good beginning, a good ending, and keep the two close together."

A week later, I was eager to see if he took my advice. I was also looking forward to introducing Jack and saying a few words before he spoke. I was somewhat of a ham myself, and since so many important people would be there, I could use the exposure in case I did pursue something else within the agency in the future.

A few minutes before it was time for me to go up to the podium, I was cool as a cucumber. I casually walked away from the main table and checked my cell phone for any messages. My daughter was supposed to let me know if her stomach was still bothering her. Sure enough, I received a text from her, which indicated that she was feeling better. She knew that I would be speaking at this important function, so she included in her text, "For the Holy Spirit will tell you at that time what to say" (Luke 12:12).

Thanks, April, but fortunately, this time I knew exactly what I needed to say.

I was on. I cleared my throat. "It is with great pleasure that I introduce someone you all know. In fact, my job tonight is easy! I could simply remind everyone that he has worked tirelessly at the CIA for twenty-five years, and he has made huge, admirable contributions to three different components of the agency before becoming the deputy director of Science and Technology. He has been a mentor to me and countless others over the years, and he has been an integral, guiding force behind the last three administrations in the White House. And here is a direct quote that I was asked to read:

"Jack Russell has been the most influential and valuable member of the CIA since its inception in 1946." I looked at Jack as I pretended to point to the paper that I held and announced, "By the way, Jack, you spelled the word *inception* incorrectly."

Luckily, I got a few laughs and some applause.

"Anyway, I will not continue talking about Jack and his accomplishments and bore you to death. I will leave that all up to him."

Now came the really hard part for me, listening to Jack tell about two hundred people everything he knew about computers.

Truth be told, Jack really did know his stuff, but I didn't think he realized who he would be stuffing tonight. I certainly hoped he would be able to stuff them in an amusing way. I also hoped that he would take advantage of some of my ideas from when I helped him last week. After all, I was a better writer than he was, and I have forgotten more jokes than he *ever* knew. On the other hand, computers were Jack's forte especially the details of supercomputers and big data mining.

Jack began, "Thanks, Tom, but I will talk to *you* later. As you all know, two years ago, the US government initiated the National Big Data Research and Development Initiative, which explored how big data could potentially be used to address some of the most crucial problems facing the government and the world. Of course, you all know that the new wave of computers can make use of data better than ever before. We need to extrapolate and draw conclusions from the information and make it beneficial to the government, but not in the self-serving ways that businesses are inclined to do. Well, we believe that the paradigm shift is now ready to take place in our favor, but we need projection and ingenuity."

I couldn't believe it, but Jack had to wait a few seconds while some of the audience applauded. Next, Jack went on about data mining and its relevance in the twenty-first century.

"Let me enlighten you with some information that is not well known. Every day we create six quintillion bytes of data. In fact, ninety-five percent of the data in the world today has been created in the past eighteen months alone. I can see that there are a lot of people here my age, so I am sure that you can remember way back when "log on" only meant something you put on the fire, and when "hacking" was simply a really bad cough."

Here we go. It was time to brace myself. Jack was now wavering from what I suggested. I hoped that April would text me again. No such luck.

"Analyzing enormous sets of data actually takes up approximately thirty percent of all CIA workers. That is a threat to American security since too many valuable resources are used up in the process. Also, consider that a few years ago, the United States Federal Government owned seven of the ten most powerful supercomputers in the world. But now the pendulum is swinging in the other direction, and out of the top fifteen supercomputers in the world, we own only three."

Come on, Jack, I thought, you're losing them. Please quit while you're only a little behind. Hit them with "Jesus versus Satan." Now is the time.

Jack continued, "Using computers and the big data to predict what the masses will purchase may help businesses, but we need to find ways that this vast capability can authentically help society in general and the government in particular. We want to employ our supercomputers to break new ground in determining how all of the access to the infinite mounds of information can be used to enlighten us and enhance our great nation…"

I stepped away to check my cell. April, where *are* you? I was hoping that my daughter would text me right about now so I could have something to take my mind off all of this. Tell me how the birthday party is. Send me another Bible message of some type. I'll take anything at this point!

I returned my attention to Jack who was now perseverating about supercomputers and what makes them super. "That's why they are so valuable. And expensive. We have supercomputers at Langley that have so much processing capability due to the interconnected racks of CPUs, tens of thousands of cores, hundreds of teraflops, and memory that is measured in terabytes."

You're losing them, Jack. Most of the people here know all of this already, and the others didn't give a flying leap about the details that Jack was supplying. In fact, they were only here for the dinner. I tried to tell him that weeks ago. I was originally worried that Jack's speech would be ponderous, but this was off the charts. The worst part of this was that I was hoping to make an impression tonight. If anyone thought for a minute that I actually helped Jack write some of this, it wouldn't do *me* any good.

"The fact is, we have supercomputers from just a few years ago that will be dismantled because they are obsolete, and they use so much energy that they are no longer cost effective."

Luckily, I got distracted for a few minutes as my cell phone vibrated. Fortunately, everyone's attention was entirely on Jack, so I walked back to an area that was away from most people's line of sight. It was April, but for some reason, all I could hear was muffled voices, music of some kind in the background, and laughter. It took me a few minutes of screaming into my phone with no response before I realized that I had been pocket-dialed by April. Those few minutes were still better than anything I heard so far from Jack. Where were the jokes?

"Data mining is now pedestrian. Phase 2 of the National Big Data Initiative has come and gone. Now the CIA has taken the lead, and we can collect and study limitless amounts of text, information, and a multitude of data to make predictions and analyze trends that no one could have done a few years ago. In fact, under the complete jurisdiction of the CIA, we are announcing the beginning of Phase 3 of the Big Data Initiative." Then I remembered that the whole purpose of tonight's dinner was that one official announcement. More applause. *Don't encourage him*, I thought.

After a few more minutes, it looked like a few people in the audience were beginning to leave. I would have taken off myself if it wasn't for the fact that Jack drove me here, and I didn't have a car. I had no choice. "Measuring big data by size is misleading. It is quality, not quantity. Size doesn't matter anymore, no matter what you have heard. Remember, it's not the *size* of the wand, but the *magic* that's in it."

Hey, a few more people cheered at that one. Luckily, we are still basically a "good ol' boys" club, and they appreciated the little touch of male humor.

Then Jack suddenly hesitated, and Henry Norris, the associate deputy director of the agency indicated that Jack should end it there. Mr. Norris could actually pull rank on Jack, so I was elated that he had to wrap it up now. "I just have to tell you one last thing, a story that I heard—Jesus and Satan were having a battle about who was the most computer savvy. After weeks of arguing, God was determined to settle the debate once and for all.

"'I am going to set up an experiment that will take twenty-four hours, and we will see who is most successful.' So for an entire day, Satan and Jesus went to war. They had to work with excel, they had to search the Internet and prepare documents, and they had to send files and e-mail. They did more research, wrote spreadsheets, and documented everything. They downloaded and scanned. They did everything imaginable with the computer. But five minutes before the contest ended, lightning suddenly struck, the earth shook, and the electricity went out. Satan stared at his blank screen and nearly had a stroke. The electricity finally went back on, and each of them restarted their computers. Satan lost everything when the power went out! On the other hand, Jesus calmly printed out all of his work from the past twenty-four hours. Satan became irate and stubbornly accused Jesus of cheating.

'How did he do it?' Satan asked incredulously.

God shrugged and said, 'It's simple. Jesus saves.'"

I couldn't believe it, but there was thunderous applause. I wasn't sure if it was due to the joke, or the fact that Jack was actually finished speaking and they could finally enjoy their dinner.

"That was great, Jack," I tried to sound sincere.

"Thanks, Tom. I thought I really nailed it tonight, especially with that last joke that you gave me. Now let's eat. Before I forget, I want to see you at headquarters first thing Monday morning. I hope that you had a nice vacation doing nothing, you bum. But

Monday *is* 'labor day' if you know what I mean. I will give you a ring early next week. Just wait for my call. I may have something special for you to work on for your next assignment."

"I was hoping to ask you if I could take a few weeks to keep tabs on the *Learning Styles Project* and make myself available to the pilot schools and monitor their progress. There have been some problems lately."

"We probably have to wait on all that. You know that's not something we normally do. We're lucky that they even agreed to it. Anyway, this next assignment should be an NSA puppy. Right now, for some strange reason, our friends there don't know about it…or want to know about it." He looked up and exclaimed, "Oh, there's someone I really need to talk to. I will catch you after dinner. Find me later if you still need a ride home."

Throughout the rest of the weekend, I couldn't stop thinking about the twenty pilot schools and how they were doing. I wanted to visit each one of them to see exactly what was going on. Everything seemed to be working out well in some schools while a few of them were having some issues. Unfortunately, I couldn't do anything until I heard from Jack. On Monday and Tuesday, I went to the racetrack and blew almost a hundred dollars due to some slow horses with catchy names. On Wednesday, Jack finally called.

"Tom, a computer will be delivered by someone from the CIA, and I will explain more about what you have to do at that point in time. Everything is still up in the air for now, but one of the directors insisted that you work alone on this."

"Which director?" I asked with anticipation.

Jack simply dismissed my question and continued, "I can't tell you any more than that. One of us will stay in contact with you, and I want continuous updates on your progress."

"But how will I know who I will be dealing with?"

"He has informed me that for now, he has to be referred to as Mr. M. He will make it very clear that he *is* the boss of this mission, and believe me, he is very powerful, if you know what I mean. Be careful. He has been evasive, even with me. And you know what they say about *boss* spelled backward, right?"

"Yes, of course. Double *sob*," I calmly stated, knowingly. Jack and I have certainly encountered many different types of people throughout our years together in Washington, DC and not just from within the CIA.

Jack continued, "He will either e-mail you or call you on the cell. That's all you'll get for now because that's all *I* have. Oh, and by the way, the level of security is merely 'confidential.' Even if it rises to the level of 'secret,' you're still covered. If it goes any further, we will have to get around it, but I don't anticipate anything like that happening. Remember, don't even go to Langley until I tell you it's okay. If anyone from the FBI or NSA find out about this, it could mean trouble. I am under direct orders to keep them out of this."

"Who have you been dealing with?" I casually asked.

"Don't worry. You just do your job, and I'll do mine!"

This sounded a little too abrupt coming from Jack. I noticed that for the past few weeks, he *was* acting a little on edge. Jack then put me on hold for a few minutes, and I took the opportunity to do something I do well—daydream. As my mind wandered, I recognized the fact that I could not let go of my real interest, and although raising the security status of a project usually piqued my curiosity, I still couldn't let go of the Learning Styles Project. My wife Sally and I have essentially organized the entire curriculum currently being taught in the public schools according to learning styles. Sally is a special education teacher, and she has been for the past fifteen years. We both came up with the idea to create several model schools, which were totally geared toward each child's individual learning style. I was very convincing that the monetary savings for the taxpayers in the long run would be huge due to the fact that billions of dollars were already being spent on remediation in public schools throughout the entire country. Furthermore, in order for the United States to compete globally with other advancing countries, enormous funds need to be allocated for gifted and talented activities as well as various enrichment programs. According to our models and forecasts, many of our advanced students would be able to excel significantly with much less cost since the programs would be naturally built into the school system we proposed.

For example, if a child had a more auditory learning style, he or she would be placed in a school that had teachers who were adept in that type of learning modality. Conversely, if the child was a visual learner, he or she would then be placed in a school that chiefly accommodated that type of learning style. The key was to match children to the learning environment in which they could best thrive and surround these young learners with the appropriate teachers who would be properly selected and trained, therefore consistently able to enhance their education by using the most ideal learning modality. Sally and I insisted that each child be placed in a school that not only had teachers adept in the learning style geared toward their strength, but we also proposed that there be a sufficient number of teachers who were proficient in and could therefore support the student's weakest learning modality. This was all a major paradigm shift in education, and we were already beginning to see many students thriving where in the past they had struggled. Furthermore, many of the students who always performed well in school in the past with traditional means were doing even bigger and better things. Some of these students were performing at a superior level, excelling in ways that their teachers never thought possible. In fact, some students were achieving success and advancing academically two or three grade levels ahead of their original status in only one year.

Of course, I attribute a large portion of this plan to reorganize the educational community to my wife and daughter. Sally is truly an outstanding, dedicated professional educator. We met at college when I was doing graduate work at Georgetown

University. It was Sally who supplied me with much of the data from her first eight years of teaching special education to children in various grades. At one time, Sally taught at the middle school level; and more recently, she taught special education students in the elementary grades. My daughter April is now ten years old, going on thirty, but when she was only four years old, I had time to work with her while I was home on a "medical leave of absence." I experimented with various approaches to learning, using April as one of the subjects. I was able to thoroughly test her learning styles, and this resulted in some interesting discoveries involving how the brain works and learns. When Sally came home from school each day, together we would look over the results of what I had tried with April as well as what Sally attempted with the fifth graders from her classes. For nine months, I used statistics and computers to analyze the results, and we formed predictions and hypotheses. Years later, some of these ideas would eventually lead to our project of reorganizing schools in the DC area. A year ago, we put together the plan and implemented it on a limited basis. It was agreed by the highest ranking educational leaders of Washington that we would pilot the program for two years, and if it proved to be successful, we would expand the pilot to the entire region including areas of Virginia and Maryland. Eventually, we hoped to spread out even further and train educators throughout the United States to restructure even more schools.

Unfortunately, we still needed another year for the initial data to be thoroughly analyzed and deemed statistically valid by the computers that I controlled. I was so grateful that Jack was able to use his influence to get the Learning Styles Project off the ground.

When Jack finally got back on the line, I spoke up right away with what was truly on my mind. "Okay, but I hope this new project doesn't take too long. Like I told you the other night, some of the schools want me to come in and check their progress. I am on the verge of suggesting that we get yet another group of schools involved because we are seeing a few kids in each school who are having some difficulty. It seems that we may have to account for yet another type of learning modality that we still have to identify. I just need some time in each building to ask some questions of the staff and gather some more data. What will I be looking for? What exactly will be delivered?" I guess I wasn't paying full attention to anything Jack said earlier.

"You'll see, Tom."

I was disappointed that Jack was being ambiguous regarding this assignment. This was unusual for him. I was also surprised that he did not suggest meeting at the office face to face.

The very next day, Jack seemed much more forthright. "Tom, here it is in a nutshell—we need you to find out as much as you can about a newly discovered special computer. This device is the only one of its type that we were able to track down. We need to find out how this computer was configured and programmed. We also need to determine what kind of power this device ultimately has and how these powers can best be utilized to benefit society."

"But, Jack, what are you talking about? We have many supercomputer s like this. I've worked with them a few times."

He abruptly responded with tenacity, "I know, but this one is not the same. It's not built with the same complexity, and it is not nearly as large. Take my word for it. This is one special device. Whoever masters it will gain tremendous power. It is different than anything we've seen before." Jack went on, "The past couple of days, I have been talking to the person in charge of this whole operation, and he feels it is best that you work alone and begin with a clean slate, no preconceived notions about what it can or cannot do. He wants you to learn everything for yourself. Experiment, run tests, ask questions the way you know how. You're the best at that kind of stuff. Do whatever you feel compelled to do. Believe me, according to him, you will realize that this makes studying big data seem bogus, like a big waste of time."

I didn't quite know what to say to that since I was a little surprised, if not confused. I remembered the adage, "It is better to remain quiet and be thought a fool, than to speak and remove all doubt," so I said nothing. We left it at that, and I was now actually looking forward to the challenge.

THE CLICHÉ KING

That night, I again woke up in the middle of the night; and for a few seconds, I had no idea where I was, or who I was for that matter. I looked at the clock, and I saw that it was 3 AM. Luckily, I didn't have any bizarre dreams like the one I had the week before. I wondered if that dream could somehow be related to the project Jack had in store for me. I went down to the basement and sat on my recliner and stared at my encased Louisville Slugger. My eyes were wide open, but I was miles and years away. I remembered some of the projects I worked on in the past such as the time when I took on the grueling task of analyzing the Washington, DC transportation system. I used statistical analysis and computer modelling to prepare an evacuation plan for the entire Washington, DC area if it ever became necessary. I eventually worked on the evacuation plan for many of the major cities in the United States. Since I became so knowledgeable on transportation, I was subsequently assigned the task of devising plans to alleviate the increasingly dangerous air traffic around many of the major US cities. Unfortunately, a major accident occurred near Chicago's O' Hare International Airport, and 250 passengers and crew were tragically killed including my younger sister Kate who worked as a stewardess. I thought I could have prevented the disaster if I began just a few weeks earlier. I was so devastated that it took me nearly nine months to get back to work, and by then, someone else had taken over the air traffic project.

I picked up a crumbled piece of paper near the wastepaper basket. It was my resume; I must have missed that bank shot after all. I looked it over, and it brought back a different set of memories. I taught math and computer science in high school for two years, went back to graduate school to earn masters degrees in statistics and computer science, and then worked for the government as a computer programmer for a few years. Finally, I acquired a position with the CIA. It was men like Jack Russell and Patrick Myers who encouraged me and allowed me to earn their unequivocal trust to a point that I got to work on a few projects that were classified as "confidential" and "secret." The degree of secrecy of any project is called its sensitivity. Confidential reports are defined as such because the information would "damage" national security if it were disclosed to the general public. On the other hand, when something was labeled as secret, the second highest classification, the information contained would cause "serious damage" to national security if released. Although it was somewhat of an honor to obtain the "secret" security clearance, I have been primarily working only on reports deemed "confidential" or "sensitive but unclassified" lately. In fact, I would never want to work on anything top secret because the level of scrutiny that my family and I would be subjected to would be unbearable and possibly even dangerous. Top secret information is defined as such because if publically disclosed, it would cause "exceptionally serious damage" to the national security of the United States. Of course, it has been a genuine privilege to corroborate with so many experts in various fields and to write reports that often appear on the desk of the president. A few years ago, I worked on an assignment with NASA involving space exploration to Mars and beyond. We concluded that manned space travel to Mars could not feasibly be implemented for at least another twenty-five to thirty years since the radiation that astronauts would be exposed to would reach terribly unsafe levels from deep space cosmic rays emitted from supernova explosions as well as cosmic rays from the sporadic solar flares of our own sun. On the other hand, it was rumored that scientists from China might develop high quality space suits and materials that would better protect space ships from radiation. Therefore, if the Chinese become partners in outer space endeavors, it could allow the trip to Mars to come to fruition in only 17.4 years according to one of our most reliable supercomputers, Henry. (Believe it or not, here at the agency, we had names for each of the high level, cutting edge computers that are available to us.)

I'm not proud to admit that for a while, I also worked on the agonizing task of playing out various war scenarios. My team and I spent months on this job, and the computers supplied every detail imaginable: the number of body bags that would be needed, the number of personnel who would need artificial limbs, and the overall "winner." The worst part was having our computers describe the outcome when various chemicals were used by other nations even though these dreadful weapons were all supposedly banned. It was one of the most revolting things that I ever was a part of, and I had terrible nightmares for weeks. I almost had to quit the agency. Luckily, my department head eagerly assigned me to other, less gruesome projects since he could see that I had remarkable computer knowledge. Unfortunately, I still have some of the horrifying images and sickening feelings thoroughly etched into my mind and soul.

It was ironic that the government supported many of these special projects only to sometimes conceal the final report, stamping it confidential, secret, or in rare cases, top secret. I also noticed that if they didn't keep it under wraps completely, they certainly didn't make addressing the controversial issues a priority. Furthermore, they were not going out of their way to make the public aware of all the findings. That's why I never worried about stepping on anyone's toes when I put together my final report; very few people ended up seeing the final draft. If I *had* to step on anyone's shoes, I was always careful not to mess up their shine. As a matter of fact, in formulating the final document, I would often embellish it with appropriate anecdotes or even personal stories. I was also known as the king of the cliché, inserting old, outdated, overused phrases or corny one-liners every chance I got. As I once told someone, "Sorry if I get a little carried away with the cliché, but I try to use the phrase that hits the nail right on the head." I first drew the attention of the president, and he chuckled when I wrote, "Let's abolish, eliminate, and eradicate redundancy!" In the beginning of my career, I noticed that the president of the United States was a big fan of the banal truism, and it was something I utilized since very early in my career. At Georgetown, I took courses such as The Way to Understanding the New Testament and Genesis to Jesus, so whatever I wrote often contained references to the *The Good Book* as Bible quotes were mixed in my writing from time to time. Again, the only reason why I had that flexibility was because that same president preferred it that way. As he once said in a meeting of his inner circle, "The Bible is the ultimate truth, and the government needs to be proponents of the truth at all costs so the people will have someone to trust." Among his own advisory committee, this same president was not reluctant to quote the Bible himself, and he happened to be one of the most popular two-term presidents ever.

The next night, I had more trouble sleeping than I'd had in a long time. At least the other night, I was able to get in a few hours of shut eye. This time, my mind was flooded with some of the incredible experiences that I remembered from the past few years of work. It was two in the morning, and I couldn't fall asleep for more than five or ten minutes at a time. I drifted in and out of sleep, constantly thinking.

Global warming is continuing to be a cause for alarm among many scientists and government leaders throughout the world.

Yet concerns about global warming are not being addressed adequately, according to many environmentalists. The level of concern regarding the impact that global warming is having on the earth depends on which side of the fence one is sitting or to put it another way, with which political party one is affiliated. The only undisputable fact is that the continual industrialization throughout the world is leading to staggering amounts of greenhouse gas emissions. We are trying to implement policies that will reduce the greenhouse emissions by twenty-five percent over a ten year period when studies call for an eighty-five percent reduction in order to prevent disastrous results. Part of the problem is that there still has not been complete agreement that humans can control the global temperature by limiting greenhouse gases. The debate rages on about how many scientific resources should be allocated to the problem, and there is no unilateral agreement as to the effect global warming will have on the overall environmental condition of the planet. Many believe that it is only a matter of time before the polar ice caps melt, and we see real changes in the earth's environment that will severely impact the world in which we live. Still, some people choose to ignore the potentially devastating impact this will have and how soon that outcome will be felt. There have certainly been more hurricanes over the past ten years. Floods have been a bigger problem than at any time in the past, and rising sea levels will eventually have a serious impact on low lying coastal areas according to the majority of computer models. Another real problem is that global warming will surely increase the spread of diseases like malaria as disease-carrying insects migrate north. These are all serious issues to be sure.

The Global Warming Project used mathematical modeling and scientific data to calculate the precise extent of the global temperature increase as well as the effect it would have on the people on earth. Of course, the most crucial thing we needed to calculate was the effect it would have on national security, which was not easy.

Another time, I had the responsibility of dealing with the world's energy supply. I was responsible for calculating how much energy the world uses and projecting precisely how long we would be able to sustain our current rate of consumption before the supply runs out. Again, the most important question was how it could potentially threaten the safety of the United States. Back and forth, I drifted in and out of sleep. This has been happening more and more lately; I knew that I would have to see Dr. Panthos soon.

I often thought back to when I was teaching high school math and computer science and how happy I was then. Fortunately, I now had the opportunity to work with many super people who were also doing vital work. I even met the president of the United States on several occasions. Regrettably, at other times, I felt that my efforts were a waste of everyone's time, and that my work was done merely to appease the politicians and powers that be. Would anyone truly read and understand my eighty-five-page report? I barely understood it, and I *wrote* it. Besides, I knew from the experience of working for the government that when all is said and done, more is *said* than done. The truth is, even when they classified my final report as either confidential or secret, only a limited number of people had access to it. This further exemplified an important aspect of statistics; the fact that what really matters is not what is revealed but what is concealed. (Much like a bikini if you pardon the rather crude analogy.) At least, all my hard work usually got me a nice vacation and some quality time with my family. Ten days in Disney World would have done wonders for the mind, body, and even the soul. Not so fast, Russo! Not this time! I didn't finish writing my latest report until January 5. Timing is everything, and this time, it was not in my favor. Sally couldn't leave her teaching job for a week since she just had time off for the Christmas break. My well-earned "vacation" ended up with me staying home by myself for one week, going to the Laurel Park racetrack a few times to play the ponies, and watching a lot of television reruns. At least the racetrack was rife with interesting characters, and it gave me a chance to recharge my batteries and see a few of my friends.

The truth is that after just a few days of what I described, I literally couldn't wait to get started on something new. I heard through the grapevine that there were some ideas out there pertaining to solar flares and their potentially devastating effect on power grids throughout the nation and the rest of the world. Unfortunately, I quickly found out that this noteworthy effort would have to wait for a while. Jack and the unnamed director had confidence in me to solve their computer problem and as one of them put it, "You're the only one who can pull this off." How flattering. Apparently, a very high-ranking CIA official specifically chose me because he came to the conclusion that I had all of the characteristics necessary including exceptional loyalty, so I could be trusted completely.

Over the next few days, I found out a little more after talking with the director, Mr. M. This computer, "Max" could somehow unveil so much information regarding anyone that it was astounding. The computers that I have personally used in the past at the agency dealt with studying much broader data regarding the masses. However, the information that Max could generate was not limited to people since it was also revealing information about certain events and places. One of the significant features driving this whole phenomenon was the fact that the more information regarding a subject initially entered, the better the quality of new information that was revealed. If you already knew some obscure facts about the person, place, or event, the details reported by Max were immeasurable. The most intriguing thing was that by definition, this was by no means a "supercomputer."

What good could come out of all of this computer capability? That was essentially what I was being asked to find out. Furthermore, I was under the impression that there were only a few people in the world who were familiar with this computer.

For all I knew, Jack had been getting information directly from the director of Science and Technology, the director of Intelligence, or someone even higher up that that. He indicated that the CIA had a reliable source and was pretty confident that most of the people or companies who ever owned any of these computers were not aware of the vast capability of the search engine, storage capacity, speed, or inexplicable potency. In fact, it was quite possible that even if more of these computers were out there, the owners were probably not even mindful of their unusual power. Instead of one thousand facts on a specific topic, a computer search might result in ten thousand bits of information; however, no one was going to search through ten thousand bits of information to get more details of a topic, place of interest, or the personal history of someone when they already had access to more facts about it than they would ever need to know. But as the old expression goes, "The devil is in the details." In fact, the genuinely noteworthy information could be buried beneath the surface. One would have to know what to look for and how to properly narrow the search. Another important aspect of this powerful computer's success was based upon knowing precisely how the questions should be asked. This proved to make a huge difference in the quality of the information gathered. Also, since some of the true power of this computer was augmented when someone already had some little known information about the topic or person involved, it was important to acquire some "secret" information and appropriately input it along with as much other information as possible.

Jack indicated that these computers, and this "phenomenon," had been brought to their attention about two years ago. I guessed that with all of the mention of big data recently someone high up deemed that now was the right time to act on it. There would surely be a lot of hard work ahead in order to resolve all the issues involved, and I was informed that some questions might never be answered. *They don't know me very well*, I confidently thought.

They weren't kidding when they promised that a "package" would be delivered. I was surprised to see five men pull up in a type of van that I had never seen before. Of course, I assumed they were from the agency, but I didn't recognize any of them. Two of the guys were huge, with shoulders about the width of a table. It took a while for them to get everything down the basement stairs, and I was shocked that it took another three hours for the computer to be assembled and configured. None of the men spoke much the entire time. As a matter of fact, even the one well-dressed man spoke very little at first. I left them alone for a few minutes and went upstairs to get them each a bottle of water. When I returned, I noticed one of the technicians was on his hands and knees feeling along the baseboard where the computer was now situated.

"What's *he* doing?" I inquired with understandable curiosity. He was moving some of my old textbooks and practically flinging them across the room.

"He's looking for an outlet," the other technician abruptly answered.

"Has he considered golf or racquetball?" I sarcastically asked, clearly demonstrating a little attitude of my own.

One of the men chuckled, and that was the extent of the emotion that any of them displayed until they were ready to leave. Fortunately, after a little while longer, they seemed to have everything in place, and I was finally in business. Or so I thought.

I guess they were instructed to take nothing for granted because they took another hour to explain everything about the computer to me. They described every wire, every piece of hardware, and every antenna attached to the machinery. Some antennae reached six feet into the air, nearly touching the ceiling.

"I get it now," I assured them. "If I have any questions, I will certainly give you a call."

I was half kidding, but just then, the so-called brains of this crew, who was quite intimidating, rushed toward me and pounded his finger into my chest a few times and warned, "No, you don't seem to understand. This is supposed to be a *covert* operation. We don't even exist as far as you're concerned. As far as *you* know, everything was just dropped off, and it was up to you to configure everything. You *are* supposed to be some sort of computer expert, right?"

"I dabble," I replied modestly.

"Well, this is labeled as confidential, and that's the only reason you are able to work from home. You will be yanked off the assignment immediately if it rose to the level of secret."

"But I have secret security clearance," I protested mildly.

"Never mind! It should be labeled top secret according to some people. If you worked on this at Langley, your butt would be under so much scrutiny that you wouldn't be able to get diddly-squat done. I guess they figured that no one would suspect anything vital was going on down here in your basement. So watch your step!"

We left it at that, and they took off, speeding away from our quiet neighborhood. I didn't even get the chance to tell them about my extensive background working with the CIA or to see if they knew anyone that I worked with besides Jack. I never expected them to take such a tone as they did, and I thought the whole experience was quite odd. At least now I could get right to work. I looked over all the equipment and hardware. Everything took up so much room, but at least most of the components were carefully labeled. There were four main external memory devices, each about the size of a suitcase. One was labeled personnel information, another historical data, another events, and the fourth miscellaneous. I quickly found out that there was no single computer anywhere that simultaneously had access to all the data that this computer had. Anywhere. I certainly had my work cut out for me, trying to sort all of this out, and I felt confident that I was up for the challenges that lay ahead. First, I decided to take a nap. The computer would have to wait. I hadn't been sleeping well lately, and I felt like I needed to rest.

THIS IS NOT GAMBLING

Jack and Mr. M supposedly didn't want to fill me in on everything that they already knew because they wanted me to be totally open-minded and unbiased. I was left to my own devices, my own imagination, and my own creativity. I quickly discovered some of the best techniques for taking full advantage of Max's power, and it didn't take me long to appreciate the fact that it was not an ordinary computer.

I was still eager to take my family to Disney World as soon as school let out for summer vacation in June. I immediately realized that I was able to easily access information that would not be found on an ordinary computer. I was able to tell exactly how many people were on any given ride at any time. I could also generate a comprehensive list of everyone who was on the grounds of Disney World (or any site for that matter) on any given day. With the proper preliminary information, a few techniques, and Max's innate ability, I could determine if anyone I knew would be there and where he was staying. I could find out information about every worker at Disney, now or in the past. I could access his family history, medical records, salary, and other very personal information. And of course, it didn't have to be such a high profile organization. I would be able to gather detailed information regarding any company in the world or any person for that matter.

A few days later, Jack was difficult to reach by phone for some reason. I wanted to share that I was able to search for any given sporting event in the past ten years and access the names of every spectator present. I could also take anyone (famous or not) and find out everything about him or her such as where he went to school, what grades he received, his various standardized test scores, and other personal information. I was able to take any movie playing in any theater in America within the past seven years and find out who attended. I certainly realized that most of this information was easily accessible by certain agencies, but I was surprised that I was able to access it all through Max. After only a few more days of dabbling, I knew that there was much more to the special ability of this computer than merely accessing data. I saw the tremendous processing power and storage capacity of this machine, unheard of for a computer of its size even though I was accustomed to dealing with some of the most powerful, sophisticated CPU mechanisms ever produced.

One day, I noticed that I was able to input the license plate number of any vehicle and find out the location of the car. I tried this out with my brother Johnny, and it freaked him out. He was driving to Atlantic City for an attorney's convention, and he just entered the Atlantic City Expressway. I called him on his cell phone after Max reported his location to me. Johnny almost drove his Lexus off the road when I told him that I knew exactly where he was, and that he was driving at eighty-three miles per hour. He informed me that he was supposed to speak at a conference and was running a little late. I also knew (according to Max) that he just drove through the EZ Pass toll lane of the expressway about a minute ago, and that he was listening to the Bruce Springstein song "Born to Run" at that very moment. I was amazed that Max was so accurate, but I was sorry that I wasn't able to tell Johnny how I knew all of this.

I also found out that Max confidently predicted the condition of any vehicle including when and how it would break down. The problem was that I didn't have the time or the patience to randomly wait by the side of the road for a car to break down and then tell the driver, "My computer predicted that!"

When I finally spoke to Jack again, he specifically informed me that what I was doing was nothing spectacular. He called it pedestrian. I was given some time and a little latitude to discover and learn for myself, but both Jack and Mr. M insisted that I should be doing more and finding out more. I tried desperately to get them to tell me everything that they knew to begin with since that would save me some valuable time. For some reason, they were both reluctant to do so. They were evasive and made excuses, repeating the notion that it would be best for me and Max if we discovered everything by ourselves.

Before very long, Jack became much more persistent and demanding. I had worked for Jack for nearly ten years now, and I had never seen him like this. He constantly pressured me to come up with "significant results" soon otherwise he would drop out of the project and I would have to deal with Mr. M. directly. He insisted that I would not want that to happen, and that I would be under even more pressure if it ever came down to that. There was something disconcerting about the whole thing, and I was sure that Jack knew more than he was telling me, but I didn't want to waste time fighting with him.

I was eager to share some of my findings with the big data experts at the CIA and even compare notes, but I was also told by Mr. M. to keep everything to myself for now. "Nothing was to be revealed to anyone at Langly, no matter what their security clearance." I found this quite peculiar, but I was in no position not to comply. "Furthermore," Jack insisted, "this has nothing to do with big data." I assumed he knew what he was talking about.

Even with the use of big data machinery, no one can tell for sure exactly what an individual's next purchase will be. The experts are able to make general predictions regarding the population at large, and they have had a staggering penchant for success over the broad spectrum. But they couldn't approach what Max and I were doing. All I had to do was enter an individual's credit card history, several details about his life, and some family information. I would not only get a description of the next item he would be purchasing but also a list of the next five items he would buy. At first, Max was not always correct. For the first few times that I tried this feature on my wife, my brothers, and a few friends that I knew closely, the computer was correct on all five items only twice. On the other hand, after experimenting and practicing, Max got more proficient, and the results seemed a little better each time.

I realized that this type of thing seemed to be the antithesis of data mining. Big data analysis studies trends and probabilities for the largest groups possible. On the other hand, what I had access to was searching the personal information of specific individuals using Max's profound ability. I still wondered if I was on the right track since I was not given a specific direction. I felt like I was searching for a single needle in a haystack, and I was among hundreds of haystacks.

Fortunately, I quickly realized that there was a very practical aspect of Max's shocking ability. I was able to go to the racetrack after doing a search on the key aspects of a particular horserace including the jockeys, and the history of each horse entered. I was able to determine with ninety-eight percent certainty, which horse would win! Additionally, I was soon able to not only use Max to determine the winner of any horserace but also to determine the second and third positions. Win. Place. Show. A "trifecta." I found this unfathomable but very fortunate as far as I was concerned. I'm also proud to report that I don't feel I have abused this little fool proof system for making a little extra spending money. In general, I am usually somewhat wary of all forms of gambling, but I didn't consider this gambling by any stretch of the imagination.

Not since I was able to use Max's insight and unflawed logical reasoning. On average, about once a week, I would venture out to Laurel Park and put a mere one-hundred-dollar wager on a trifecta, and that would be enough to satisfy me for a while. I felt justified because every time I won at the track, I always gave a good portion of my earnings to a few of my favorite charities such as Tomorrow's Children and The United Way. I also took comfort in remembering an old horse racing adage from years ago that helped me overcome any feelings of regret that arose. "No one ever committed suicide with a good two-year-old in the barn." Max may have been more like ten years old, but I thought it still applied. I do admit, I was a little ashamed of myself for using Max in this way, but I soon realized that I would eventually be involved with way more important issues.

On February 5, a key turning point in my escapades with Max occurred. It seemed creepy and surreal, but it really would begin to change everything. I implemented a finely tuned search on myself. I entered my name, social security number, and some general background information including some obscure personal facts about myself. I asked Max about a particular date, time, and place from my past that I distinctly remembered. I was nine years old, and it happened near my old neighborhood on Hillwood Avenue where I grew up in Falls Church, Virginia, a suburb just outside of Washington, DC. It actually happened at the Liberty Ave Community Carnival, and I remembered the event that occurred as if it was yesterday. During this local carnival, I was walking around with some of the older kids from my neighborhood, and they were talking about some of the girls from the neighborhood who were good looking and others whom they couldn't stand. They also went on about which girls they thought were "weird."

The name Joanie Wilson came up as being "totally out there." As they spoke, I remembered seeing her earlier that night near the carnival listening to music with some of her friends. I broke away from the older boys, or more likely, they broke away from me, probably to go to the woodsy area of Larry Graves Park a few blocks away to have a smoke. I found myself alone and drawn toward the lights and music of the carnival. As I got closer and closer, I noticed that Joanie Wilson was suddenly a mere ten feet in front of me. She had her back to me, and she was dancing with her friends. "Boy is she weird," I remembered one of the older boys saying with disdain. *I* didn't see anything weird about her. She actually had gorgeous brown hair that seemed silky smooth. She was having a good time with her friends, drinking a coke and dancing. She was really quite attractive, or at least that's what I can remember thinking (not that a nine-year-old boy has any clue about what makes someone attractive). Although this was more than thirty years ago, I vividly remember hearing the music, smelling the buttery popcorn and sweet cotton candy, and walking right up behind her, and slapping her butt while she was dancing. *What was the big deal?* I remembered thinking. That's probably exactly what my older "friends" would have wanted me to do anyway. Well, I wasn't going to stay and wait to see what Joanie's reaction would be. I turned and ran away as fast as I could, figuring that I would make it to the woods before she even knew what (or who) hit her. The woods were only about one hundred yards away, and I prided myself in the fact that I was the fastest runner of any nine-year-old boy I knew. Little did I know that Joanie was to go on to become a varsity soccer player in high school, and that she was *really* a fast runner. Well, she quickly caught up to me, grabbed me, turned me around, and slapped my face so hard that I saw stars! My cheek hurt, and I was mortified, but I desperately hoped that no one saw anything. I surely never told anyone about what happened that night. I essentially learned my lesson. Treat girls with respect, and you will spare yourself a lot of heartache and cheek ache. I always remembered that little life lesson. What a shame it would have been to feel the pain but miss the actual lesson.

Max informed me that Joanie Wilson went on to become an all-state soccer player for Paul VI Catholic High School in Fairfax, and she then played soccer for Duke University. That was easy to verify on an ordinary computer, but no ordinary computer could ever dream up the details of the carnival incident. Clearly, I was privy to a device that was no ordinary computer. Using Max, I was shocked to find the entire story of the carnival, Joanie Wilson, the slap on my face, and the older boys smoking in the woods all in more detail than I could ever have remembered from over thirty years ago. I was in total shock, and I thoroughly racked my brain as to how the computer could have come up with this factual information from such a long time ago. I was absolutely sure that I never told anyone about the incident that night. Why would I? Maybe some of it came up when I used to see Dr. Panthos on a regular basis, but he was certainly not at liberty to ever talk to anyone else about something that I told him in confidence. Could Joanie have recounted that story and written about it for some type of school assignment? If that was the case, then I would have thought that a traditional search on a standard computer would have found the same information. However, even with diligent checking, I could not find any account of the incident even after a thorough search on my laptop. I even tried a top-notch computer at my office at Langley even though I was specifically told to stay away from there until further notice. I found no information about anything that happened that night.

I was reluctant to do any other searches on myself for fear of what else Max would be able to reveal. My past might be filled with incidences that I was not particularly proud of, maybe even ashamed of. I knew that some things are simply better off not remembered. Nevertheless, I couldn't resist letting Max search for information regarding my "first kiss" as a high school senior (so I was a late bloomer). I remembered that I was alone with Carla DeFranco in a stairwell of my high school. I supplied Max with a few facts about Carla, and I asked Max about the date, the time, and the location. I was shocked to discover that a complete account of the incident came up. Max seemed eager to share precisely what took place. It was as if either Carla or I somehow supplied the details to this incident. I know for sure that I never told anyone what happened that day, and I don't think that Carla could have told anyone either. You see, this took place at about 2:25 PM just before school let out for the weekend. After I left Carla at two thirty, she got into a fatal car accident on her way home. I was devastated. Carla was the sweetest girl I knew. She was intelligent and extremely talented in art and music, and it took me about two years to really get over her untimely, unfortunate death. In fact, I didn't have a serious girlfriend until my second year in college. Carla could not have told anyone about our "encounter," and I certainly wasn't one who would kiss and tell. In any event, Carla's passing was certainly one of the most devastating things that ever happened to me.

When Jack or Mr. M called, I was now the one who was evasive. I no longer divulged everything that I discovered since my intuition told me to not completely trust either one of them anymore. It was difficult for me not to be able to confide in anyone, especially my staff or even my wife. As far as Sally was concerned, all that I was dealing with was some aspect of computer programming involving cutting edge technology. I knew that I would eventually fill her in with some details, but for now, I wanted to spare her from this mess that had the potential to get even more complicated. The truth of the matter was that I was surprised that the "powers that be" would even trust me with all of this since Max was potentially too valuable to take for granted. Didn't they realize that anyone would be tempted to find a way to use this special device for his own good? Or that he would be eager to sell it to a business, or even another country? I knew that I could never consider such a perfidious act of blatant dishonesty, and at this point, I was determined not to dismiss the trust that was placed in me. Besides, I was so intrigued with this device and what I might be able to eventually find that I had not even considered making any kind of profit for myself. I did have a few minor issues with the ponies, but I would hardly consider wanting a little extra spending money a major crime. I wondered if either Jack or Mr. M monitored my work with Max on a regular basis. If they did, I'm sure they would have known that I was not totally forthcoming. I know that the time I spent doing horse racing analysis would have been brought to my attention and would not have been appreciated to say the least.

MIND READING MAYHEM

My office was in the basement of my house, and I often worked on my official assignments from home whenever their level of sensitivity was low enough. The best part of working from home was that it allowed me to spend more time with my daughter, April, who was now ten years old and in the sixth grade. She actually skipped first grade because in some areas of learning, she is extremely advanced. She has a keen photographic memory and a love of classic literature, including the Bible, and she always looks for connections between the Old and New Testaments and to the real world. One time, April brought in her Bible to school for "show and tell" with her class. She spent an hour talking about it, telling her classmates about some of the stories in it, and what the Bible meant to her. That was when she was in the third grade!

After school, the bus dropped April off right in front of our house, and I was usually there waiting for her. We would hang out for a while and play, work on a craft or puzzle, or do her homework. Sometimes we shot baskets in the backyard or played catch with our softball gloves. She would eventually write in her journal because she was extremely passionate about writing. She had pages and pages of stories, daily events, prayers, and Bible quotes.

From time to time, I vividly remember back to the period when I was having trouble concentrating after my sister died. I had to take off almost an entire year. The only thing that got me through was the support of Sally and the fact that it gave me the opportunity to be with April who was four years old at the time. That's when the idea of the Learning Styles Project first took root. I worked with April every day for nine months. Or, I should say, I played with April every day for nine months since everything was a game of some type as far as she was concerned. I constantly recorded data on what she learned, how she learned, and where she thrived in just about every aspect of cognitive reasoning. I tracked how the different learning modalities affected her understanding of colors, shapes, language, spelling, and many aspects of math. I recorded everything that I discovered, formulated ideas, and passed everything along to Sally. She did similar work with her entire class of twenty-five students. The information that we collected at the end of each day was enormous. It was through my computer ability that I was able to write programs that would totally organize the information, and we were able to make sense out of everything. We experimented with six or seven different learning styles including kinesthetic, auditory, and visual modalities. We even accounted for some children who were musically inclined who were receptive to using music to enhance their learning ability. For some of the students, we had a song for everything that they were to learn. Each day, we concentrated on a different skill such as math facts or parts of speech for the children in Sally's class. We constantly examined the optimum approach for each child to learn each skill. Not only that, I also set up "play dates" with about ten children who we knew and who trusted me and Sally. The parents knew that their children were having fun while they learned, so they unequivocally gave us permission to play and work with their children. Thus, it basically amounted to me having one or two of April's friends or other children approximately her own age for about three or four hours each day to work with and experiment with some aspect of the learning styles being tested. Sally and I formed all sorts of conclusions that we put together into a sixty-page paper that summed up all our findings. This piqued the interest of the commissioner of education, and we outlined a plan that would enable us to test our findings and hopefully go forward to revolutionize education in America.

I was delighted to have had the opportunity to be with April and have fun watching her grow and learn. Fortunately, the bond that we established has never been broken. By keeping busy and focusing on something worthwhile that year, it helped me to take my mind off the guilt that I felt for not being able to prevent my sister Katherine's unfortunate death.

I cleaned out a few things from the basement to make room for a small bed in case I worked late and fell asleep down there. I often worked on my reports after Sally and April went to sleep. I noticed an old computer tucked away in the corner, so I decided to bring it out to the trash. I went through the backdoor and saw April on the swings. When she saw me, her eyes lit up. "Hi, Dad, long time no see. Why are you throwing that out? It looks fine to me."

I tried to explain, "That's what happens when technology gets obsolete. It makes way for something new. Even with some supercomputers every so often, we completely destroy them, and new ones take their place."

"That sounds pretty insensitive," she remarked compassionately. "Almost inhumane!"

"Well, if you saw the energy bill that an inefficient supercomputer generates when it gets older, you would probably change your tune." I continued. "Just before we turn it off for good, we ask it to come up with something beneficial for us—anything."

April didn't seem interested at first, but she asked with a little more enthusiasm, "Dad, what makes a supercomputer super?"

"What? That's really hard to explain. What did you say?"

"You heard me," she insisted. "Will the witness please answer the question?"

"Why can't you ask me questions that most kids your age ask their dad, like why is the sky blue?"

"Because I know that already," April confidently announced. "It's because of the way the molecules in the air scatter the sunlight."

I responded with an air of false confidence. "Oh, sure, I knew that too." Then I tried to dismiss her question, hoping for some divine intervention. "My boss, Mr. Russell, can tell you the next time you see him."

"But I'm asking you *now*."

I paused for a few seconds. "It's all about speed, hon. Let me put it to you this way. Suppose we gave a calculator to every single person in America. That's over three hundred million people."

"Even babies?"

"Yes, even babies. Work with me here. And suppose they all did one calculation every second for six hundred days straight, nonstop. A supercomputer could do the same amount of computations in one second."

"They should call them super *fast* computers. I think I actually get it. So then supercomputers have speed and power. That's it."

"That's plenty. It's like me saying that all Mom has going for her is great looks and a wonderful personality. Isn't that enough? It's enough for me!"

"Okay, so you want to marry a supercomputer?"

"What? Funny April. You had me going there for a while."

"Just kidding, Dad. I actually understand it better now."

"Good, not many people do. It *is* hard to wrap your brain around something like that."

"What do *you* do with them? Supercomputers."

"They hardly ever let me use the supercomputers. So I have to be more efficient with more traditional computers. With my work, it's about knowing what to look for, and that's why it usually takes me a long time to complete an assignment."

I enjoyed telling April about my career working for the government and hearing about the times when people referred to me as loyal. I would always tell her about the time Patrick Myers, who was the head of the center for technology management, mentioned me in his retirement speech. I was only thirty years old, and I worked for his department for five years. He really appreciated the quality of my work, and he clearly valued my ambition as well as my loyalty. In his retirement speech, he stated, "…and I won't fail to mention Tom Russo who has worked tirelessly for me and the department for the past five years. And it is not only his work habits and energy. He has a creative mind and a marvelous sense of humor, and he will be doing some great things in the future, but it is his *loyalty* that is second to none." I remember whispering to Sally who was sitting right next to me at the time, "Do I have to sit here and take this garbage?"

Anyway, he went on to say "And if you look up the word *loyalty* in the dictionary, you will simply see a picture of Tom."

As much as April used to love it when I repeated that story, this time she commented, "Dad, the corn is falling off the cob."

Nostalgia isn't what it used to be, I thought to myself.

"Dad, why did you originally decide to work for the CIA?" April did seem eager to talk, probably because she hasn't seen much of me lately.

There wasn't one single reason, so I tried to encapsulate, and I simply told her that, "I wanted to help Uncle Sam solve problems before they became bigger problems."

"Why do people refer to the United States government as Uncle Sam?" April eagerly asked, full of questions on this night.

I thought for a few seconds, trying to come up with the best way to explain it to her. "That's a good question. It's called a metonym, like when we refer to the movie industry as Hollywood. It's just another informal way of referring to something. When I call the CIA 'Langley,' it's almost the same thing."

"Oh, I get it, Dad!" April eagerly exclaimed. "'The pen is mightier than the sword' uses the word 'pen' to mean words, right?"

"Absolutely!" I answered.

"So 'the sword' must really mean fighting or taking something by force."

"You got it!"

Just then, April and I both flinched as two eerie shadows came toward us. "Hi, Elise," April loudly and enthusiastically called out to a girl whose backyard met up against ours. Her friend Elise was thirteen years old, very intelligent, and April totally looked up to her. During the summer, we often included Elise on trips to the shore, and the girls were extremely close. Their personalities just seemed to click; they both had enjoyable senses of humor and were always kidding around, acting things out, and giggling. They had a plethora of inside jokes and always seemed to know what the other was thinking.

Elise was with her five-year-old brother, Kevin, who often tagged along with her, and sometimes Elise and April included him when they played in the backyard or if they played a board game of some type. We invited them both over to our yard to play on our jungle gym equipment that included climbing ropes, slides, parallel bars, swings, and more. Elise began leading them in a "follow the leader" type game. Kevin noticed a few new pieces of equipment on the jungle gym that we recently added. He was quite eager and enthused. "Wow, you guys have a lot of new pieces of 'quipment," Kevin beamed.

"Boy Kevin, you're so observant!" I responded sarcastically. "You huckleberry!" My voice faded imperceptibly, and he had already run off to the other side of the jungle gym. He stopped for a few seconds and was clearly intrigued with the special type of rings that we recently added.

Kevin turned to April and asked curiously, "April, what are *those* rings for?"

April casually replied, "They're for doing flips, Kevin."

"I can't do flips," he replied in all seriousness.

"Well then, don't use those rings," April nonchalantly responded. A logical piece of advice from a ten-year-old. April and Elise both burst out laughing for some reason. They all played for a while, and I was glad to see them having such a good time. At least for a few minutes, I was distracted enough to forget about all the excessive work that I had ahead of me, trying to sort out the mystery of Max. There is something special about children playing and laughing—it is magical.

Right about then, Elise came up to me and eagerly asked, "Mr. Russo, would you be able to come into my school and talk to my class for career day?"

"Are you sure you want *me*? I have a very boring job." I was a little surprised.

"Are you kidding me? Some people at my school think that you are a spy because you work for the CIA."

"I guess I *better* come in then. They have to realize that not everyone who works for the CIA is an undercover agent with deep, dark secrets. There are many positions for people who are trained in science, technology, analysis, and engineering who don't live secretive lives. Ordinary people, lawyers, secretaries, office workers, you know."

"Okaaaaay. Let's go with that." She sounded skeptical.

"Not everything is all glamorous and exciting. For everyone who works undercover, there are twenty who work in more traditional roles. Let me put it this way—it's like a parade. Not everyone is actually *in* the parade. You have to have many hundreds and thousands of people on the sidelines cheering and applauding as they go by, right?"

I could tell that she still wasn't quite buying it, so I responded, "I will try to come in and talk to your class, but it may have to be in a few weeks, okay?"

"Sure, thanks," she replied, now a little disappointed. Elise then perked up suddenly and arbitrarily informed me, "Mr. Russo, you look like someone I know. You remind me of my uncle."

I responded with, "Who is your uncle, Brad Pitt?" Elise thought I was funny, and she and April laughed hysterically while Kevin was still trying to figure out the rings. "Hey, girls, it wasn't that funny." At least I was in pretty good shape. I ran three or four times per week and played golf and tennis. I even completed a triathlon last summer. That seemed like ages ago, and I realized that I haven't been exercising these past few weeks. What a coincidence, that's exactly when I started working on this project to sort out the enigma of Max.

"Dad, can I have a sleepover with Elise?" April called out to me casually. She must have forgotten that it was a school night, and she had to actually sleep at night.

"I don't think so, honey. Your mom would never allow it on a school night and neither would Elise's mom," I reasoned with her. I liked the way that I cleverly diverted the blame.

"You know, I haven't had a sleepover with Elise in five years!" she exclaimed, clearly getting annoyed at my flawless logic.

"Now, April, come on, don't stretch the truth. I must have told you a million times not to exaggerate," I joked.

April and Elise both laughed. April turned to Elise and asked if they could get together on Saturday instead and possibly spend the day together.

To which Elise replied, "No, I'm sorry, April. I can't. I have to do four more hours of community service."

"What did you *do*?" April asked innocently.

"No, not that kind of community service. It's with my youth group at church. We are going to the Senior Citizens Home, and we read poems to our adopted grandparents."

Just then, Kevin fell from the equipment and hit the ground with a thud; surprisingly, instead of crying, he laughed. *That kid is a real nut*, I thought to myself. "Kevin, you are one incredible kid! But I think you need a checkup from the neckup," I joked, hoping that he wouldn't take me seriously.

"What's a neckup?" he asked innocently.

"Never mind, as long as you're all right."

April quickly seized the opportunity and jumped right in, "Dad, can I go to Elise's backyard to play? There's absolutely nothing to do back here."

"Why did I spend money on this jungle gym and all of the additional equipment if you always want to go to Elise's house? Sure you can go, but it's getting dark. I'll come out and get you in half an hour. Your mom will worry about you out in the dark."

"Dad, tell her not to worry. Can any one of you by worrying add a single hour to your life?"

"I know." I was on to her this time. "Matthew 6:27. I'll tell her."

I went back down to the basement to resume my cleaning and more importantly to continue my adventures with Max. I was disappointed that I was working on this project for weeks now, and I was feeling a great deal of anxiety, but I was still resolute to use my adept computer knowledge to discover the arcane powers of Max. I was generally enthusiastic and optimistic about what I was doing and where it all might lead. Regrettably, at other times, I felt pessimistic and depressed. A few times I would actually be so discouraged that I was afraid I might revert to when I had a major battle with depression, and I had to be hospitalized for a few weeks. It was then that I realized that I was over all of that. I had a sensational family and a good job with an opportunity to really make a difference. My wife Sally and I were best friends, and my daughter, April, was a super ten-year-old. I also knew that if I ever totally lost interest, or worse yet felt like I was on the verge of a major breakdown, I could simply spend a day or two at the racetrack to earn a boatload of money and be done with this atrocious rat race once and for all. I would return Max to Jack and tell him that I decided to retire from the agency and be finished working for the government. Fortunately, I resisted this temptation as I remembered the quote from Winston Churchill who said, "A pessimist sees the difficulty in every opportunity. An optimist sees the opportunity in every difficulty."

Whenever I did a search of someone, something, or a particular event, I first investigated it traditionally in order to find out as much as possible by conventional means. I would use this as preliminary information along with any other facts that I happened to know. If I was personally aware of some obscure facts or private information about the person being researched, especially some hidden thoughts that I happened to know about, this almost always resulted in more specific information, sometimes resulting in fantastic deductions. Of course, this all took some experimentation at first; but I finally got the hang of it, and I was able to collaborate with Max for a real eye-opener. Collecting information on the subject's close friends, associates, and family members enhanced my searches and invariably resulted in detailed, unusual, and intimate information. The computer fed on knowledge, and the more information I could give it, the better it performed.

One of my goals was to see how close I could actually come to getting into someone's thoughts without him knowing. Even though I am quite convinced that we will never get to the point where we can truly read each other's minds, with this computer, I sincerely believed that I would be able to come close.

I first thought about trying out Max's "mind reading" prowess on Jack Russell, but he wasn't exactly approachable these days, so I abandoned that idea. Instead, Sally seemed to be the ideal candidate since I knew her more deeply than anyone besides myself. I gave Max a great deal of information regarding many different aspects of her life. I included every fact that I knew about her; some that were documented and some that only I knew about. Not only did I input fundamental information such as her social security number, credit card numbers, and her family history, but I also supplied facts about her schooling, her medical history, her hobbies, and her interests. I entered the last four books she read. I even entered the names of some of her coworkers. I supplied Max with the names of all her students, as well as the names of everyone she encounters throughout a typical day such as the custodians in her school, the secretaries, and the waitress at Starbucks where she picks up her coffee every morning. I included some information about the school nurse whose office is near Sally's classroom. Somehow all of this detailed information resulted in some bold statements that Max generously supplied pertaining to Sally. Inexplicably, I was made aware of some interesting estimations regarding what was on Sally's mind. After April went to bed, I confronted my dear wife, and I began by gently rubbing her back and shoulders.

"Sally, do you know this computer that I've been dealing with lately?"

"How can I not?" she replied.

"Well, I'm supposed to find out what makes it so special. I want to see if it was on target when it said that it can read your mind." I hoped she wouldn't notice the magnitude of what I was alluding to.

Sally did notice. "What in blazes are you talking about? If who is on target?"

"Max. The computer."

"Max is the computer?"

"Yes. It's been telling me things, and it has been correct every single time."

"This is getting weird. Even for you. Let me get this straight. Max is the computer in the basement? I thought I heard you talking down there in the middle of the night, but I assumed you were on the phone."

"Not only that, but he speaks seven different languages." I have to admit, this was easier than I thought. Sally was being a real team player. "Of course, I keep it set on English."

"Naturally. I'm sure your Latin is a little rusty."

"I usually have it automatically print out the information it comes up with. I usually keep it that way, but sometimes I like to hear its voice in the middle of the night or during the day when no one is around. It helps me keep my sanity."

"I'm not sure it's working."

"Ha-ha. Very funny."

Finally, Sally cut to the chase. "Then what did you want to talk to *me* about?

"Max indicated that it can read minds, so I checked it out on you."

"You *are* losing it! But I'm willing to help out…in the interest of science."

"And don't forget, national security."

"*What*ever." Sally sighed. I could tell she was exhausted from a long school day. She continued, "I'll play along, but remember, I'm very skeptical. Will that affect how well it works?"

"No, dear." I chuckled. "I'm not about to hypnotize you."

Sally laughed too. Then I continued, "First of all, don't be frightened if any of these are correct."

"Go ahead," she huffed. "Please hurry, I have papers to grade and lesson plans to write!"

I put the paper up to my forehead as if I was using furtive powers of my own mind. "You want flowers for Valentine's Day this year. Roses. Sent to your school."

Sally didn't seem impressed. "That's no secret. I hope for that every year, and you still haven't come through. Next."

I jumped right to the next thing on my list. "You want to go to Italy for vacation this year instead of Disney World."

"Hey, that's pretty good. I never talked to you about that. I may have mentioned it to my sisters, but that was months ago. What else you got?"

"You are secretly disturbed that I leave crumbs all over the place and clothes around the house. You actually think that I am…sloppy."

"Now there's a scoop!" Sally seemed to be getting a little perturbed. "I never said anything about that all of these years because I know that you're always under a lot of pressure with work. But that should have been axiomatic for your friend Max."

"So you *do* think that I'm too messy?"

"Let's face it. Cleanliness is next to godliness. But with you, cleanliness is next to…impossible."

I felt a little insulted. More importantly, Sally didn't seem too impressed. "Oh, that hurts! I think we're done here."

"Not necessarily. I *am* quite intrigued. Is that the best that you and Max can do?

"Okay, how about this? You are planning a surprise party for my birthday in December."

"Hey, how did you know? Do I talk in my sleep or something?"

"No, but you *do* snore."

Finally, Sally showed some real emotion, almost passion. "This is really pretty amazing! I have to admit, you were right every time!"

"Are you ready for one more?" I asked with more confidence now.

"I guess so, but why don't you just quit while you're ahead?"

"I am willing to roll the dice. You know what a gambler I am." I hesitated for a few seconds and gave Sally a chance to get a drink of water. I kept thinking about how Max came up with everything. Even if Sally talked about any of this to anyone from her school where she worked or in her daily routine, I am sure that Max would not be aware of it. People must have better things to do than to run to the computer and type in the details of conversations that they had with Sally. I found it amazing that Max was able to dig up this kind of information on its own.

The last thing that I brought up was the notion that Sally really hated having such golden blonde hair. Sally's consternation was that due to her blonde hair, good looks, and good-natured personality, some of her colleagues considered her vacuous, and that she lacked substance. In fact, she rarely socialized in the faculty room at school, and she always ate lunch by herself in her classroom to save time and get some planning done. Sometimes she would use the time during lunch to give extra help to some of her needy students. When I brought up this last prediction from Max, Sally seemed at first to take it in stride.

"You're right! I do feel that a few people at work don't always take me seriously, or that my opinions don't matter as much as some of the less experienced staff members." Then her tone changed dramatically. She really seemed upset and confrontational. "Do you think that any of this is true? You seem to have all of the answers tonight!"

I compassionately reassured her that she was doing admirable work at her school, and that in a couple of years when our Learning Styles Project comes to fruition, everyone would know that she was a huge part of it. I surely wouldn't have been able to get it off the ground without her.

Sadly, Sally ended up storming away, and she slammed the door to our bedroom, with me on the outside looking in. I took the opportunity to go down to the basement and get some sleep. I was confident that Sally would be back to her jovial self in the morning. For some reason, she was prone to frightening mood swings lately, but I didn't have the time or the patience to try to figure her out. I actually *thought* about sending her flowers for Valentine's Day, but I again missed my opportunity. Well, it *is* supposed to be the thought that counts.

By now, I typically stayed up late every night to try various ways of inputting data and to see what other surprises Max would produce. I was getting so little sleep that I was usually fatigued an hour or two after dinner to a point that I would have to force myself to stay awake. Regardless of my physical exhaustion, I tried desperately to stay awake until at least midnight or one o'clock and then still be up by five the next morning. One night, after dinner, I was working down in the basement, and I could barely keep my eyes open. I was double-checking a traditional search on my regular laptop computer when I fell asleep. It was only 8 PM, but I had been working until 2 AM for a few nights in a row. April came downstairs to the basement to say good night before she went to bed. She really wanted to talk for a little while, and she must have been curious as to what I had been so intent on doing the past few weeks. The time that I usually spent with April was precious, but the past few weeks hadn't been so pleasant since I had so little time for her. April saw that the computer was still on while I was asleep, and she apparently tinkered with it. Of course, April didn't know that Max was not ordinary, and she didn't have any idea of what she was dealing with. Still, she was quite handy with the computer and Internet searches. There was no telling what she could find.

It was about 8:30 PM when Sally tracked April down and told her to get ready for bed. I woke up and was still quite groggy at first, so I told Sally that April would be up in a few minutes. April must have been working on the computer for almost thirty minutes, but I didn't think much of it. After all, it usually took me a few hours of searching through everything to come up with anything significant. I was ready to take her up to her bedroom when she asked me in an excited voice, "Daddy, will I be getting a baby brother or sister?"

"What are you talking about? Mom isn't having a baby. Whatever gave you that idea?"

She informed me of her search on the Internet, which was all set up to look for information on me. Like always, I began with some basic information to help facilitate the search. I had left off trying to decide what day, month, and year to explore. That is when I fell asleep.

While April was using the computer, she changed the search settings to a "Marks" search. I haven't used that particular search engine in years. Buried in hundreds of pieces of information were some true facts about myself. The fascinating part was what April stumbled upon inadvertently. It was hidden, but April was able to pull up a chronological listing of recent events of my life, and they all seemed plausible except that one thing stood out.

The fact that Sally was now going to have a baby, and she was already four months pregnant. What kind of bogus nonsense was Max now coming up with? I convinced April that it was all just a big mistake, and that she should know better than to believe everything found on the Internet. I got her off to bed and tried to persuade her to not mention any of this to anyone, including her mom. Especially her mom. Of course, before she went to bed, April had to write in her journal, and I was sure that she would include this intriguing revelation that there would be a new baby in the family. Fortunately, Sally never read April's journal; so at least, I would have some time to sort it all out.

As soon as I was convinced that April was asleep, I rushed back down to the computer to see what was going on and how Max could have been so wrong. I did confirm that what we found was my complete profile with a great deal of information about me that was clearly true. I felt a little flushed and then almost panicky as I kept scrolling frantically on and on, past the current date and into the future dates that appeared. It was something that Max seemed to have compiled based on whatever access it had to my personal data as well as anything that was out there in cyberspace. At a future date, it clearly mistakenly described me as married with two children, April and Ryan. Sally and I never talked about having more children, especially since we were so busy with our careers. Besides, April was the greatest kid anyone could ever hope for, and we didn't want to push our luck. On the other hand, I vaguely remembered that we did mention before we were even married that if we had a boy, he would be named Ryan.

I would probably have dismissed this unusual occurrence as totally erroneous, even preposterous if it wasn't information from Max. How did it come up with this kind of fiction? The hardest thing to swallow was how wrong Max was in this case considering its track record. I realized that this was the first time a Marks search was done with Max, at least since I took control. I wasn't totally convinced it made the difference. After all, coming up with a profile on someone that spilled into the future might have been interesting, even mind-boggling, but it would be a total waste if the results provided were incorrect.

This whole ordeal turned out to be a pivotal turning point in my efficiency to solicit crucial information from Max. It took me a few days to perfect the technique, but I was eventually able to set it up so that I could directly ask Max virtually any question about any time in a person's life. The results it provided were not always that dramatic. It would take anywhere from three seconds to thirty minutes, but Max would always get back with a definitive answer, every single time. Whether the information was valid or not remained to be seen.

THE BANK ROBBER

The next day, I temporarily forgot about what happened the night before. I actually decided to get some sleep during the day while Sally and April were at school. I woke up from a long nap in the afternoon feeling refreshed. I stayed away from the computer for a few hours, ran some errands, and went to the drug store to pick up some essentials.

That night, I asked Sally how she was feeling. Sally worked exceptionally hard, and she took her teaching responsibilities very seriously. She was a dedicated professional educator, but that never stopped her from being an outstanding wife and a sensational mother. Sally told me that for a few weeks something didn't feel right with her body, but she dismissed it as stress and as she put it, "A lot is going on at school." She continued telling me about some mandatory testing that was going on at her school district and how hard she was working to prepare her kids for it.

"Some days, they do great. And other days, they seem totally out of it. Almost clueless." Sally continued, "I have been trying to fully take advantage of the various learning styles, but on certain topics, a few of the children are having trouble no matter what I do."

We talked about the fact that this is unfortunately consistent with some of the preliminary results that a few of the other pilot schools were reporting. There might have been a few children in each school who were having difficulties in some areas, but no one should be drawing any conclusions at this point in time. We were instructed to let the study play out. We suspected we might be missing something, but we had to wait and see.

Somehow, I managed to nonchalantly ask her to take a pregnancy test. First, she laughed, then she cried, then she ended up laughing again. I couldn't believe it when she actually agreed to take the test. She was quite shocked when I pulled out a pregnancy test that I bought at the drug store that day. She did mention that she missed her period last month, but she dismissed it as irrelevant since it has happened several other times in the past few years.

"Sometimes there is a great deal of stress due to all of the work and anxiety from teaching, and the body can respond in various ways," she casually explained. Stress and anxiety from teaching was understandable. After all, I did have some tension throughout *my* two years of teaching high school math. Anyway, the results of the pregnancy test were quite definitive—positive.

Sally subsequently went to her doctor two days later, and the results were confirmed. She was in fact almost four months pregnant. How could Max have known this? How could it yield valid results when no one else on the planet knew this at that time, not even Sally? And how could changing the search engine matter so much? I decided to test out the theory that the Marks search engine was the key. I put out another search of my own life and included a few obscure facts about whatever I could think of, including my own health history, my hobbies, and a few personal bits of information including some of my favorite charities. It took a while and a lot of reading through pages and pages of information that Max was providing. Initially, most of what it was showing was nothing noteworthy. Finally, I did come across a few things that were new. In fact, one of the troubling things that it came out with was that my minivan had faulty brakes, and I would soon be in a terrible car accident. I didn't think this was possible because I recently traded in our old van, which needed brakes, among other things, for a new Toyota Sienna. This was done less than one year ago, and my new van was working fine. We were probably the only family of three who owned a van, but it came in handy, especially the way Sally packs, even on a weekend trip to the shore. In any event, the results pointing to my accident troubled me a great deal. How in the world could Max now be "predicting" the future instead of merely reporting the past? Could it be yielding ingenuous results by simply processing every bit of information and wisely foreseeing events due to flawless logic and powers of deduction? There was still no way to explain everything that was going on and determine what was valid or invalid. How could I hold any credence to something that has not been completely tested for accuracy? Yet.

Just to be safe, the very next day, I went right down to the Toyota dealer where I bought my van, and I had them check it out. They laughed at me right to my face and mocked me as being paranoid, but I really didn't mind since I was used to being the butt of jokes; after all, I did have two funny, sarcastic brothers who would constantly deride me whenever they got the chance. I was eager to get to the bottom of everything and finally prove that Max could be wrong after all. Fortunately, at the dealership, they did humor me; and while they had their mechanics check out the car for anything that was potentially faulty, they did some research as to when and where my van was manufactured. They had some very sophisticated computers themselves although I was convinced that their machinery wasn't even close to being in Max's league.

As I sat by the waiting area, there was a small couch, and I didn't want to pass up the opportunity to sit back, relax, and stretch my legs. Fortunately, there were no other customers waiting, and I was able to fully recline and make myself at home. I closed my eyes and almost fell asleep. After about thirty minutes or so, one of the managers casually walked over and nudged me a little. He must have thought that I was sound asleep. He asked me in a soft, friendly tone, "Mr. Russo, are you comfortable?"

I replied equally friendly, "I make a good living."

He seemed taken back at my poor attempt at humor, "No, no, I meant are you feeling okay? You looked a little tired, and I didn't want to disturb you."

"You don't even know the half of it. But what about the van?"

"Well, we did some checking, and we found out a few interesting facts about that particular vehicle."

It turned out that with that particular model, manufactured on that exact day, there was an incident where a worker had to be sent home ill. The brakes were never tested, and in fact, it was confirmed by the Toyota mechanics that it was only a matter of time before the brakes were defective and hazardous to drive. They kept the car and guaranteed that they would work on the problem and get the situation rectified by the end of the next day. They would even throw in a free carwash.

"Gee, thanks," I stated. "You should throw in a free Jacuzzi spa to make up for the ten years of my life that I just aged."

Not surprisingly, they didn't agree to that; and when the manager became a little curt, I had someone drive me home. I also decided that I would be taking the bus or walking for the foreseeable future. Now it did seem that Max was indeed showing signs of predicting the future based on having access to enough information about the subject. It just might have been a case in which Max had access to everything it possibly needed to determine that there would have been a brake issue. On the other hand, there certainly was no way to tell for sure that I would have been in a serious car accident like Max foresaw. I needed incontrovertible evidence, absolute proof that Max could *predict* something that would positively come true. I realized the vast amount of information and data that Max must have had access to was colossal. It must have been privy to everything that the dealership had access to and much, much more. It was bordering on illegal or at the very least unethical. I would have objected if it wasn't for the fact that it seemed that my life might have been spared due to the information that Max provided. It was certainly plausible that Max had the ability to logically deduce or even predict some future events with all its reasoning ability.

Nothing noteworthy happened for a few days, and I found it hard to concentrate after what I considered a near death experience. At dinner that night, Sally and I had to help April with some homework. She was assigned what at first seemed like the arduous task of finding a few puns and then *explaining* them. She also had to put in her own words why the play on words was funny or ironic. I easily generated her a list of ten puns that I had collected over the years. I was surprised that Sally knew a few right off the top of her head.

"Don't waste your time looking them up," Sally suggested. "Here's one. It was raining cats and dogs. There were poodles all over the road."

April groaned, "Oh, Mom! Let me hear the ones that Dad found."

"How about this?" Sally tried to quickly redeem herself. "Two Eskimos sitting in a kayak were chilly, but when they lit a fire in the craft, it sank, proving once and for all that you can't have your kayak and heat it too."

"That's pretty good." I was quite impressed. "But how about this one. I remember using this one when I taught high school. A rubber band pistol was confiscated from algebra class because it was a weapon of math disruption."

April clearly was not impressed. "That's okay. I'll do it myself."

Sally wanted one more crack at it. "How about this? Two boll weevils grew up in Cornwall. One went to Hollywood and became a famous actor. The other stayed behind, drove a tractor, and never amounted to much. That one, naturally, became known as the lesser of two weevils."

I pretended to laugh so hard I fell off my chair and onto the floor. While on the floor, I managed, "That reminds me of a guy who entered a local paper's pun contest. He sent in ten different puns, in the hope that at least one of the puns would win. Unfortunately, no pun in ten did."

April had no trouble telling why all the puns were witty or paradoxical. It gave us a few laughs, and she did a great job without help from either one of us.

Then April broke the news to us. *We* had homework that night. April explained that Sally and I were assigned the depressing, almost humiliating task of writing a letter to the teacher telling her "Why my child is not working up to her potential." We were totally surprised that our gifted, hardworking child whom we loved and supported in everything she did had been singled out for such a devastating label. Sally and I sent April to her room, not as a punishment, but merely so we could talk about it by ourselves for a short while. We didn't know how to respond. Of course, she *could* work a little harder. On the other hand, even though April was only ten years old, we knew that she was precocious in many ways, especially academically and socially. She had stellar grades in school and numerous accomplishments. She won the spelling bee at her school for the past three years. She had all As on her report card for the past four years. She read all sorts of books on her own that were usually several grades ahead of her current grade level. She read the Bible on her own for goodness' sake! We tried to think of anything that April could have done that prompted this unusual request from her teacher. April did miss a few homework assignments this year when her stomach was bothering her. She also missed her share of days at school when she wasn't feeling well, but she always made up the work that she missed. We had to strain our brains to think about anything inappropriate that April could have done. Finally, Sally and I realized what was going on.

"April, darling," Sally called out. "Can you come in here please?"

"Yes, Mom?" April called back with a slight quiver in her voice.

We could clearly see that April had been crying when she was alone in her room. She seemed devastated by our reaction to the news that the teacher, Mrs. Garrett, singled her out. Sally and I both hugged April and kissed her and told her how much we loved her. She was a precious child. She was bright, gifted, compassionate, and special. However, April simply did not make it clear to us at first, and both Sally and I misunderstood her originally. It took a while, but we finally figured it out.

"April, who was that assignment for?" we asked.

"It was for the whole class. It was a writing assignment, and the teacher wanted to see a sample of our parents' writing. I guess I should have mentioned that in the first place, right?"

"That's okay. April, you know that we love you very much," I told her. "We are extremely proud of you, and we love you no matter what. You are talented and blessed. And *we* are both very blessed and privileged to have you as our daughter. We both know that you are working to your highest potential. Remember, what you are now is God's gift to you. What you make of yourself is your gift to God."

This was all the motivation that she ever needed, and April was quite satisfied and content. It turned out that April's teacher, Mrs. Garrett, was doing a project for a graduate course that she was taking. Mrs. Garrett did in fact have the assignment of comparing the writing styles of children with their parents' writing to see if there was a correlation with style, level of vocabulary, and grammar. The fact that we were so defensive and sensitive shows how eager we were to see April go on to do special things with her life. We all had a good laugh, but April took a while to get over the trauma of upsetting her parents even though we weren't disappointed in her at all. Sally and I should have used a little more common sense. If you see hoof prints in North America, think horses, not zebras.

The next day, I decided to call Jack. Surprisingly, he seemed to be in a hurry. I suggested that we all meet somewhere face to face, meaning him, myself, and Mr. M. He again refused to accede to my request, and I could see that something was off with him, almost sinister. I tried to dismiss that notion, and then Jack unexpectedly snapped, "You should be doing this all by yourself anyway." He was actually flippant, and that was unusual for Jack. He continued, "You are supposed to be the freakin' expert. Do your freakin' job. You're just lucky that the person in charge of this whole escapade insists that *you* are the one. I'm not even sure why that is."

"Who are we talking about?" I eagerly asked.

"Never mind! I've got to go!" Then he hung up. Now I was totally convinced that something was peculiar, but I could not waste time trying to figure it all out. I was on a mission, and I felt sure that I would not be able to trust anyone now. Then I remembered what I wanted to talk to Jack about. I was not receiving any paychecks! *Where's the coin?* I was thinking, a line my brother Dave was noted for. I was tempted to call Jack again, but it was clear that it might do me more harm than good. If it weren't for the pile of money that I saved from my jaunts to the racetrack, I would have *really* gotten angry with Jack.

Anyway, I finally had to break down and take the van out for a ride. I needed a diversion, so this seemed like a good time to take a little break. I had been collecting used bikes, and it was time to bring them to St. Therese School, which is located in an impoverished part of DC. They really appreciated me stopping by every few months with five or six bikes for the children of their school. In our town, sometimes in one year, a child will outgrow his bike; and if there were no other kids in the family to hand the bike down to, they either had to be thrown out or kept in their garage collecting dust. I kept the bikes in my own garage until I accumulated at least five of them. Then I would load the bikes into my minivan and make a trip to the school. Sometimes April would join me and help me get the bikes out and walk them over to the office of the school. Even on a Saturday, the school would be open. Sister Noreen was the principal of the school, and she was the most dedicated educator I have ever known. Sister Noreen was extremely hardworking and caring. She not only ran the school with a very limited staff and budget, but she also taught classes herself and monitored the after school program for children who had to be picked up late. I always threw in a few hundred dollars of my own money that was intended for bike helmets, knee pads, or whatever else the children needed. I wouldn't have been surprised if they used some or all the money that I gave them for books, paper, pencils, and other essentials needed to run a school, considering how poor they were. Sister Noreen and the children were certainly most appreciative, and I always received a letter of gratitude a day or two later that essentially was the most sincere thank you note imaginable. It always ended with the line, "We will pray for you and your family."

On this particular day, April did not accompany me because she was at a friend's house. I had six bikes stuffed in the van as well as some money that was intended for whatever Sister Noreen saw fit. This time, I had a little surprise for her. I took some of my winnings from my last horse racing endeavor and put the money in an envelope. Along with the six bikes, I would be giving Sister Noreen $3,500 to use however she decided.

Unfortunately, I couldn't find a parking space anywhere near the school entrance where I would need to unload the bikes. I drove around the block five times, and it was getting late. Sally was out of town with her parents, helping them with some errands. Every weekend, she would get up early and stop over to their house, which was thirty minutes away, and help them with some paperwork, shopping, or whatever else needed to be done. I promised to meet Sally in front of the bank, close to our home. We were going to transfer some money from a certificate of deposit at one bank and go across the street to another bank where the interest rate was half a percent higher. To me this all seemed like a waste of valuable time. On the other hand, I was in no position to argue with her considering I was not much help at home lately. I promised Sally that I would meet her exactly at noon. After we completed the banking, we planned to go over to April's friend Francesca's house at one and bring them to their school where they were having a car wash to raise money for neglected animals. The timing would work for all of this only if I could be depended upon to do my part and meet Sally at the bank in time.

I was getting quite anxious since it was almost eleven thirty, and I still couldn't find a close enough parking spot. I was losing my patience. Desperate for a parking spot, I made a deal with God. I decided that I would abjure all gambling with Max and all horse racing for my own personal profit from now on. No, better yet, I promised that I would continue to go to the racetrack once in a while, and I would give one hundred percent of my winnings directly to St. Therese's. I even spoke out loud, "And if I find a parking spot within the next minute, I will give *all* of my horse racing winnings to St. Therese's from now on." Like I said, I was desperate. Before I even got all of the words out, I noticed another van pulling out right in front of the school where I needed to park. I quickly retracted my agreement with God. "Never mind, God, the deal's off. I just found a parking spot." What a coincidence. A parking spot appeared just when I needed it.

I quickly dropped off the bikes and handed the money to Sister Noreen. She thanked me about ten times and kept saying what a wonderful person I was. I drove away smiling, but in reality, I knew something was wrong, and I wondered what was happening to me. All the pressure I was feeling as well as everything going on with Max and its predictions were affecting me in ways that I never deemed possible. I should have slowed down right there and thought about how to get my priorities straight again. Instead, I knew I didn't have the time or focus to even try to sort it all out, and I simply had to get to Sally in time. The fastest way for me to get back home, or in this case to the bank, was by taking a steep, winding road that was nicknamed dead man's curve. As kids, we used to ride our bikes down this hill with reckless abandonment, and we sure had a blast. However, that was thirty years ago when the traffic was not what it is today. I was already late, so I drove quickly not remembering that they recently changed the configuration at the bottom of that hill to include a traffic light. As the road curved sharply to the left and I turned through the last part of the winding road, I looked up and saw a red light. I had to stop quickly, and I skidded ten feet, just in the nick of time! The oncoming truck blew its whistle, other cars beeped their horns, and I actually had to back up a few feet while I waited for the light to turn green. This would have been the grave accident that I would have been in that Max foresaw! If my brakes were the least bit faulty, and I now knew that they were substandard before they were recently fixed at the Toyota dealership, this surely would have been the time and place that I would have been in a terrible, possibly fatal accident. I guess this was exactly when the magnitude of everything finally hit me like a cold slap on the face even more stinging and painful than years ago when Joanie Wilson slapped some sense into me as a nine-year-old boy. Now, I finally saw what was happening, and I was overwhelmed with the actuality that I had to deal with Max. This was not an ordinary computer issue. Throughout my entire adult life, I dealt with computers one way or another. This was the first time that I ever had a computer challenge and didn't know precisely how to handle it. What I was dealing with here was simply incomprehensible, and I knew that I had to get to the bottom of all this quickly before I totally lost my mind as well as my perspective. Could all these really be coincidences? I thought about the parking space opening up right when I needed it. I thought about the close call at the red traffic light. I snapped back and regained my focus. It was already twelve fifteen, and I was late. I called Sally on the cell phone and told her that I was on my way. She told me that she was already parked in the bank's parking lot. Needless to say, my dear wife was very annoyed with me.

I arrived at the bank at about twelve twenty-five, and by then, there were two police cars parked in front of the bank. Each police car had its lights flashing, and they were both parked next to Sally's Toyota Corolla. Sally did not look happy to say the least. It turned out that the bank manager noticed this suspicious-looking person parked outside their bank for more than half an hour, and he was worried that something was amiss. He called the police who happened to have two squad cars nearby. They pulled up to Sally simultaneously, and they must have scared the wits out of her. One of the officers was just handing back Sally her license and registration. When I pulled up and saw what had happened, I was sure that I was going to be blamed for all of this since I was so late. Fortunately, Sally was in a good mood, and she laughed along with everyone involved including the bank manager, the officers, and a few random customers. One thing I knew for sure was that Sally was not a bank robber.

Hypothetical Free-For-All

It was now five full weeks since I began the project. I was down to about three or four hours of sleep each night, and I managed to spend only about one hour each day talking to Sally about her school day and how she was feeling. For some reason, the news of having another baby had not really hit either one of us yet. It was almost as if we both were in some sort of "denial stage" due to everything that we both had going on in our separate lives. We even decided to hold off on telling the news to anyone in our family including April.

Sally was preoccupied with the needs of her special education students and finding the right prescription for their success. I often found myself helping April with her math homework. Of course, she totally enjoyed having my attention one–on–one, so she purposely or subconsciously didn't do her best unless I was right there with her. I was not a psychology major, but it seemed like that was certainly plausible.

I was finding it more and more difficult justifying to Sally, and myself for that matter, the terribly long hours that I had been working. No project that I had ever worked on was this demanding, and Sally knew it. When did I ever have to work eighteen to twenty hours each day? In the past, I would have so much time for my family since I could do much of my work on the computer at home, often at night when everyone else was asleep. The three of us always had a lot of great times together. We loved each other, and we knew how lucky we all were. Often we each wrote out a list of all the things that we were thankful for, and we always thanked God for everything that we had. We were also blessed since in less than five months, we were going to have an addition to the family. I am almost ashamed to admit that what happened over the course of the next few weeks was arguably even more miraculous than the birth of a baby.

I finally received another call from Jack. This time, I happened to be at the racetrack of all places, so I was not in the most ideal position to discuss anything with him. Of course, I fully expected him to be in a bad mood, contemptuous as usual, so this time I was prepared for him.

"I am calling to see how you are doing, Tom," he opened almost too casually. "It seems like you are doing some wonderful things with Max."

Now *that's* the Jack I knew. He had never been stingy with his compliments and words of encouragement until this project got underway. Still, I felt compelled to change the subject.

"Never mind that," I complained. "I haven't gotten paid yet. I have bills to pay too you know. I've been dealing with your friend Max for over five weeks now, and I have been working almost twenty hours every day lately."

"I know you're moving forward, but at this rate, it will take you a month of Sundays. We never should have given a boy an assignment that was meant for a man!" Jack was a huge guy, about six feet, two inches, and he weighed at least 290 pounds, probably more like 300. I certainly didn't want to get into it with him if we were standing face to face, but since he was on the phone, I had a little more nerve than usual.

"Jack, I *have* been making progress. And if you ever sit down with me, and you know who, I will be glad to fill you in." I was really raising my voice now. "But if you want a preliminary report, I need to see Mr. Green. Remember, money talks, everything else walks."

"Tom, you are dealing with something here that you don't seem to be able to comprehend. It's too much for you, isn't it?"

"No Jack," I protested. "I can do this."

"Then you'll be getting the checks in the mail from now on. Just stay away from Langley. I'm just about done." Then he hung up. I had the distinct feeling that I wouldn't be hearing from Jack for a while. In fact, from then on, I received a check in the mail every week, but almost no contact from Jack. Surprisingly, it was not a typical payroll check. But considering the astronomical amount of money involved, I was in no position to complain, inquire, or be concerned. I continued to work long hours, but I now had some monetary incentive for pushing myself. In reality, my curiosity and complete obsession with Max was the real driving force, more than I would care to admit to anyone. Regrettably, it was very disconcerting to me that there was still no end game in sight.

My sense of reality was getting more distorted each day, fueled by the lack of sleep and the pressure to keep learning more about Max. I kept trying to learn how to narrow my searches, tinker with some special coding techniques, and come up with better ways to help Max perform. I was delighted that I was able to directly ask Max questions. If they were worded properly and contained the right amount of specificity, Max would always respond after a reasonable amount of time, depending upon the complexity of the question. Max continued to get better and better as *I* learned more. I was so fixated on finding out additional things Max would be able to reveal that I was sometimes on the verge of being delusional. I found that it was actually better to force myself to stay away from the computer—any computer—for a couple of days at a time. This type of discipline usually restored my rational thinking as well as my relationship with my wife and daughter. In fact, if it wasn't for this coming back to reality at least two days each week, usually on weekends, Sally would have been even more suspicious that something was wrong.

We usually tried to spend Sunday together. First, we would go to 9 AM mass at St. Luke's, then we would either go for breakfast at the diner or bring home fresh bagels. Later in the day, we often walked a trail or went for a bike ride in the park across town, which had a fabulous bike and jogging path. Every month or so, we would get together with my mom who was a spry eighty-one years old. We often hooked up with at least one of my two brothers, usually for dinner somewhere at a nice restaurant.

Sally was now so occupied with her own job, caring for April, and taking care of herself that it took us a few weeks to finally come to grips with the fact that she was actually going to have another child. I was shocked that Sally didn't complain about my preoccupation with my work, which was now closer to an obsession for me. Maybe she *was* aware, and she was purposely playing it cool for some reason.

It could have been a dream or television advertisement that prompted my next idea. I heard the words, "You can count on the computers at Find a Match website to hook you up with the person of your dreams, your soul mate if you will." I thought I would give Max a crack at this type of thing. Not necessarily for me of course, but for controlled research. I was curious about how Max would handle this type of analysis, which was a little less scientific. Once again, I found that the more detailed information I supplied, the more interesting and precise the results seemed to be and the more confident Max was. Especially when it included extremely personal details. It was about now that I noticed that the hype of big data was clouding my thinking all along. Much of the success that I have been having with Max was due to what I would refer to as individual data or even unique data. This first seemed like the antithesis of big data, but I eventually realized that it was more of a supplement to it, working in unison to make a huge difference. At least some of Max's success was due to the fact that it used some of the features of big data analysis, but I was able to combine that with the individual bits of information unique to the subject or person at hand. This was like having the best of both worlds. This concept worked again for us because I was able to use Max to find a mate for anyone. In fact, Max could be set up to provide what amounted to a top ten list of compatible partners. Max also supplied the names of people to "stay away from." (Let's see a dating service do that.) I first provided all the typical information about myself including the type of information any online dating service might ask. I entered a physical description, which included a recent digital photograph, hobbies, education, and what I was looking for in a mate. I also took into account the general geographical location, so Max didn't match someone from our area to someone in a far off place such as Albuquerque, New Mexico. I was very pleased that by entering a basic, honest, and complete description about myself including some information that was unknown by anyone else, it did result in a list that included Sally among the top ten. Some of the people that it warned me to "stay away from" were so logical that it hardly caught my attention. *Thank you, Captain Obvious*, I acerbically thought. Additionally, when I entered, some of my friends, especially some who were already married, the results were a little disheartening. In every case, those who were happily married were listed as compatible or "an excellent match." On the other hand, those who were having some marital difficulties or were on the verge of divorce came out on the list as "incompatible" or "avoid at all costs." Unfortunately, according to Max, some who were married with no obvious problems were also doomed for an inevitable marriage meltdown.

I persisted in experimenting, wondering, and inquiring. If Max could predict what would eventually happen with relationships, what else could it foresee? I also wondered what would happen if I entered even more detailed information about my subjects. I continually used a combination of the big data approach and some obscure facts about the subject. I kept gravitating to the idea that if I entered information that no one else knew I might be able to successfully peak ahead into the future! I knew this might be opening up a Pandora's box and prove to be a slippery slope that I needed to avoid if I was to have any chance of success in using Max for its real purpose. Unless this *was* its real purpose. Either way, it was very tempting to use Max for this type of hypothetical free for all. After some thought and speculation, I finally broke down and gave in to this temptation. I entered a profile about myself that included ten hidden facts about my life that very few people, if any, knew (aside from Sally and Dr. Panthos, of course). I set up Max to answer the question, "What would have happened if…" This took some time to formulate, but eventually, the results were most prodigious.

Something occurred when I was fourteen years old while I was hanging out with some friends who were considered the "cool" group. We were walking along the train tracks after a Saturday of doing absolutely nothing (I did say they were considered cool, not necessarily ambitious). One of my friends had a cigarette and passed it around. I chose not to partake. They ridiculed me, but I shrugged it off. After that day, they stopped letting me hang around with them. I actually didn't think much of it at the time, and I hooked up with other friends. From then on, I never regretted it.

In this case, I changed only one bit of information, kept all other facts about myself the same, and waited to see what the computer would predict. I merely included the notion that I actually did smoke a cigarette with the others when I was a fourteen-year-old boy. I subsequently asked what would have resulted due to the alteration of what indeed happened. The results were astounding! According to Max, much of what actually happened to me in real life seemed to be erased! I did not go on to college and graduate from Georgetown University. In fact, it seemed as if I never went to college at all. I didn't get married nor did I have any children. Instead, I would have died of lung cancer at the age of thirty-five! I was skeptical and intrigued at the same time. The one comforting fact was that here was a situation that Max could not be proven right (or proven wrong for that matter).

I reluctantly tried again to alter something, and this time, I changed the college that I attended. At one time, I considered attending Northern Virginia Community College where I was offered a full scholarship. I turned it down to attend Georgetown. In my search, I claimed that I accepted the scholarship and went to NVCC. The result was that I met the "girl of my dreams" and dropped out of college after only one year. I married her and got a job as a manager at the local Shop Rite grocery store. This didn't work out and neither did my marriage. We got divorced after two years, and supposedly, I was married two other times within five years. I bounced around from job to job before I enrolled in… you guessed it—Georgetown University. And then I *majored* in governmental studies. Unfortunately, there would be no jobs in this field, and I was unemployed for quite a while until I found a government job. The problem was that I would have gotten a job as a toll collector. (Not that there is anything wrong with that.) In fact, I would still be working there now, according to Max. This was all an interesting bit of fiction, and I am totally glad that it did not happen that way. I truly cherish my life. I wouldn't alter a single thing. Of course, there was no guarantee that I would always feel this way.

I tried another adjustment in my computer search. In my "current" life, I had the opportunity to teach math at a high school and then return to college to earn master's degrees at Georgetown University where I met Sally. She was a freshman elementary education major. I was a graduate student, and the rest is history. What if I didn't go into teaching in the first place? Even though I only taught for two years, the whole teaching experience dictated a great deal of who I was and who I am today. What if I decided to major in governmental studies like I had originally planned? I programmed Max and provided the information as if I never went into teaching in the first place. What would Max have to say about me now? According to Max, when I graduated from college, I would have gone on to work on the staff of William Henning, who was the senator from Virginia at the time. I would have moved on from there after six years, and then I would have worked as an aid for the president of the United States. I still would never have married Sally, and I would never have had April.

This computer phenomenon allowed anyone to virtually relive his entire life by changing one or two facts about his personal history. The amount of details that Max provided were staggering. I figured out a way to pose it all to Max so it would provide pages and pages of specific facts that played out in chronological order. This could all be finely tuned to provide as much detail as I wanted. Of course, it would not have actually changed one's life, but I could find out how a single hypothetical alteration would have determined the course of the rest of the person's life. That is, if you could believe that Max had any validity beyond pure speculation. What if you did not meet your current husband or wife? How would everything have turned out for you? Would you have met someone else? What if you said no instead of yes back in high school? What if you chose religion instead of sin? The possibilities were endless. One could literally spend the rest of his life imagining the possibilities of how things might have been and then read about it in fabulous detail that a computer such as Max would readily supply. Then someone could go on to change something else and see how *that* modification would have worked out. Each alteration would result in totally different circumstances, which Max would eagerly and confidently outline in exceptional detail. It was then that I again realized I was getting way ahead of myself here. Why was I so trusting in Max? I kept trying to tell myself that we should trust only in God. To hold any credence in what Max would hypothetically propose would be totally foolish. Still, I could not stop myself from pondering the fascinating possibilities. Unfortunately, we simply cannot go back in time and choose another possibility and see if it matched the outcome that was foreseen and reported by Max. What I needed was some way that Max could be put to a test that could determine its credibility once and for all.

That night, it occurred to me from nowhere. Why couldn't Max be used to predict the future beginning from the current moment in time instead of from some precise instant in the past? Then I could easily test it out for accuracy. What I did so far was take information from the past combined with one piece of misinformation to determine hypothetical results. It was certainly based on logical reasoning, which was something Max undoubtedly possessed. On the other hand, what good would that really do someone? They would never know if the altered detail would truly have led to the predicted change. On the other hand, the real advantage would be if Max could report the possible outcome when someone had to wrestle with *current* problems or upcoming decisions. For example, suppose that next week you had to make a choice between two or three job opportunities. Or perhaps someone needed to answer yes or no to a marriage proposal? They would simply enter both scenarios, see the possible outcomes, and then decide. On the other hand, would everyone want to know? Isn't life better when there is an element of uncertainty? I am sure that some people would want to know while others wouldn't. I thought, *Shouldn't people be able to decide what is right for them?* I was getting a little ahead of myself again, putting the proverbial cart way before the horse. How could I prove that I would have died of lung cancer if I had chosen to take a single puff of a cigarette back at the age of fourteen? It seems like it was a viable possibility. I might have smoked a few cigarettes, gotten addicted, and found a new hobby. Nothing unbelievable there, but there was no way to actually go back in time to test any of these hypotheses.

On the other hand, now I was hoping to enter all the current information in as much detail as I could possibly manage including a single decision that had to be made soon. Where would it lead? I would have Max determine the outcome. This could be it. This could be the ideal purpose for Max. I could see someone wanting to try various possibilities then decide which path would be the best to undertake after seeing how each one of them would play out. Would Max be able to accurately tell what is best? Therein lies the dilemma. All of this would again totally depend on Max's credibility. None of this would matter to anyone unless he could believe wholeheartedly that Max was accurate in what it predicted.

I decided that I would need to lay out a situation currently in the works right now. I would enter all the facts as they currently existed. I would need to enter every bit of data available, not just the axiomatic. I had the perfect idea. This plan would help me decide if using the computer in this way was valid or bogus. At the same time, I could use the next few days to get back my declining role as husband and father. I remembered that Sally was administering an important diagnostic test to her class the following Friday. It was a benchmark assessment that would determine the quality of work her students were producing as well as her own level of success as a teacher. Sally frantically groomed her special education students by giving them an abundance of prep materials in class and for homework. She diligently applied many of the techniques geared toward addressing various learning styles. Furthermore, she built up the confidence of her students every chance she got and had them really thinking that they would do well. I tried to assist Sally, and I prepared review worksheets for the math skills that would be tested, which would account for about half of the test. I spent at least three hours with her each night, and I was even able to help her prepare some language arts material that she used.

After a few days, I finally went back to the computer after staying away for all that time, which seemed like an eternity. This was going to be a real test for Max. I gathered as much information about each of Sally's students, and I included all the information that I had access to including their family history and the students' documented learning disabilities. I uploaded each student's Individual Educational Plan, which in itself was a ten- to twelve-page document. I also added in their grades on weekly tests since the beginning of the school year. In addition, I included every single piece of review material that Sally provided her students over the past two weeks.

Finally, it was time for Sally to administer the test, and I had Max provide us with the results before the students took the test. Even though it was a full week before the results of the test would be available, Max had no trouble coming out with its "predictions." Of course, to Max, it did not seem like a prediction. It was more "matter-of-fact." The students who would be taking the test were listed, and the results appeared alongside each student's name. Only a week's wait would be needed to tell us if we had a veritable crystal ball on our hands. Even though I was extremely skeptical, the frightening thought came upon me that if Max was successful in predicting test scores for second graders, it could also predict other things like the gain or decline of a particular stock. This has never been done before by any computer with one hundred percent accuracy. Stock prices have always been an enigma because the price of individual stocks as well as the stock market in general are determined to a large degree by human emotion. And there are so many other variables involved, worldwide factors that drive the buying and selling of stocks and establish their price. The human emotion factor that drives the stock market is simply not able to be measured by any ordinary computer. Even a supercomputer could not weigh the collective human emotion necessary to take on such a task. How could it measure fear and greed, the two key components that drive the stock market? Of course, if this could be done not only for the long term but on a daily basis, it would completely change the entire business world. What if only one person had use of such a computer? If he was the only person with access to the "Max factor," that would be an entirely different situation. I wondered why the original owner of Max would give it up to let others work with it and discover all these possibilities. Could it be because they had no idea that Max would ever be able to do some of these extraordinary things? Perhaps they had plans to use Max for even bigger and better things? I got so lost in my work that I wasn't even thinking about Jack or Mr. M until now. I also wasn't planning on contacting either one of them at this point in time. Part of it was because I didn't know who I could trust, but I was also getting to a state where I wasn't even sure that I could trust myself. Anyway, I decided to wait for the results of our little second grade trial before I experimented with the stock market. Besides, I had access to the winner of any horse race, and Laurel Park was a relatively short drive away.

THE PRINCIPAL'S OFFICE

I found myself again thinking about the list of people who Max decided were best suited for me. Max predicted that if I married someone other than Sally, eight out of the top ten people on the list still resulted in divorce or heartache. (This was not very encouraging to me since these were the ten *most* suited for me!) I knew that Sally and I had a strong, genuine, rock-solid marriage, and we were totally compatible. Where we *did* differ, it seemed that we filled gaps. She is organized; I am not. She is irrational and gets excited easily; I am cool, calm, and collected. Usually.

The only scenario I did not play out was regarding the person who was listed as the *most* compatible to me, and this person was *not* Sally. There was a graduate student whom I knew at Georgetown University, and we were very good friends for one year. I was a little curious to see what would have happened if I felt the same way about her that she felt about me. I was flattered at the time, and I now wondered how my relationship with her would have played out, especially considering this revelation that we were supposedly extremely compatible and "meant for each other." She invited me to join her for a cup of coffee one day, and that's when she told me about the feelings she had for me. I insisted that I really just wanted to be friends with her. How could I not have seen the potential for us? Other than the fact that the academic area she was most interested in was biology, we had so much in common according to Max. She was born in China and moved to the United States with her parents at the age of three. I seemed to forget how close we had gotten back then. I used to call her May, and Max conveniently refreshed my memory regarding the dynamics of our relationship. Her full name was Meihui Lee. (Meihui means beautiful wisdom). At first, I could barely remember her; and ironically, Max had us living happily ever after. I was curious, but I decided not to find out the details regarding what would have or could have happened. I was completely happy with my life, my family, and my career. Well, almost completely. I loved Sally and April more than anything in the world. At that point, the only thing in my life that I was not happy about was getting involved with this draining computer assignment. I was getting concerned that it could seriously affect my relationship with Sally and April, not to mention my own health. It basically had taken over my life, and I was totally obsessed.

I continued for the next two days playing out scenarios of my life by entering alternate possibilities. With a few changes at various times in my past, I wanted to see what the outcomes would eventually lead to. In every example, I could see what was predicted, and it was astonishing how the hypothetical scenario that played out was so remarkably plausible. It was intriguing but my fixation was something that I found troublesome. There were now days that I got only two or three hours of sleep, and I wasn't sure which reality was currently mine.

Very often, I would dream about one of the scenarios that I just read about on the computer, and I saw and felt how my life would have played out. Often, my entire personality and career were totally different from what they were in reality.

One night, I had Max explore some things that happened in my two years as a high school teacher. This really gave me a chance to remember what actually transpired back then. I was only twenty years old when I received my undergraduate degree in mathematics education from Georgetown University. I earned a myriad of college credits for work that I did in high school including Advanced Placement credit in biology, physics, calculus, and history. In college, I essentially earned a double major in mathematics education as well as computer science. When I entered the world of teaching, I taught some upper level math courses such as calculus as well as some computer science classes. I thought that I had a very good sense of humor, and in fact for two years in a row, the senior class voted me the teacher with the best sense of humor. My picture appeared in their yearbook along with teachers who were voted most influential, best dressed, strictest, and nicest smile. I did have some funny moments in the classroom if I do say so myself.

For example, when a student went on and on about an obnoxious teacher, the amount of work they had, or some other problem, I would say, "Here's a quarter. Go call someone who actually cares." The other students always got a chuckle from that sort of thing, as long as *they* were not the butt of the joke. Of course, if a student had real problems or wanted to talk about any serious issues, I would always be able to lend an ear. I would never turn anyone away.

I recalled something else that was a big hit in the classroom. I would start to say some curse word by accident but then catch myself and tell the class how in all honesty, "Don't worry, I really never curse, drink, or smoke. I never have and I never will. Furthermore, I never gamble." Then came the immediate punch line, as I exclaimed in a matter of fact way, "Oh dagnabbit! I left my cigarettes at the bar in Atlantic City." Not only did most of my students think that I was extremely funny, but they also thought that I was a fantastic teacher. Sometimes, I can't believe that I gave that all up.

There was a time in my second year of teaching when I was dealing with a function in calculus class, which was not defined over a certain interval such as -2 to +2, and so we would write "No Graph" along that interval. After a few of these types of examples, the students should have known how to handle that type of graphing problem quite well. The next day, while going over the homework, which included a few examples of that type, a senior named Billy asked what the NG stood for in the middle of the graph that I had sketched on the board. I turned the question around and asked him what *he* thought the NG stood for. He exclaimed, "No girls?" I knew he was merely trying to be funny. I replied rather emphatically so that everyone in the class could hear, "No, Billy, this is calculus class, not the story of your life." Everyone laughed. Immediately, a girl named Tracey asked, "How can that be?" She was obviously referring to the unusual fact that a graph could be missing a part, and there is literally no graph in that section of the coordinate plane.

However, I persisted in getting the most out of my joke at Billy's expense. As soon as Tracey asked "How can that be?" I replied, "Well, it's probably a combination of a bad personality, someone who is not very good looking and not very friendly, basically someone who is not very appealing to the opposite sex." Again, the class roared with delight, at poor Billy's expense. I couldn't resist the opportunity to push the envelope even further by adding, "No, everyone, I am only kidding. I'm sure that Billy here is actually a real 'Don Juan' with the ladies. They don' wan' to have anything to do with him!" Fortunately, Billy seemingly took it all in stride and laughed along with everyone else. I finished the lesson, and that should have been the end of it. I had ribbed many students during my first two years of teaching, but I don't think anything went as far as that. That night, I started getting worried that Billy secretly took offense at my tasteless jokes at his expense. At that point of the school year, I didn't know for sure how secure Billy was. Maybe he was not popular at all. Was he a loner? Did he *ever* have a girlfriend? I was a late bloomer myself and never had a girlfriend until the end of my senior year in high school. Everyone is different, and my imagination ran away with me. I had trouble eating dinner that night because I was so worried. I was ashamed of my own insensitivity. I hated the fact that I was willing to make a joke about someone and even take a chance at insulting him merely to try to be funny. I continued to worry about that incident throughout the night, and I couldn't fall asleep. I finally slept for only a few hours, and I woke up with an intense feeling of anxiety. How *had* Billy taken my comments? I wondered if he went to his guidance counselor or another administrator to complain about my harassment and lack of judgment. I had some theories of my own about raising kids, and they all allowed for having compassion. On the other hand, my ideas also included the notion that kids of all ages, from tots to teens, needed to sometimes be immersed in the frigid waters of reality. Hopefully, no one took my kidding around too seriously.

Sure enough, near the middle of the first period of the next day, I got a call on the classroom phone from the principal's secretary, Mrs. Wiggins. She informed me that instead of going to my lunch duty at 12:05 PM, I should report directly to the principal's office immediately following my fourth period class. She did not tell me what it was about although I reasoned that it must have been regarding the incident with Billy in yesterday's calculus class and my insensitivity. I noticed a few of my calculus students giving me a funny look that morning in homeroom, and they seemed to be discussing something secretive. Every time I looked their way, they abruptly stopped talking. The morning dragged on. A guidance counselor even popped her head into my classroom during my second period class and reminded me to be sure to meet at the principal's office later on. She would be there as well. I wondered if she was *Billy's* guidance counselor, so I checked my files that I kept on each student. She was in fact his guidance counselor. I tried to think of what I would say.

I was ashamed of my inexcusable behavior, and I thought of an appropriate apology. I also thought about what I would do if I got fired that day. I was a nontenured teacher who had very few rights. It was only my second year in teaching, and I had been in trouble my first year even though I was under the impression that the situation had been totally resolved. Although I was establishing myself as an excellent, personable math teacher with a lot of potential, I could see the seriousness of what I had done. I put the self esteem of a student at risk. I could have damaged him psychologically, and I was feeling quite terrible, almost nauseous by the time it came to meet in the principal's office. Also present was Billy's guidance counselor and Billy himself. Sure enough, Dr. Riggio, the principal got right to the heart of the matter.

"Mr. Russo, I want to talk about what happened in calculus class yesterday. Billy brought something to my attention, and I thought it was necessary to hear your side of the story. Ms. Fisher, his guidance counselor, is also here on Billy's behalf."

I stammered. "First of all, I just want to say that I am terribly sorry for what I said." I meant to continue, but I was interrupted by Billy covering his face, trying to hide what I first thought sounded like sobbing. He was certainly taking this all very hard. It was a joke for crying out loud. All these people needed to get a life, *especially* Billy. Why in the world was he crying? However, I realized that my poor attempt at humor at his expense obviously affected him significantly.

"Well, sorries just don't cut it in this situation, Mr. Russo," the principal chimed in. He really looked angry with me. He tried to scowl in my direction, but even *he* couldn't hide his laughter any longer. Four or five of my calculus students came into the principal's office from right around the corner. They were listening the whole time. They were probably laughing the whole time. This was all a big joke all right…on me. They were all in on it, and they got me good. Billy did mention what happened in class to his guidance counselor. He essentially told her about the entire incident in a complimentary way. He was actually so impressed with my teaching ability and my sense of humor that he explained to his guidance counselor, Diane Fisher, that he was thinking of majoring in math in college and becoming a math teacher himself. He told her about some of the other things that I did in the class that he was totally in awe of. Ms. Fisher was also quite impressed with my teaching, my personality, and my rapport with the students. She and I actually went out for a while. We had a lot in common, and she was a very positive influence on me. The fact that it didn't work out between us was partially due to the fact that I left the teaching profession at the end of that school year to attend graduate school.

Anyway, they all had a good laugh at my expense. I couldn't believe how nervous and apprehensive I was prior to that meeting. In the end, I felt truly grateful that everyone actually appreciated my sense of humor and whimsical personality. Furthermore, they respected the fact that I could take a joke myself and that I had a warm and friendly disposition.

The very next day in my calculus class, I was preparing to derive the formula for the derivative of the tangent function. This time, I very sternly demanded that they all put their water bottles or soda completely away. Some of the students in the afternoon section had lunch just prior to my calculus class. They reluctantly put away whatever drinks they still had leftover from lunch. I knew they deserved an explanation, so I told them, "Class, you had to put away all drinks from your desk. The reason is because I am now going to derive an important formula in calculus. Even *I* have to put away my water bottle. After all, everyone knows that you shouldn't drink and derive at the same time."

A lot of people liked my style, and it wasn't just the humor that my students appreciated. The students could relate to me. I was encouraging, and I tried to make them feel good about themselves. I learned at a very young age that people will often forget what you said or did, but they will always remember how they felt when they were with you.

As it turned out, toward the end of my second year of teaching, my seniors were getting harder and harder to motivate. They all knew what college or university they would be attending the following year, and they had a massive case of "senioritis." It got to a point where I had to actually tell them a joke before class began just to get them to pay attention that day and agree to take notes the entire period. I tried to justify it by reasoning that it was a small price to pay for fifty minutes of them actually working. Fortunately, I had a huge assortment of jokes, puns, and riddles that I used with them. Ironically, my all-time favorite joke was the very last one that I told in class. I remember it being a warm spring day, and in my calculus class, no one was in the mood for learning about integration and finding the area under a curve. *Surely, everyone would appreciate this little tale*, I thought.

I began, "Morris was an eighty-four-year-old man who went to his doctor for a checkup. He left the doctor's office, and the very next day, his doctor saw Morris in town walking along, looking very happy with a beautiful twenty-two-year-old woman walking arm in arm next to him. When the doctor confronted Morris and asked what he was doing, Morris casually replied, "I am simply taking your advice from the other day when you told me to get yourself a 'hot momma' and 'be cheerful.' The doctor quickly responded, 'No, no, no, I said you got yourself a heart murmur, be careful.'"

For some reason, that joke got me called on the carpet, which basically meant that I had to meet with the principal. This time he was *not* kidding. In fact, I vividly remember the day Dr. George Riggio came up to my classroom on the third floor. (I did get a substantial raise in my second year of teaching; I was assigned to teach my classes on the third floor instead of the second floor.)

Anyway, Dr. Riggio came up to my classroom while I was alone eating lunch and grading some papers, and he greeted me with a pleasant smile. I pushed aside my half-eaten roast beef sandwich and water bottle and tried to act glad to see him. He was there to give me some advice. After all, he was a man with over forty years of experience in education, and I was all ears.

"Tom, you're a good kid with a lot of potential in this field. You're sharp, enthusiastic, and you have an excellent rapport with the students. You are truly an excellent teacher. You could probably teach a polar bear to be whiter!"

"Thanks, Dr. Riggio, I think," I replied softly and humbly.

"But you have to drop the comedy routine in your classes. Save the jokes for the faculty lounge. You can be entertaining in class without telling off color jokes. Everyone likes you for who you are—a caring, focused professional educator."

"Yes, sir," I promised. "No more jokes."

For some reason, he was not satisfied with that. He continued, "And I want you to neaten up your appearance. You should come into school clean shaven. And get a haircut. Your hair is much too long."

Now he was hitting a little too close to home. I did have a small goatee, and my hair was long, but it was by no means out of control. I was feeling a little perky and brazen, so without thinking, I decided to challenge him. "With all due respect, Dr. Riggio, the greatest man who ever lived on the face of the earth was known to have long hair as well as a beard." Of course, I was referring to Jesus Christ. I continued, "Jesus Christ had a beard and hair that was much longer than mine."

As I alluded to earlier, Dr. Riggio was in education a long time. He had seen it all and done it all, and he seemed to have an answer for everything. He nonchalantly got up from the desk that he was sitting in, casually took my water bottle and raised it into the air. The sunlight glistened directly through the window into the classroom and reflected right through the clear bottle of water, creating a prism, a spectrum of brilliant colors. "Tom, as soon as you can change this simple bottle of water into a bottle of a magnificent Chianti Italian red wine, you can wear your hair any way you please. Until then, get a haircut and a shave!"

From then on, I came to school clean shaven with a crew cut. Message received.

Furthermore, I cooled it with the jokes in the classroom for a while, and I stuck to teaching math. I liked teaching, and I would be up for tenure at the end of the subsequent year.

I remembered that near the end of that year, with only a few days left in the school year, I was ready to accept my contract as well as my teaching schedule for the following school year. I would be teaching two more sections of calculus, computer science, and two freshman classes of Algebra 1. These were all nice classes to teach. There was a variety of upper level classes as well as some basic classes that required very little planning. I was looking forward to this schedule and working with such a wide variety of students. On the other hand, I also had the option of taking all my savings and putting it toward the tuition for a graduate program at Georgetown University. I loved teaching, but I felt a strong desire to get a master's degree in statistics, computer science, or perhaps both. I also had an interest in getting involved with some aspect of the government, and Georgetown did have some courses in governmental studies. Unfortunately, I had only two days to decide what to do—graduate school or back to teaching the following school year, which began at the end of August. If I chose to continue another year of teaching, I had to sign my contract by Monday. If I wanted to go to graduate school, I had to send payment the very next day or risk losing my spot. I double-checked my finances and verified that the tuition would cost me my entire savings.

It was a Friday night, and Diane Fisher asked me to come over to her apartment. She planned to cook dinner for the two of us, and she hoped we would watch a movie and talk. For some reason, I decided to stay home alone and think about what I should do for the following year and my long-term future. She took it as a sign that I was not interested in including her in any of my important decisions. Our relationship was never the same after that, and we officially broke up a few weeks later. Coincidentally, that also happened to be right around the time when I told her what transpired with a student Heather Thompson from the previous year. And I didn't even tell her everything; I just didn't have the nerve to make known to her all of the details. In a way, I was sorry that it did not work out with Diane. On the other hand, graduate school was where I met Sally, and my life would not be the same if it were not for her.

Back then, it was usually not a high priority for me to think and reflect on anything that I needed to make a decision about. Then again, for some reason this time, I felt the urge to reflect seriously as I stayed at home alone and read the Bible. I thought deeply about what I should do with the next phase of my life. I certainly had a lot of fond memories of teaching. I loved the people, the students, and all my colleagues. The following year, I would also have had the opportunity to take on the role as school treasurer. This position took the place of lunch duty and study hall duty. It required that I keep track of all club and activity accounts for the entire school. The role also included keeping tabs of all bills and accounts for the athletic department, which was headed by my friend Lou Monahan. He assured me that being the school's treasurer was not that difficult, and he would help me learn the ropes. After all, most of the other accounts in the school that would be under my jurisdiction were minor. For example, the math club had about eight hundred dollars in their account for sweatshirts, calculators, and that sort of thing. The Foreign Language Honor Society had $1,200 for various activities and international parties held at the end of the year. There were about ten accounts all together. Understandably, the athletic director, Lou Monahan, had control over a great deal of the money; and for most years, it was a total of about 1.2 million dollars. I would need to record all transactions and account for all the money during the course of the year. It would actually be fun working with Lou during my free periods, and I wouldn't be saddled with lunch duty where I would have to monitor the eating habits of uncouth adolescence. Lou was one of the nicest guys I ever knew. He was sincere, sharp, and funny. If anyone had a conversation with Lou whether it was for thirty minutes or for thirty seconds, you could be sure that three things would happen. Guaranteed. He would bust your horns, he would make you laugh, and you would walk away feeling better about yourself than before. He was a marvelous, special man.

On the other hand, I really wanted to go back to Georgetown. I had a feeling that I had some "unfinished business" there waiting for me. That's what I really hoped to do. I also enjoyed teaching, and I felt that I would truly be able to positively contribute to the school and make a difference in many lives over the years. I had a real connection with numerous students as well as many of the other faculty members. Once again, I drifted in and out of consciousness. I was sitting up on a reclining chair. As I reflected, I vividly remembered a conversation that I had with a science teacher Steve Jordan.

I was alone in the teacher's lounge, reaching into my front pocket for a tissue, and I was having a little trouble getting my hand out because of the mess in there. I also kept my watch in my pocket as well as a few pieces of chalk, cough drops, and other teaching necessities. Steve walked in, and seeing my hand fumbling around in my pocket couldn't resist the temptation to ask, "Tom, what are you doing down there, playing a game of pocket pool?"

"No, Steve," I quickly retorted back. "I was reaching for a tissue. My allergies are bothering me something fierce today."

"That's okay, Tom. You *are* allowed to play a harmless game of pocket pool once in a while. As long as you don't decide to play any *away* games." Then he started laughing. He was quite the comedian, and as Billy Joel would have said, "He was quick with a joke or a light up your smoke." Well, Steve was also a lot of fun at parties, so I liked to use the line, "He was good for a laugh or to share a carafe."

Ironically, Steve could also be serious and reflective at times. Steve approached me on more than one occasion and asked me something to the effect, "Tom, why are you always so cheerful and enthused? You really seem to like coming to work everyday. Aren't you merely on step two of the salary guide? What do you make?"

"I make a difference, Steve!" I replied. "For me, teaching is an awesome profession, an opportunity to have a positive impact on the lives of young people. The high school years can be a very trying time for teens. I had my own share of ups and downs during my high school days, and I always appreciated having someone that I could relate to and talk to."

"Oh, let me get out the violins, Tom," he replied facetiously.

Try to understand this about Steve. He was very knowledgeable, intelligent, and had a captivating personality. Then again, he was a cynic. Someone once claimed that he overheard Steve respond to a question at a party, and the dialogue went something like this.

"Steve, I understand that you are a teacher. What do you teach?"

To which Steve immediately replied, "Animals...I mean kids!"

Steve simply didn't get it.

"Sorry, Steve, but that *is* how I feel. That's how it is for me."

"You huckleberry!" he bellowed. "Well, here's how it is for *me*. My five classes are a nightmare. Teaching chemistry is like pulling teeth. And earth science? I'd rather dig a ditch than to deal with some of the jimbonies that I have to teach."

"Well, Steve, I'm sorry that you feel that way," I said sympathetically. "Why did you go into teaching in the first place?"

"I went into teaching for two reasons."

"And what were they?" I asked reluctantly.

"July and August!" He smiled.

"To each his own." That was the only comeback that I could muster. He had me on the ropes.

Steve continued, "Tom, for me, teaching is like performing a series of five one-act plays in front of a hostile audience, for very little pay."

It was too bad that Steve was having difficulty appreciating his teaching career. He made it clear that he was looking forward to retiring in a few years anyway. The way he put it, "I put in my time. All I have is three years left. I hate working with these teenaged lunatics. They simply have no idea of what to do."

"Steve," I reasoned, "there wouldn't be any need for us teachers if kids always knew the right thing to do. We would *all* be out of a job!"

I then snapped back to reality. I was getting lost in thought, probably because it was such unfamiliar territory for me. Usually, things came natural for me especially with important decisions. I usually didn't need to think my way through it this much.

And what about the money? I thought. Going back to graduate school would prove to be a very expensive endeavor. It would cost almost every penny that I had saved over the course of the past two years, and then some. I was reluctant to use the fact that I didn't want to spend all my hard-earned money from the past two years of teaching to be the sole factor in deciding what I should do. I took a break for a few moments. I reopened the Bible, and I found my answer. It was right there in front of me. "No one can serve two masters. Either you will hate the one and love the other, or you will be devoted to the one and despise the other. You cannot serve both God and money" (Matthew 6:24).

Therefore, I chose to leave the teaching profession and pay for the graduate program at Georgetown University. At that point in time, I was officially "broke."

All I had to do was change that one decision and "ask Max" what would have happened if I had accepted the contract offered me in teaching. Max was able to reconstruct the past and supply as much detail as I requested. In the new scenario, I would have stayed in teaching all these years, and I never would have gone to graduate school at Georgetown. Instead, I would have waited a few years to get a master's degree in mathematics education at George Washington University. The problem was that I often made these types of changes, and some nights I took hours and hours to read everything that Max indicated would have happened in the altered scenarios. I was able to get Max to supply so many details regarding how my life would have played out that it was astonishing. I usually fell asleep thinking about and dreaming about what my life would have been like, and these dreams seemed so real. Years of my life played out in exquisite, dramatic detail, consistent to the narrative that Max generously supplied. Furthermore, when I woke up, I could remember so much of what happened in the dream, including how I felt.

Sadly, I could not leave well enough alone. I had to find out more about what would have happened if I stayed in teaching. I discovered that I would not have had the positive influence of such a caring, special person, namely Sally. It turns out that I would have gone on to become the school treasurer for five years, and there would be a slight problem with some of the records that I had been keeping. Well, saying there was a *slight* problem was like saying that the Washington Monument was a pedestrian landmark.

Here is what would have happened. I hate to refer to it that way. Here is what might possibly have happened according to Max.

One day, when working with Lou Monahan, the athletic director, I realized that as treasurer, I could tap into the school's athletic account and easily modify his records. At first, it was merely a thought that raced through my mind for a split second. Then I gave it a little more consideration and the idea seemed to take hold. I realized that if I altered his account a little at a time for the entire year, I would be sitting on a pretty good amount of money. The athletic director's budget was slightly more than one million dollars since he was in charge of all referee fees, coaches salaries, all sports equipment, and the upkeep of all gymnasiums and fields for the entire district. If I helped myself to a mere one hundred dollars each week, by the end of the school year, I would have made an extra $3,600, and no one would ever notice the missing money. In fact, this would have continued for a total of five years before anyone detected anything. I would have actually increased the amount of money that I earned (I hate to use the word embezzled) to about two hundred dollars per week. At the end of five years, I would have accumulated over thirty thousand dollars! Not only that, I covered it up so well that the district's business administrator took a full five years to eventually realize what had happened; however, it was Lou who had to mistakenly take the blame. Lou would have been fired, made to pay back the money, and gone to jail for eighteen months. How could I have let this happen? This simply wasn't me; but according to old reliable Max, it definitely would have happened. I woke up in trepidation, in a cold sweat, and I wondered not only how Max could declare these types of things but also why it affected me so greatly. I went back to sleep just to get the awful feeling out of my head. I first had Max play out something different, just so I would forget about the terrible nightmare about the school treasurer turned corrupt.

In contrast, there were times when my life worked out quite well, even though it invariably played out much differently based on the changes that I fed the computer. For example, there was the time I asked Max what would have happened if I actually stayed with the music that I loved as a child. I played the alto saxophone, and it was a passion of mine for two years. If I would have stayed with the alto sax another year or so, I would have joined a band when I was seventeen years old. I know it seems propitious and far-fetched, but our band would have eventually gotten a record contract. We would have been world famous, and

I could read about many of the astonishing details. How could I not be drawn to this captivating device that allowed me to practically relive so many intriguing scenarios?

THE FIVE-DOLLAR BILL

My interest returned back to my days at Georgetown. I finally let Max help me to remember everything that actually happened. It was a few weeks before the end of my second semester of graduate school. I remember Mei Lee sending me a note, informing me that she was going to forgo her last two semesters of graduate school and go to a medical school in California. There was a special program that incorporated the latest advances in medicine and alternative treatments that she was determined to pursue. She told me how much she admired me, and that she wished it would have worked out between us. She clearly would not enjoy seeing me spend more and more time with a certain freshman education major that I was beginning to grow very fond of. Mei was very perceptive, and she must have realized that even though Sally and I were just friends at the time, things would work out nicely for us. Sally and I were married four years later, and the rest is history. The real history. I felt badly for Mei. I had always hoped that everything turned out well for her, and that she found success and happiness in the medical field as a homeopathic physician.

That night at dinner, my mind wandered as Sally told me and April the story of Manual Cruz who was in Sally's second grade special education class last year. The progress that Manny made since the beginning of that school year was truly inspiring. He could not even read at the beginning of the year, and now his case manager was considering having him declassified. As Manny entered class one day last year with only two weeks remaining in the school year, he was dragging his backpack, looking listless and dejected.

Sally asked compassionately, "What's wrong, Manny? Why the long face?"

"Mrs. Russo, this could be the saddest day of my life," Manny said in earnest. He was clearly broken up about something.

"Why, Manny? Do you want to talk about it?"

"I just found out that after this year, I won't have you as a teacher any more. Oh, what a terrible thing."

Sally choked back a tear while she reassured Manny that she was so proud of how well he had done since the beginning of the year. Sally worked with Manny for thirty minutes every day during lunch. Equally as important, Sally always showed Manny that she cared about him. Manny's home life was not pleasant at all. His parents were divorced, and he sometimes didn't even know where he would be staying on any given weekend. "Next year, you can still stop by after school and visit me often. You can even show some of my students how to read! You have become a terrific reader, and I would love to see you help others who might benefit from your excellent reading ability." This all reassured Manny and made him happy. He beamed as Sally continually spoke words of encouragement to him, giving him more and more confidence.

My mind continued to drift, and I wondered if Max had a way to access every written article, every document that was known to man, every principle of psychology, and every mathematical rule. If it could process all of that along with every law of chemistry, physics, and human nature, it might explain at least partially what was going on. The storage capacity as well as the processing capability of Max were two of its unbelievable features. I was still confident that if I didn't physically break down, I would somehow be able to piece it all together. I also concluded that it was taking too much time. I hated to admit it, but Jack and Mr. M were right. I needed to hasten the pace. Unfortunately, I allowed myself to be distracted by playing out various scenarios that Max was so willing and able to supply. Discovering how my life would have turned out was intriguing, but I was spending too much time and energy on that and it was preventing me from making substantial progress.

I certainly didn't need a computer to tell me that how we treat others in our lifetime as well as the decisions that we make certainly do have a profound effect on our lives.

The next day, I played out a scenario based on an encounter I had with a homeless man years ago. I wanted to help him, but all I really did was give him a five-dollar bill, which I suspected he ended up using for a bottle of wine. I asked the man his name and then practically threw the money at him as I scurried away to my first job interview out of graduate school. Ironically, I have come to know him well within the past year or so, and I have become friends with him lately. The man was Henry Davis, a marine veteran from the first war in Iraq. I figured out a way to ask Max what would have happened if I would have shown Hank some real compassion back then. What if I would have taken him home, cooked him a meal, and shown some real interest in him? I wasn't the least bit surprised that Max was again bold in its predictions. It reported the rest of the story as if it actually happened, again with confidence and certainty. According to Max, if I would have taken Henry home to my apartment and given him some clothes and cleaned him up, that would have been the turning point in his life. Through Max, I also found out his entire history and the story of how he originally enlisted in the marines years ago. He did two tours of duty and worked his way up to captain. In fact, Henry Davis was a pilot who was responsible for flying troops out of danger zones and piloting planes that supplied food for US soldiers and many of the refugees. He even won the Purple Heart for bravery, flying over enemy lines under fire on many occasions to bring wounded soldiers to safety.

Unfortunately, after the war, times were tough for some veterans returning home from this controversial war. In fact, Hank Davis was a mess. He had a severe case of Gulf War Syndrome due to exposure to depleted uranium and serin gas during his tenure in the Middle East. He had a variety of ailments, and he ended up jobless, homeless, and penniless. Hank was in this pathetic state for a total of three years, but if I would have befriended him, that would have given him some hope. He would have been motivated to get his commercial pilot license and work for a passenger airline in the States. He would have worked his way up from piloting planes that delivered freight to go on and become a highly accomplished commercial airline pilot. Max claimed that one day, Hank would be flying a plane to Chicago that needed to make an emergency landing. The engine trouble was very similar to something he encountered in Iraq in the war. Back then, he had to make an emergency landing in the desert while piloting a C-141 Starlifter cargo plane, and he saved the lives of 113 American soldiers. This time, however, he would have been flying a plane that held 250 passengers, all civilians. Among them would have been my sister Katherine. Henry Davis's experience and clear thinking would have landed the plane safely. According to Max, no one else would have had the presence of mind to land the plane on a field adjacent to a nearby highway. In fact, if Hank had been the pilot, not a single person would have been injured, and my sister would still be alive today.

The moral of the story—a little bit of kindness can go a long way. The only problem is that in reality, it did not happen that way. Someone else was flying the plane when that ill-fated airline disaster occurred. Hank Davis did not get rehabilitated and go on to use his expertise acquired in the military to save lives. I failed to show a real interest in him beyond giving him a meaningless five-dollar bill. And my sister was still dead. I was feeling pain and guilt similar to how I felt seven years ago when Kate's plane did go down.

This clearly showed me a very real example of something that I had to come to grips with. Every action we do or fail to do has an impact on our lives, as well as the lives of others, sometimes many others. I could have helped to prevent the terrible tragedy of my sister's death without even knowing it at the time. Years ago, I was upset only because I thought that if I began my work with the Chicago air traffic controllers sooner, it might have prevented the plane crash there. After all, most of the blame was focused on the fact that the air traffic controllers never suggested landing in a nearby field. Now I concluded that I surely would have changed history if I actually showed a homeless man an act of kindness that was meaningful and genuine. The emotions I felt were taking a serious toll on me, and I was developing a sort of antipathy toward Max. This is exactly what I did not want to happen, but I again realized that we learn much more from our failures. Hence, I am a huge fan of second chances.

Ironically, about a year ago, I was reintroduced to Hank Davis at the racetrack through some friends there. I was determined to take an interest in him and show some *real* compassion. Unfortunately, I also knew it might have been a case of too little, too late, like closing the barn door after the horse already escaped.

These days, whenever I went to the track, I was confident that Max wouldn't let me down. I brought three hundred dollars, some of the winnings of my previous jaunt. Talk about playing with house money. I liked to call it playing with "horse" money. I realized that I wasn't only enjoying my time at the track for the extra money that I was gaining; it was also because I loved seeing my friends Louie, Tony G, and Pete. They all hung around the track so often one would think they worked there. Still, whenever I saw them, they provided a certain level of comfort for me. Louie and Pete were retired and now had all the free time in the world while Tony Giordano probably never had a real job in his life. It was a little odd, perhaps even scary that I considered them among my best friends. We talked a little about horse racing and Langley, but more importantly, they were always willing to listen when I had a great deal on my mind to unload. They all knew about my sister passing away, and they tried to help me to steer Henry Davis on the right track. After all, they were the ones who formally introduced me to him a year ago. Of course, I didn't share with them the surreal saga of Hank including the potential comeback that Max revealed could have happened. They did know about Hank's demise and how depressing things were for him at his lowest point a few years ago. They could certainly relate to Hank's plight after his military service since Louie and Pete were both also in the armed forces many years ago. (Even though the only "action" they ever saw was when they were on official leave.) Years ago, they were the ones who convinced Hank to get to the Washington, DC VA Medical Center where he could receive desperately needed and deserved treatment for his many symptoms related to Gulf War Syndrome. I constantly worked with Hank to improve his self-image by reminding him of all the positive things he did throughout his lifetime, and I tried to convince him that there were sure to be many more opportunities for success and happiness.

"Hey, weren't you here already this week?" Louie shouted as I tried to make my first wager.

"No, you must have me mistaken for my brother. I haven't been here for two weeks." So I lied. I started to remember that I was there twice already this week. I guess I needed this place more than I cared to admit…just to clear my head.

"Who's looking good today?" Louie asked eagerly. "You've been on a heck of a roll recently. Are you sure you are on the up and up? Maybe you got your CIA pals to take care of some of the jockeys."

"Keep it down. I'm not supposed to be here," I pleaded.

"That never stopped you before! I'll only keep it down if you tell me who looks good in the first race. You must have *some* connections lately!"

"That's the way lady luck dances. You didn't see me two weeks ago when I lost a couple of yards. No, stay away from me. I'm due for another losing streak."

Then Tony G walked over to us and the stale, powerful smell of his old cigar overtook me. Dutch Masters Corona. I could tell that foul scent anywhere. I started coughing for a full minute, and I almost didn't get my wager down in time.

Tony bellowed, "What are you doing over here at the fifty-dollar window? Your old lady will kill you if she saw you there." He started laughing hysterically, and he almost choked on the smoke of his own cigar. We called him Talking Tony for obvious reasons.

I didn't even notice Pete at first, but he came over and shook my hand. "Long time no see, you bum."

"Yeah, since yesterday," Tony joked. He wasn't that far off. In all seriousness, I couldn't distinguish the times I went to the track any more. Days seemed to be blending in together.

Pete added, "Hey, Tommy, are you sure your old lady knows you're here? You better check your cell phone. Remember that time when she was looking for you and she left you four or five messages?" Then he made his voice go high in mockery. "Thomas Russo, you better get your butt home right away. You have chores to do around the house."

Just then, the smell of beer filled the air even before Hank came over with a huge cup that overflowed with froth. I shuttered to think that his lowlife "friends" probably bought it for him. I thought Hank was wise enough not to spend the little money that he had on a frosty cold beer when he could be using it to get further out of the financial mess he was still in. Among the sweet aroma of beer was mixed the delightfully fresh grass scent and clean, crisp air. I suddenly detected the foul, pungent odor of horse manure that seemed to smother all the other enjoyable scents. It was right about then when I realized I had to get out of there. Who were these people? More importantly, who was I? I was working on something that could actually be vital this time, and I was wasting my time with a bunch of…I couldn't bring myself to say it. They were good people; I was the one who was falling apart and missing what's important. Hank Davis seemed to be looking over to the bleachers where his other friends hung out. Hank finally looked well, and he was on the right path. Who knows for how long? Not long ago, he seemed to be getting a little too close to some of the real shady characters at the racetrack. I knew that sort of thing couldn't be good for him. There were four guys in particular who were big gamblers, and they were lobbying to get Hank to join them and do some work for *their* boss putting money out on the streets. The man they worked for was a notorious loan shark who also took numbers and racing bets on the side. I tried to steer Hank away from all that, and he convinced me that he wasn't stupid enough to get caught in their trap even though he met their boss on several occasions. It was frightening to think that at one point, Hank was close to working with them. One time, I came right out and gave him a piece of advice that I remembered from my father. "Hank, when you lie down with dogs, you wake up with fleas." I was hopeful that he knew exactly what I meant.

"Hey, look who's here," Hank hollered enthusiastically as he approached me. He was wearing a crooked grin that showed a couple of teeth missing. "Are you here to pick us a winner? I hear you've been cleaning up lately. Who's giving you tips? This guy named Max, the one I've been hearing you mention on the cell phone all the time? Were you here the other day?"

Pete suddenly stepped in and added, collaborating Hank's claim, "If you *were* here, you could have at least stopped by and said hi, Mr. Big Shot."

I awkwardly retorted, "Come on, guys, give me a break. I didn't come here to take abuse. I could have stayed home and gotten it."

They laughed, and we walked down to the finish line to get a better view of the first race that just began. Hank was a little more chatty than usual, and he kept asking me about the assignment that I was currently working on. I usually shared my stories of space exploration, climate change, and other topics; but this time, the more I insisted that I was not able to share much with him and the others, the more Hank kept pressing me to tell him some of the details. The first race was actually pretty close, and this acted as a minor diversion for a few minutes. In fact, when it was over, I pretended that I didn't win; and to be more convincing, I threw down an old racing ticket that I still had in my jacket pocket from a few months earlier, before I found my foolproof system for picking winners. I had to wait around for a while because I bet a ton of money on the Daily Double. As soon as my horse won the second race, I decided that I would collect my winnings and take off. I vowed to stay away from this place for good. Unless of course, they were true to their word and eventually put in slots. Bringing in those one armed bandits would definitely be a game changer.

While we waited, I told the guys a few jokes and had them practically going in their pants. As soon as I saw my second horse come in, I pretended to lose for the second time, told them I was already out of money, and said that Sally was looking for me. *That* they could believe. That's when I handed Tony my racing form that had the winners to the remaining races, according to the remarkable perception of Max. I lied and told the boys I would see them next week. I looked at Hank one last time. For me, he was quite a reminder of my sister Kate. Hank Davis had no idea that Max predicted his life would have turned out so very differently if only I showed him some real compassion years ago. Even now, Hank's life was only a few notches above the pitiful state that it was in when I first met him. At least now he had a place to live. Still, he bounced around from job to job and at the end of the day, usually ended up at the track where we invariably found him scrounging for a horse racing tip that would once again, "turn his life around." Up until today, the only real tips I ever gave him were to trust in God and to stick with one job even if it only paid a little above minimum wage. I also suggested that he work at the gas station as a mechanic since he was always handy with cars.

"Keep busy, Hank. That's the key. An idle mind is the devil's workshop," I often told him.

All in all, I helped Hank to get on the right path; and in return, he unknowingly helped to guide my own sense of right and wrong. I often used my dealings with Hank to determine if I was truly conscientious and compassionate. I tried to walk away once and for all, but Hank couldn't seem to be able to let go of my sleeve. Hank seemed to want to tell me something, but I really needed to go. I was now determined to make that day one Hank and the boys would remember for a long time. I temporarily stopped trying to get Hank to release the sleeve of my jacket, and I spoke quietly to him, "Hank, remember that God always gives you another chance."

"Are you sure?" He wanted some sort of guarantee.

"Absolutely. You'll see. Do you have any money on you?"

"No." He sounded discouraged as he held up his beer. "I just spent my last few dollars."

"Take this five-dollar bill. It will be enough. I won't see you for a while."

As I began walking toward the exit, with Hank now a few feet from me, I called back to Tony, Pete, and Louie, "Oh, hey guys, I just remembered a good horse in the seventh race if you're still here." Suddenly, I noticed the seedy foursome, Hank's pseudo-friends who were originally standing about fifty feet away in their own private area. They were creeping a little closer. Their heads lifted a little as they were drinking beer, throwing down their losing tickets from the last race, and scouring their racing programs for their next wager.

"What is it?" the boys all asked in unison, checking their programs frantically. "What horse are you talking about?"

I replied, "It's called *Toilet Seat*." They continued pouring over the program for a few seconds, still believing me. "Put all you can on it," I shouted back as I hurried to a window around the corner where they wouldn't be able to see me collect my winnings, about four thousand dollars. I could have stayed longer and parlayed that money into a whole lot more. Instead, I knew I had to get out of this place. I needed this lifestyle like a moose needs a hat rack. I also yelled back to the boys, "Take a good look at the program I gave to Tony. Make sure that Hank gets part of the action. Bet on those circled horses and consider that my going away present to you all, in case I don't see you for awhile." Hank was still only ten feet away from me, so I softly spoke to him, "Go with God, Hank."

The boys all looked dumbfounded, and even Tony was speechless. They noticed that in the program, I circled all the winners for races three through seven as well as two trifectas for the eighth and ninth races. Hopefully, they would all stay until the end. By then, if they followed the program, they surely would have been convinced that somehow my selections were all valid, and that every one of the picks were winners. By the eighth race, they should have amassed a boatload of cash, and they would probably be ready to trust putting all or most of their money on those two high-paying trifectas. Hopefully, this time, the five dollars that I gave to Hank would actually do him some good; mostly because included with it were my best wishes, kindness, and compassion.

I hoped that I would be able to check on them in a few weeks as I assumed that by then, everything would calm down with my own hectic life. I knew that I would miss all of them in the meantime, especially Hank. At this point, I saw Hank as someone who reminded me of my own disinterest and lack of compassion from years ago. I was determined to learn from that experience and to never let it happen again. Maybe in some way, this would help to make it right; hopefully, it would at least show Hank that someone really did care about him. Right now, however, my moral compass was guiding me toward the exit and far away from this place. I realized that deceiving Sally about coming here so often was not what I was all about. I also knew that some things in my life would have to change from now on.

The next day, Jack Russell contacted me on my cell phone. Fortunately, I wasn't at the racetrack "cleaning up" when I spoke to him. I was losing track of my conversations with him as they were usually so brief and inconsequential. Sometimes he sounded calm and relaxed as if he was talking to me from a tropical island without a care in the world, but other times, he was quick, abrupt, and distant. When he unexpectedly asked me if I had been to the Laurel Park Racetrack, I was worried that he was on to me. If I admitted using Max for wagering, I am sure that he would excoriate my indiscretion.

"Are you kidding me?" I shouted over the phone. "I have been working eighteen hours every day. I need to take a couple of days off and spend some time with my family otherwise I'm in danger of losing them."

"That's not exactly *my* problem. Just tell them that you are working on something top secret for the government. I am sure they trust you." Jack was quite direct when he wanted to be, or *had* to be. He continued, "I have a certain protocol that I have to follow and important people to answer to. I tried to warn you right from the beginning! I am hearing rumblings from the NSA and the FBI, and if they find out about any of this, they will surely want to get involved. And we *can't* let that happen."

I honestly had no idea what Jack was alluding to. I *was* surprised that we weren't working with the NSA on this from the beginning. In any event, I decided that there was no way I could be forthright with him or Mr. M until I figured this all out. If they knew exactly what was going on, and I mean *everything*, this project would surely be classified as top secret; and without a doubt, I would be "relieved of my duties." Now more than ever, I could not let that happen. I desperately wanted to see this to the end.

EATING LIKE A PIG

It was Sunday, and I was looking forward to going out to dinner with my mom, my two brothers, and Dave's wife, Sophia. My mom was eighty-one years old and still going strong. She has lived alone for the past five years ever since my dad died from cancer. My older brother Johnny had no children of his own, but April and Dave's children, Hannah and Benjamin, certainly had a great affection for their Uncle Johnny. Benjamin was seven years old, and Hannah was nine. On this particular night, Hannah did not join us because she had committed to a sleepover at her best friend's house. April was disappointed that she didn't have her cousin to pal around with at dinner and share secrets like they usually did.

We were running a little late, and I hated it when we were the last ones to arrive at the restaurant. With everything that was going on, I was not in the mood to be harassed by my brothers even if it was all in fun. I was looking forward to getting away from it all for a few hours and starting out fresh in the morning. In fact, I was so busy with Max that entire day. I forgot to eat breakfast or lunch, and I was now literally famished. I was definitely in desperate need of a good meal, and we were going to the perfect place. I just didn't want to be late.

"April, please hurry," I called up to her room. "We should have left five minutes ago."

"I'm coming, Dad. Just a minute, I'm almost ready. Oh, by the way, what should I wear?"

"I thought you were dressed already." I was getting a little angry now. That was not typical of my demeanor. I tried not to sweat the small stuff. We were going to a fancy Italian restaurant, so I hoped that April knew she had to dress accordingly. "Wear something nice." I was hoping that she would come down from her room wearing a nice dress or at least a skirt. No such luck.

April came down a few minutes later wearing torn jeans and a tee shirt that had a stain on it. I was livid. "April, you've got to be kidding me. Go back up there and get changed. We are going to be late. Put something on that is *nice*! We are going to a fancy restaurant. Grandma will be there, and she doesn't want to see you dressed in *that*!"

April calmly went back upstairs. I'm not sure if she even noticed the tone of my voice. I rarely had to raise my voice with her, and I was surprised at how loud my voice could elevate. She came back down about two minutes later wearing an old sweatshirt that said, "Phelps Phan," referring to Michael Phelps, the record-setting swimmer. The shirt was a little torn, but at least it didn't have any stains. It still would not do.

"April, we are going to a classy place." I annunciated each word carefully and loudly for effect. "You are making us late. Go put something on that is nice!" It was not easy to hide the fact that I was irate now. I was ashamed that I was not quite myself, and I couldn't understand why I was so unusually petulant.

Now April stormed upstairs, probably wondering who abducted her dad and replaced him with this imposter. At least she did come down in less than a minute this time wearing an old tee shirt that I had given her years ago. It didn't even fit properly. This time, I didn't care. The tee shirt read, "I Have the World's Greatest Dad."

"Now that's more like it, April!" I announced. "That's a perfect selection."

It took that to snap me back to my old self, at least for a while. Fortunately, we arrived only a few minutes after all the others got to the restaurant. When I first saw Johnny, I noticed that he was wearing a beautiful gold Rolex watch. It was quite stylish, and I was surprised since he usually was not at all pretentious in what he did or wore. "Nice country, America!" I shouted to him as I pointed to his left wrist. He shrugged it off and pointed to the gray hair on the top of my head. Every time he saw me, it must have seemed that I was getting a little grayer on top.

"They have something for that," he quipped. "On the other hand, it's better that your hair is turning gray. It could be worse. It could be like mine and turning *loose*."

"Come on," I said as we took our usual places at the table. "Are we here to mangia or to break each others' *cogliones*?"

"Now stop that kind of talk," Mom quickly interceded. "Let's not have that language in front of the kids."

Whenever my brothers and I got together, we always had a good time. The kidding came early, and we often recalled stories of our youth growing up in Virginia. Even though we lived our own separate lives, we had an inextricable bond that never seemed to fade. Unfortunately, we are all so busy with work, and our own families that we only saw each other all together once every month or two. Sometimes we met at our mom's house, kept her company, and filled her in on what was going on with our lives. It was also gratifying when we took her out for a nice meal every so often.

My older brother Johnny was a very prominent attorney. He worked in Washington, DC for the government as a consultant and virtually called his own shots. He had many friends and many noteworthy accomplishments. Years ago, he was the lead attorney for the prosecution as he and his team tried the very first homicide case in the nation that relied on DNA evidence as the main source of testimony. Johnny spent days convincing the jury of the scientific validity of DNA evidence. Today we take this type of forensic evidence totally for granted since it is so commonly used and known to be valid. Years ago, DNA evidence was so new that the jury had to be properly instructed in the science of DNA. From time to time, Johnny was put in charge of many special assignments for certain agencies of the government, including the CIA. In fact, some of these were top secret. As he put it, "I could tell you what I'm working on, but then I would have to neuralyze you." Not very original, but Johnny certainly did know many important people had a lot of connections and had a stellar work ethic. Senators and congressmen often sought his advice and legal interpretations before they made a move. Moreover, Johnny had unparalleled charisma. He was the type of person who might be in the process of being run out of town by an angry mob, but he could make it look as if he was simply leading a parade. Now that's class.

Now, if Johnny was all finesse, my younger brother Dave was "brute force." First of all, he had a no-nonsense look that projected confidence and poise. And when April asked me, "Dad, what does it mean when you say Uncle Dave is like a horse?"

I simply replied in all honesty, "It means that he's strong... strong like bull." He did work his way through college as a bouncer. He broke up a lot of fights, and he broke some noses along the way. He worked out with weights ever since he was a teenager, and to put it bluntly, he now has muscles in places that most people don't even *have* places.

Dave earned an MBA and had a lot of impressive jobs over the years in various aspects of financial services. His philosophy was to always take the direct approach. "Tell it like it is and let the chips fall where they may." He would have had some terrific ideas regarding dealing with Jack and my overwhelming task of figuring out Max, but I decided not to reveal my dilemma. Dave's wife, Sophia, was a registered nurse, and she fit in with us extremely well. She was generally happy-go-lucky but very serious when it came to her kids and their school work.

As I smelled the food from the various tables in the restaurant, I was like a pavlovian dog, saliva literally dripped down from the side of my mouth in anticipation. I quickly took out a tissue from my pocket and wiped my mouth before anyone noticed. While the others were looking over the wine list, I interrogated Benjamin about his favorite subject. I always tried to force Ben to admit that his favorite subject was math, and I threatened to get some math worksheets from the car for him to work on while we waited for dinner. For some strange reason, he preferred to play with a handheld electronic game that he brought along. While the others were ordering drinks and appetizers, I reached across the table and grabbed his upper arm and shoulder. Although Ben was barely seven years old, he clearly had powerful arms, shoulders, and upper body strength. He surely was going to be incredibly strong just like his old man, Dave. After I let go of his arm, I couldn't miss the chance to ask him a few challenging brainteasers while April was catching up with her aunt Sophie and grandma about her time in school.

I remembered a few riddles, and I tested them out on Benjamin who was a super kid, and he was certainly bright and creative. For now, sports were his thing, and he played soccer all year long as well as basketball in the winter and baseball in the spring, often juggling two sports effectively each season. On the other hand, Ben was no match for my riddles. Not too many seven-year-olds are.

"Hey, Benjamin, what occurs once in a minute, twice in a moment, but never in one thousand years?"

"I don't know, Uncle Tom," he quickly responded, hoping that I would give him the answer immediately so he could get back to his game.

April turned away for a second from her own conversation and said, "The letter M," then went right back to grandma, and continued telling her about her latest stellar report card.

I had to take a few minutes to explain the answer to Ben. I continued harassing the poor kid, and I couldn't leave well enough alone. I asked him another riddle.

"Ben, when does *Thursday* come before *Wednesday*?"

Ben put his head down for a few seconds, clearly thinking. He seemed to be in some sort of a trance. When he looked up, his eyes were wide open, and he didn't blink for what seemed like a minute.

"Come on, Ben, you know this one," his mom encouraged. "Think of the words."

After another minute or so, he caught on and proudly responded, "In the dictionary."

"Nice going!" I exclaimed. "Good job!"

I persisted, "Okay, Ben, try this one. What is more evil than the devil, more powerful than God? Poor people have it, but rich people need it."

This time, Benjamin didn't have a clue, so now, Dave interrupted his conversation with Johnny and announced in a rather perturbed voice, "Nothing!" I wasn't sure if Dave was more upset about how his conversation with Johnny was heading or by the fact that I was hitting Ben with some difficult riddles, so I changed the line of questioning to a "lighter" sort.

"Now, Ben, I have another one for you. Where does the *finger* go on vacation?" I pointed my right index finger toward him and gently poked him with it. He still didn't know the answer.

"To the Poconos," I said as I poked his nose.

Dave looked over at us with a scowl that he is famous for, and Johnny merely rolled his eyes. Just then, Dave closed his hand and let it drop nonchalantly and gently to the table. So much for gently. His subtle tap made the entire table shake, and the wine glasses tremble with fear. That was the end of my riddles for the night.

It turned out that Dave and Johnny were discussing a real estate venture that they were considering going in on together. They would have tried to include me, but they knew that lately I couldn't be bothered with that sort of investment. The last two deals they made together barely turned a profit, and I had other things on my mind, "bigger fish to fry" as I once put it to them. Johnny must have been a little reluctant to shell out his hard earned cash this time. "Last time you got me into this sort of mess, it was supposed to be a *flip*, but it turned out to be a *flop*. No thanks," Johnny said in all seriousness.

Dave countered with, "But that's because we should have stayed with it for the long haul. We would be sitting on a profit right now if we stayed with it."

"No thanks. Not this time," Johnny insisted.

Dave seemed extremely confident with this particular venture, and he persisted, using everything in his repertoire. "Come on, you've got to *spend* money in order to *make* money," he emphasized. That line is probably as old as money itself. Dave continued, adding his own little subtle twist, "It takes *money* to make more. Any hesitation will keep you *poor*." *Now that's salesmanship*, I thought. "This is going to be a sure thing!" Dave's voice rose emphatically.

They continued talking for a while, and I proceeded to fool with Benjamin, and I tried to grab his electronic game. I also pretended to fall asleep, and I always got a kick out of how he screamed "Wake up, Uncle Tom!" as if he actually believed that I was sleeping. This was a game we played ever since he was about two years old. The entire restaurant seemed to look our way, and Dave again gave us both the evil eye, so we cooled it for a while.

At that point, Dave must have given up completely with Johnny, and he turned to Mom, interrupting enthusiastically, "Mom, have I got a deal for you!"

Surprisingly, she was on to him and quickly responded, "Sorry, hon, but this ain't *Let's Make a Deal*, and you're not Monty Hall!"

That seemed to quiet Dave for the time being. Fortunately, the appetizers arrived just then, and it was about time. My stomach was growling like a bear after a long winter's hibernation. I wasn't sure where to start since the appetizers all looked and smelled so savory. That was one thing I could always count on whenever I went out with Dave and Johnny; they knew how to order a wide assortment of lip smacking, mouthwatering appetizers that would make it seem like you died and went to heaven. I couldn't decide between the sizzling, fried calamari, the jumbo shrimp broiled in a luscious wine sauce, or the delicious mozzarella and tomatoes that you could dip in olive oil. So I put a few samples of each of them on my plate, and I wolfed down several pieces, one right after the other. I nearly choked on my food, but I simply couldn't help myself since I was famished, and the appetizers were all delightfully succulent.

"Cafone!" I heard someone call out. I couldn't tell if it was Johnny or Dave. They were still wrapped up in their conversation, but every once in a while one or both of them paused to say something relevant to whatever the others at the table were discussing. In this case, one of them apparently couldn't resist the opportunity to comment on the rather large portions of appetizers that I took. I guess I did procure a little more than my share.

"Mangiare come un maile," Dave said under his breath, half kidding I hoped.

How rude, I thought. Rudeness personified. I then realized that I hadn't eaten in almost twenty-four hours.

Dave was still somewhat engaged with Johnny, but the appetizers were going quickly, and they both knew that they wouldn't last too much longer at the rate I was devouring them.

"Hey, that was uncalled for," I responded after I finally swallowed, trying to defend myself. I know my Italian is a little rusty, but I could have sworn that Dave compared me to someone who was "eating like a pig."

Dave temporarily ended his unproductive conversation with Johnny about his guaranteed real estate adventure. "Send me a check by the end of the week, or I will have to make the offer to someone else." He ended with the phrase, "Money talks, everything else walks." That reminded me of another good line that I might try to use on Jack if the checks ceased to get to me for some reason. Fortunately, the checks have been arriving regularly at the end of each week. Even though the money was quite substantial, it was not nearly enough compensation for what I was going through. I would need something more than monetary remuneration to keep me working at the pace I was going. For now, I was determined to enjoy the evening and the appetizers.

Later on, surprisingly, Dave asked about last summer's whitewater rafting trip that I took with Sally, April, and some of our friends. Of course, he heard the story before, so I was pleasantly surprised that for some reason he wanted to hear it again. He probably wanted to take advantage of the opportunity to break my chops one more time and let his son Benjamin hear the story and observe what a "turkey" his Uncle Tom was.

Of course, as with all tales, the story grows and grows every time it is told. (I *have* been known to embellish an event, and I have been cited for rambling on and on about certain incidents that have happened in the past.) "We got to the roughest part of the river. We were in the raft for about three hours already, and we were all sore and exhausted. It was me, Sally, April, and our friends, the Millers, who also had a girl who was about April's age. Sadly, they were about as useful as this salt shaker when it came to paddling and maneuvering the raft. We had to get through one last maze of rocks, and the current was at its strongest at that point. There were a few dozen other rafts nearby, weaving their way through the minefield of boulders, but it was every group for themselves at that point. It took twenty minutes for us to get completely through it all, but we finally made it. At least I thought we did and so did everyone else. Sally was sitting at the very front of the raft when she saw the last rock coming right toward us. She tried to call out to everyone, but her voice was drowned out by the rolling water as well as all of the cheering in the raft from the rest of us. She even tried to stand up to get our attention. Then *wham!* We hit that huge rock, and Sally went flying out of the boat and down into the cold dark water, descending into the jagged rocks below! If she banged her head on the rocks, she could have been seriously injured and swept away by the powerful current. Unfortunately, I never even saw what happened since I was daydreaming at that moment. All I remember is everyone finally paddling like crazy toward Sally where they lifted her up into the raft. Why didn't I help? I was in the back of the raft, and with all of the commotion going on, I made the mistake of standing up so I could see what was going on. I lost my balance, and I fell out of the raft backward. I too could have cracked my head open or got swept away. Down *I* plummeted, but somehow I survived!

"Land the plane already," someone blurted out. It was probably my brother Johnny this time. I finished the story by claiming that I didn't fall out of the raft at all. I tried to sound believable when I claimed to jump in the cold dangerous rapids to save Sally. Not surprisingly, no one was buying it, not even little Benjamin.

This must have been my night because most of the jokes that took place from then on were at my expense. There were comments about my gray hair, comments about my being cheap, including the notion that I still had my confirmation money, and comments about how I dressed. I thought that I could afford to throw in a little humor of my own. Unfortunately, my bizarre sense of humor sometimes got me in trouble at times in the past; but I was among family now, so I was willing to take a chance. Somehow I changed the subject to marriage. When the time was right, I quipped, "You have two choices in life. You can stay single and be miserable, or you can get married and wish that you were dead."

Well, that didn't go over as well as I had planned, and I remember sleeping on the couch that night. I also had to spend some of my hard-earned horse racing winnings on some expensive chocolates for Sally the very next day, but I learned my lesson.

Thankfully, before I got further into even more hot water, Dave interrupted by getting back to my thrift, "Leave him alone. Tommy is a real carefree guy. As long as it's free, he doesn't care."

Even our mom chimed in when my thrifty spending habits were brought up and exclaimed, "He *is* a cheap son of a gun." My own mom. She added, "Sally, does he still hold onto his pennies so tight that Lincoln cries?"

In reality, I sincerely believe that my frugality was unfairly exaggerated. Evidently, no one cared about my opinion. I was just grateful that we could all enjoy each other's company, laugh, and not think about missing our sister Katherine. She was one of the sweetest people I ever knew. Katie was never married though she certainly had a few men very eager to make her a part of their life. She was about five feet ten inches in height, and she had a smile that was made for a glamour magazine. She loved to travel, and when she got the opportunity to work as a stewardess for an airline, she had her dream job, and she never looked back. I missed her so much it was painful, so did everyone else in the family. I actually started getting close to Kate, probably closer than either one of my brothers when I was seventeen years old, and she was only fifteen. When my girlfriend Carla DeFranco died, Kate was the only one that I felt comfortable talking to, and she was better than any counselor or psychiatrist could ever be. Kate prevented me from having a major meltdown back then, and since then we had a special bond. My mom seemed to be in some sort of denial about Kate's passing, and she rarely mentioned her anymore. Whenever we all got together, I was a little disappointed that no one felt compelled to broach the subject unless mom brought her up.

After a while, I couldn't resist taking a few of my own shots at my brother Dave. After all, I remembered stories about him and our younger days growing up that would make everyone laugh and forget about my own shortcomings. If we all helped each other to recall some of the classic stories, we would surely have a blast, all of us except Dave of course. For example, one time when our dad wasn't home, Mom had to call the fire department because Dave got his head stuck in a kitchen chair. There was also the time when Dave, who was known to ask for any type of food on the table even if he didn't like it or know what the heck it was, was told by our aunt Frances, "Dave, you eat with your eyes," and on cue, five-year-old Dave stuffed his roast beef sandwich into his eyes and blinked several times. Of course, Dave's son Benjamin would get a kick out of that and some of the other old stories about his dad. At least it would take away from the pounding that I was receiving.

I jumped in, "Now let me talk about some of the ridiculous things that Dave did when he was growing up."

To which Dave simply responded, "Let's not and say we did!"

"Give me one good reason why I shouldn't?" I asked sarcastically.

Dave sternly replied, "Because if you do, I will put your face in this salad and throw you onto the floor right here in the restaurant!"

I laughed. "I asked you for a *good* reason, not a *great* reason."

Needless to say, I decided to forgo any attempt to bring up stories about Dave as a youth. Instead, I couldn't resist the opportunity to share a story about Mom that just occurred a few weeks ago. This was the first time that we were all together since it happened.

Mom began by telling us what she had for breakfast two Saturdays ago, the day she got pulled over by a police officer for not signaling before a right hand turn. Yes, I know that it's hard to believe that Mom still drives, but she is still a pretty good driver. Well, let's put it this way, she certainly always stays within the speed limit. Why she needed to tell us what she had for breakfast is beyond anyone's logic, even Max I am sure.

She proceeded to tell us how she cleared the oatmeal bowl that she used for breakfast and continued to get herself ready for the day, which included a trip to the grocery store. Mom often tells her stories in excruciating detail. And I thought that *I* was bad and dragged a story on and on. Mom is the classic case of a person who, if you ask them what time it is, you will hear the complete history of the clock including the sundial and hourglass.

Mom finally got to the point where she was wiping a chunk of oatmeal from her seatbelt. "I still can't figure out how that oatmeal got there, and I must have forgotten to signal my upcoming right hand turn. I always use my signals whenever I turn."

"So that's when the fuzz stopped you, Grandma?" Benjamin asked with genuine interest.

"If you mean the police officer, yes, young man," Mom replied.

Johnny quickly interrupted, "I heard this same story from the officer who I happened to know. You might as well continue. By the time you are done, it might be time for us to close the place." He pointed to his Rolex. It *was* getting late, but I didn't care. I was having an enjoyable evening with no worries for a change. Max would have to wait.

Mom continued, "When the officer knocked on the window of the car, I got all nervous. And when he asked to see my license and registration, I got totally flustered. When I opened my pocketbook, everything spilled out, and I do mean everything including all of my pills!"

Mom does have a lot of medications. Pills for high blood pressure, high cholesterol, medicine for her stomach, and of course several antianxiety pills to help her "relax."

"Well, I felt it necessary to explain the purpose of each medication to the officer. I didn't want him to mistakenly get the impression that I was some sort of drug dealer."

Dave quickly responded sarcastically, "Of course, Mom, that was sensible of you."

Mom continued, "The last three pills were Lexapro, Xanax, and Valium, and I like to have all three of these pills on hand just in case..."

These drugs, of course, are classic examples of antidepressants and tranquilizers.

Just then, we realized something. I couldn't believe it. Mom actually wore herself out with the story. She was trying to catch her breath and took a sip of water. It was perfect timing since the main course was beginning to arrive. I acted quickly and finished the story, "After seeing all of these medications, especially the last three antidepressants, the officer replied 'Ma'am, what exactly is it that you are so nervous about?' Mom replied confidently to the officer, 'Not a *darn* thing.'"

I think Dave is still laughing his butt off.

At one point toward the end of the evening, Johnny motioned for me to follow him outside where it was much quieter. Johnny didn't waste any time indicating why he brought me away from the others.

"So, Tom, what's going on with your latest assignment? I heard that you were working with some clandestine computer technology project, and that it is driving you bonkers."

"It's just a real pain. I have no team with me this time, no support, and I have trouble contacting my superiors. The whole thing is extremely vague. Who told you all of this?"

"Mom tells me everything. She said that you hardly call her anymore, and that whenever you do, you are very quick on the phone. That's not like you. And when was the last time you stopped over to her house to see her or to check up on her?"

"It's been a while. I can't even remember."

"You see what I mean. No project is worth it if it makes you lose your priorities and slip back to when…"

"I know, I know, but I can handle it," I reassured him.

"Do you want me to make a few phone calls and find out whatever I can? I know this place and the people who are running it. Remember, I was *born* here, not *brought* here."

"I know, but I'm okay. There's a lot more to it," I replied. I wanted to tell him everything. I wanted to confide in him the fact that there were some mysterious happenings occurring, and that sometimes I felt that I was in way over my head, but that wouldn't have been the entire truth either. I simply did not know what the truth was.

Johnny persisted further, "Don't let Langley dump everything on you as if you were some *mamaluke*. Is that guy Jack Russell still calling the shots? I thought he was set to retire. I met him a few times. He never did impress me. You probably know more than that *jujule* does.

"Johnny, did you just call my boss a cucumber?"

I realized that Johnny was on a roll now, so I thought it best to just let him continue. He seemed to be trying to build my confidence. "You know, Tommy, you probably know more about computers in your left pinky than he knows in his entire six-foot body!"

I interrupted him, "Thanks, Johnny, but I will see what happens in the next two or three weeks. Besides, I am getting paid very well." I *was* getting paid handsomely, but that wasn't what motivated me to go through all this torture and pressure.

Johnny came right back, "Just let me see what's going on with this guy. I hate to see this *stroonze* give you a hard time!"

"Don't worry. I will talk to you in a few weeks. Hopefully, I will find out what I need to know by then. But thanks."

"Just remember, you don't have to die on this hill. Promise me that you won't put too much pressure on yourself."

"Absolutely," I lied. I could only hope that his counsel was not too late. I was already at risk of falling back to that miserable time in my life when the stress of work did get to me, and I almost lost it all.

Johnny and I then rejoined the others. They were laughing hysterically at something or someone, probably me. I secretly hoped that everyone would skip dessert so I could get back home and continue working with Max. The evening provided a diversion and gave me the chance to clear my head, but I now had some ideas that I was hoping to try out. Fortunately, everyone was so full, and our stomachs ached from laughing that we were content to get the bill and leave. As a polite gesture, we asked my mom if she wanted anything else besides coffee.

"Mom, how about something for dessert?" Dave asked.

"No, I don't think so. I don't want to keep you all out so long. I had a good time, but it *is* getting late."

"Oh, get *something*," Johnny insisted. "How about a nice piece of cheesecake?"

I quickly jumped in, reminding everyone, including Mom herself, "No, she really shouldn't. She is lactose intolerant!"

To which Dave commented, "That's no problem. She'll bring it home."

And *I* was the one who usually took the ribbing.

Terrifying Prediction

The results were in. Sally's students got their test scores back: Amanda Jones received 203 points out of 300 with a predicted score of 203. James Santaro received 245 points out of 300 with a predicted score of 245…

The list went on and on. It was unimaginable. All nine of Sally's students had official test scores exactly equal to the score that Max predicted. Max again delivered some phenomenal, indisputable evidence that no one could imagine or deem a fluke. Now I was left with the unenviable task of pondering the profound mystery, sorting it all out, and conjecturing about the ramifications.

I kept thinking about all the incontrovertible evidence that was piling up that Max could somehow predict the future. I actually got chills thinking about it. I was committed to find out how this computer could work at such an incomprehensible level without all the resources (not to mention the power bill) of a true supercomputer. It had only a tiny fraction of the sophistication of even our most basic supercomputers, yet it managed to come up with astounding results and "predictions." Max and I have certainly come a long way from when all I could get it to do was divulge some past events that were not widely known. As mystifying as that was, its ability to uncover true facts from the past was like child's play compared to what it had just accomplished. I still didn't trust anyone, so on my own, I knew that I had to probe more deeply to see what Max was all about.

Of course, I had to pretend that I was at least a little surprised at the sensational results Sally had with her special education students. The truth is that I was very impressed with what she accomplished. All of her students passed the test, and some achieved a level referred to as "high proficiency." Sally beamed with delight for days.

The next day, I checked my e-mail and noticed that buried within my scores of messages were two from April. She often sent me e-mails or text messages that included a Bible verse or two. I always looked forward to her notes and Bible verses since they were often so timely regarding my everyday life that it was uncanny. This time I didn't have time to inspect either one of them. I noticed that I received a message from RJM@sinclair. net and it seemed so irregular that I felt compelled to read it first. When I opened the e-mail, I was shocked to read, "You are close now…congratulations…please do not give up."

I responded by asking, "Who are you, and what exactly do you want from me?"

I immediately got a reply, but not quite the one I was hoping for.

"Never mind right now. You are doing stellar work. You will find out everything shortly." I remembered the last contact I had with Jack was something about him threatening to terminate the project or at least his support unless I came up with something real fast. At this juncture, I might not even need Jack or Mr. M any more. I was in contact with someone who might actually *know* something. I couldn't believe how much time had gone by since Max was first delivered to my house. That was January 15. It was now March 7. I tried to get my thoughts together. I reviewed everything that happened over the past two months. It was clear that this was not an ordinary computer, and it indeed represents a tremendous leap forward in technology. It did have the capacity to predict the future in many instances, and the case of Sally's students' test scores was truly profound. Everything was so surreal and mysterious that it seemed almost supernatural.

A package was sent to me the next day. It was a radar gun and a digital video camera. I received another message from RJM, which instructed me to go to a particular section of Maple Ave, right here in Vienna, a portion of the road, which was extensively travelled. I was to collect as much data as possible and upload it into the computer. I stood out in the cold for about forty-five minutes. I noted the speeds of cars and trucks. I also took about thirty minutes of video footage and then recorded the number and types of vehicles that passed by, and I even noted the weather conditions. As soon as I arrived home, dinner was ready, so I was able to enjoy being with Sally and April for the first time in a few days. I usually loved the time that we spent together, but lately, I haven't been able to appreciate my own family since I was so preoccupied with work. April was having random aches and pains more often than usual. Ever since she was four years old, she would get headaches about once a month. Now, they seemed to occur more regularly. Originally, her pediatrician dismissed it as "her imagination."

If that wasn't bad enough, Sally was working very hard teaching and taking care of April and herself. I couldn't believe that she was going to have a baby. I should have been overjoyed. Even April, who was initially elated when Sally and I first told her the news about the baby, had recently been less emotional about it all.

Sally and I played our weekly game of scrabble while April wrote in her journal, which she did every night for at least twenty minutes. Sally used the dictionary at least five times throughout the game of Scrabble. We both did things during our scrabble sessions that annoyed the other. I disliked the fact that she took a long time to spell a word whenever it was her turn. She hated it when I rubbed it in whenever I was able to use a word that earned me a high-point value, or when I won the game. Sometimes I was a little excited because I won when I thought that I was going to lose. The fact of the matter is that I usually lost. Oftentimes we would get tired of playing, dinner would be over, and we would simply call it a tie. That was a moral victory for me as far as I was concerned. Anyway, we always had a lot of fun. More importantly, we were quite distressed due to the fact that April was not feeling right, but she didn't complain. April had such a positive attitude, and she usually played Scrabble with us since she always completed her homework so quickly and was free to do whatever she wanted afterward.

"That's *not* a word!" Sally protested vehemently.

"*Lipitor* most certainly *is* a word!" I exclaimed. "It is a drug that is used to help lower cholesterol."

"I know *that*! I'm not an idiot. But you can't use a name brand of something. You know the rules." Sally was getting a little more perturbed now. She really hated to lose.

"What rules?" I exclaimed rhetorically. "There are no rules. We make up our own rules."

I had her there. We stopped playing Scrabble with the seven tiles the "rules" called for. We always used ten letters each, and that significantly increased the quality of words that we produced. We have been playing our own way for years. I added, "Last week, I let you use the word *Kleenex*, that's a name brand. If you *don't* remember, you must have selective memory."

"That was different," she smirked, trying to hide her laughter. "I asked permission, and you agreed to let me use that word."

"I had no choice back then. You said that if you couldn't use it, then the game would be over. And for the entire week, I would be completely on my own for dinner, among other things."

At that point, April lifted up her head from the table and asked sarcastically, "Can we all just learn how to get along?"

"What do *you* think, April? Who would *you* say is right in this case?" Sally was getting desperate now, hoping that her bond with April would tip the balance of power in her favor.

But I was equally as confident. I would take my chances that April would see reason and agree with me. "Go ahead, hon, you can tell us what you think."

"No, sorry. I know better than to take sides. I'm like Switzerland!"

We all burst out laughing. We were having fun, and we definitely were only half-kidding. April knew that. If there were ever two people who were meant for each other, it was me and Sally. We were friends, and we loved each other. I think that a little couch pillow that we had said it all. It was red with fancy white lettering, which said, "Happiness is Being Married to Your Best Friend." Sally and I both agreed that in any marriage, it is very important to be friends first and to have trust and honesty. We had all that and much, much more. We tried not to take anything for granted. Our marriage and family were special, and we knew that.

Although April did not join in our Scrabble game, Sally and I included her in our conversation, so she wouldn't feel totally left out. Since the deadline to sign up for softball was coming up in two days already, my thoughts were on the upcoming season. I reminded April of the time when she was in the fourth grade, and I coached her softball team. We had a lot of fun that summer, and we made it to a tournament game. I recalled the time when April was up to bat in the last inning with two runners on base ahead of her. We were trailing two to one, and we could sure use a hit. With the count two balls and two strikes, I was just hoping that April would try to swing at the ball. At that level, it was so tempting for the girls to wait for the perfect pitch, and they often walked or struck out without ever taking the bat off their shoulder. At the time, April was not a great player since it was her first year that she played organized softball. Nevertheless, she did have the uncanny knack of getting on base through a walk or by making contact and getting down the first base line fast enough to beat the throw by the time the other team got the ball to first base.

At the time, I could tell that all the girls were nervous since they were facing a really fast-throwing pitcher for the first time all year. A few of the girls got on base only because the opposing team's pitcher was a little wild with her pitches, and she walked quite a few of our batters. On the other hand, she was good enough to strike out a lot of our girls as well.

April could have done what a lot of us would have done, just hope that she kept from swinging at a pitch out of the strike zone twice more in order to draw a walk. Of course, by not swinging, she would risk striking out. To her credit, April did swing, and she made contact, hitting the ball high in the air a few feet behind the first baseman who back peddled and made the catch. Still, I was very proud of April for not taking the easy way out. She swung. She took a chance and I always bring that up when I want to commend her for at least trying and not being afraid. Softball, basketball, or life—it was the same message, and I thought that it was a good life lesson. "You can never make a shot if you don't take it." April understood that principle.

We recalled another time during the winter last year when I coached April's basketball team. April was too sick to play in an important game against our cross town rivals. She had a sore throat, runny nose, and aches throughout her entire body. Her mom would never let her play under those circumstances, but to support the team, Sally reluctantly agreed to let her watch the game in street clothes. Sally and I disagreed about a lot of things. For example, she was cautious while I took chances. Anyway, I believe that the quote attributed to William Wrigley applies to a lot of things. He said something to the effect that when two people in business together always have the exact same perspective, one of them is unnecessary. It seems to be true about marriage as well, in particular, regarding the raising of a child. I strongly believe that April benefitted from having two parents who, although compatible in most of the crucial areas, had opposite outlooks on some issues. This created a nice balance. April could see both sides of any position, and she was often exposed to varying points of view, making her a very well-rounded person.

On that night, even though April was quite ill, she attended the game to support the team. Little did Sally know that April put her uniform on under her jeans and sweatshirt. It was a good thing that she did because when we got to the gym, we were surprised to find out that two of our girls besides April had to stay home because they were also quite ill themselves. If April didn't play, we would have to compete with only four girls or forfeit the game. Well, April *did* play. After all, she had her uniform on, and we desperately needed her. I didn't force her to play, and if Sally knew what April was doing, she would not have allowed it. April scored six baskets that night, and we won the game. When we told Sally, she was quite angry for a while; but after she calmed down, she also told April how proud of her she was that she did not let her teammates down.

An amusing incident came to mind when we were coming home from a softball game last summer, and we were also taking home two of April's friends who were on our team. It was a hot summer night, and the girls were a mess, sitting in the backseat of the van. They were all covered with grass and dirt and extremely hungry. We stopped at a fast food place and got a huge bucket of French fries for the girls to share. We thought they would wait until we got home to get cleaned up before they partook of the fries. Instead, after only a few minutes, we looked back at them and saw that they were devouring the fries, dirty hands and all. After less than five minutes, the fries were all gone. I couldn't believe it, mostly because they never even bothered to clean their hands with a paper towel or a wet-nap. After a few minutes, April informed us that they were all still hungry. Fortunately, we had some fruit in the front seat from earlier that day. We had apples, pears, and a bunch of grapes. We offered the girls some of the fruit.

Sally asked, "We have some fruit up here. Would anyone like an apple?"

To which April asked, "Is it washed?"

We ended the scrabble game. I ended up not using the word *Lipitor*, and I even helped clean up after dinner. April was feeling a little better now, so she went up to her room to finish writing in her journal and to listen to her favorite music, which lately has been some old classics from Johnny Cash.

Later on, I went down to my office in the basement to read, or so I said. So much for honesty in a marriage. Somehow, I knew that I would eventually have to tell Sally more about what was going on with me and this computer project. I was troubled that I wouldn't know where to begin and how to fully explain everything that was happening. Sally would understand if I couldn't share anything with her, although in the past, I have to admit that I confided in her on some of my work that I never should have. I would have loved to tell her about the experiments that worked and about reliving the past. As much as I was sure that Sally would be supportive of my work, I felt that it would be way too creepy. I decided not to say anything to her until I found out everything that I needed to. I wanted to put closure on all of this, and for some reason, someone out there was confident that what I did today with the traffic data would be very beneficial in helping me to figure this all out.

At about 9:00 PM, I finally entered all the traffic information that I gathered into the computer. It didn't take much time for Max to disclose the fact that something tragic would happen where I was "stationed" on Maple Ave. A major traffic accident would take place. This was not totally inexplicable considering the fact that many of the cars on that particular section of the road notoriously travelled faster than the speed limit on a regular basis. Some motorists apparently consider the speed limit there to be a mere suggestion. Max was as clear and definitive as ever: "Ten car pileup results in three dead and twelve injured." If it wasn't for the blasted computer's track record, I would probably have dismissed this as nonsense. Predicting a car accident is one thing. For Max to claim three fatalities and the exact number of injured people involved was downright irresponsible. Max even reported the time of the accident, 11:03 PM. I was sure that it simply had to be a sham. Still, I felt compelled to go directly to the intersection since it was only ten fifteen, and I still had some time. I also could have called the police, but I simply did not know what I would say. I was so tired that I decided to rest my head on the pillow of the bed for a few minutes to think about the options.

I woke up at about 1:15 AM. I missed my opportunity to do anything preventive because according to Max, the accident already occurred more than two hours ago. I tried to fall back asleep, but I was very worried. I thought I heard sirens in the distance, but it was probably my imagination. Some of what Max has come out with so far can never really be substantiated since we cannot change the past and see how it would have played out. Max was certainly right about various test scores, faulty brakes, and Sally's innermost thoughts. Max also had ridiculous success predicting the winners of horse races, but at least it had substantial data as a basis for its calculations. I was really hoping that this was an opportunity to finally prove that some of Max's bold predictions were completely bogus. Even if there was some sort of accident on Maple Ave within the next day or so, it could be entirely coincidental. How could Max emphatically declare the exact number of people involved as well as the precise time of the collision?

I could not sleep the rest of the night although I was totally exhausted. I stayed in bed, tossing and turning. Once again, my mind was racing wildly as I tried to come up with other "questions" for Max to ponder. I needed something simple and much less controversial. I wanted something that would be easier to check. How about this? What would April have for breakfast tomorrow morning? She always asked for something different. Toast with butter or jam, oatmeal, cereal, eggs, pancakes, frozen waffles were all possibilities. Since Sally left for work early lately, I usually helped April get ready for school and supplied her with a good breakfast.

To give Max a reasonable chance for success, I decided to enter everything that April had for breakfast for the past week. This was actually easy for me since Sally and I recorded everything that April ate for all of her meals since her doctor has been monitoring April's stomach issue for a few months. April has had some problems with stomachaches, even more lately than ever before. The doctors are still trying to pinpoint what combination of foods worked for her and what foods could be potentially troublesome. I entered the information and waited a few minutes. I did not see any pattern to what she wanted to eat even though I am a trained and experienced statistician. The computer predicted pop tarts. Not apple, but strawberry. April hasn't requested strawberry pop tarts in over a month. The report by Max went on to include orange juice and blueberry yogurt.

I continued to worry that Max was so precise with its predictions and so exact with the earlier accident details. This might undo all the other significant results that we had, especially if Max was finally wrong. On the other hand, if Max was correct again, I didn't know what I would think. Between the car accident and the breakfast choices, two completely different situations, this could either derail our progress or confirm the unimaginable. Could Max be right about both predictions? I might have my answer sooner that I bargained for.

To make matters even worse, Max claimed that April would be sent home from school the next day at 10:00 AM with a stomachache. I was skeptical, but I was also ready for anything.

The next morning, everything went a little haywire. It was totally dreamlike, as if I was in a fog. At the same time, my heart raced as I saw the headlines of the morning paper. I felt the beginning of a panic attack overtake me, but I tried desperately to fight it off. The newspaper read, "10 Car Pileup Kills 3 and Injures 12." I felt sick. I was at that exact location the day before! Max also had the time right as the newspaper reported that the accident occurred a little after 11 PM. The guilt I felt was overwhelming since I remembered that instead of acting upon my suspicions when Max first revealed its prediction, I inadvertently fell asleep. I was so disconsolate that I almost shed tears right then and there. It seemed so ironic that many of my dreams felt like I was awake, not dreaming at all, and now I knew that I was awake but it seemed so surreal, almost as if I was hallucinating. On the morning news, I could hear the announcer mention that the combination of slick roads, mist, and fog contributed to the pile up.

I needed to tend to April who had just woken up. I was scurrying around more than usual, helping April get ready for school by myself because Sally already left for an early morning faculty meeting, which she mentioned yesterday. I forgot all about it, and I realized that I wasn't scoring very high on the attentiveness scale lately.

April immediately greeted me in the kitchen and answered my question before I even asked.

"Pop tarts, Daddy," she groggily announced.

"What? For breakfast? How about toast?" I tried to think of other options just so Max would be wrong.

"No, pop tarts. *Strawberry*." She was adamant and seemed to switch from being half asleep to completely wide awake.

"How about eggs?" I coaxed.

"No, pop tarts."

"How about apple pop tarts? We don't have any more strawberry."

April proved me wrong as she reached into the cabinet and pulled out a single strawberry pop tart. She poured herself the last four ounces of orange juice, but she was still hungry and understandably so. I suggested fruit. She insisted upon blueberry yogurt. Anyone who wasn't aware of Max's ability would have been shocked out of their mind by all of this, but I took it all in stride. At least for now.

Later that morning, I got a call on my cell phone to come to the school immediately. The nurse called to inform me that April had a stomachache and needed to be taken home right away. When I got the call, it was nine forty-five, and I was already waiting in the school parking lot because I knew what was supposed to happen. I would have been trembling even more if it wasn't for the fact that I was well aware of Max's ability and power, and I wasn't surprised that it was all playing out the way it did, clearly unfolding exactly how Max foresaw.

When I got April home, and after she unpacked her backpack, I let her just relax for a while and watch television. She found an old DVD of something called VeggieTales, and I remember hearing her sing something about a character called Larry Boy. She sounded pretty good for someone who left school ill, less than two hours ago. Surprisingly, she was soon hungry, and I gave her some toast for lunch, something light. I noticed that she gobbled up the two pieces of toast as if nothing was wrong with her. In fact, she talked me into taking her out back to play on the swings. It was a little damp and cloudy, and it appeared as if it might even rain soon. April looked and sounded okay, so I agreed.

"Wear a warm jacket," I urged.

"Of course I will, Dad. I'd hate to catch a cold and miss school."

I thought to myself, *This looks awfully suspicious*. If I didn't know any better, I would have guessed that April was not really sick at all; that she just wanted to spend the day with me. After all, how much time have we spent together like this in the past few weeks? Even on Saturdays lately, I had so little time for April. I couldn't even remember the last time we had a day to spend together, just the two of us.

April casually brought up the car accident that occurred late last night. "Dad, did you hear about the terrible car accident late yesterday? I heard some of the teachers at school talking about it." I could hear a quiver in her voice even though she tried to give me the impression that she was not broken up about the incident, and that she was able to freely talk about it. I was surprised what she said next. "Dad, where was God? He said, 'I will never leave you nor forsake you.'"

"I don't know. All I can tell you is that it might have been even worse. People should know that Maple Ave is extremely dangerous. Some people drive way too fast on that road. Maybe God repeatedly warned them, and only some of the people listened."

April wasn't satisfied with my answer. "But, Dad, what about all of the other tragedies that happen? How about the hurricane last year when thirty people along the coast died? Did God just look the other way?"

"Now, April, you of all people should know better than that!"

"Sorry," she apologized.

I then told her a story that hopefully made some sense out of it all. "April, here is a story I once heard that helped me realize that sometimes God provides a path, but we have to be open enough to follow his way. And God's way is not necessarily our way or what is most convenient for us." I tried to hide the fact that my entire body was shaking due to the magnitude of everything that happened as well as how Max predicted it all in advance.

So I paused and took a deep breath before I began. "There was a great flood in a city, and one man got up on the roof of his house so he wouldn't drown. Needless to say, the flood waters kept rising and rising. The man constantly prayed, 'God, please deliver me from this terrible flood,' and he basically put it in the hands of God. After about an hour, a rescue boat came by and offered to take the man out of there. The man declined, saying, 'Oh no, thanks, God will rescue me.' About an hour later, another rescue boat arrived, and again the man refused to accept help. This happened twice more, and the man always declined help from the rescue boat, claiming that God himself would deliver him from the terrible flood. Well, since the flood waters continued to rise, the man died. He did go to heaven where he confronted God. 'God, I thought you would rescue me?' God said, 'Well I tried to. After all, I did send the rescue boat past your house four times!'"

April apparently understood the message and seemed to be somewhat satisfied.

After using everything on the jungle gym and climbing a few of the shorter trees that were in the backyard, April made her way to one of the tallest trees back there.

"Hey, April," I called out to her as she scampered up that tree. "Do you want to catch a squirrel? Then climb up that tree and act like a nut!"

I was surprised that April laughed since she was so zoned in to climbing higher than ever before on that particular tree. *So much for being sick*, I thought. I let her climb for a few minutes until I could take no more. I was getting a little nervous now. "April," I called up to her with a seriousness in my voice. "Come down, it's raining!"

She called down trying to convince me that there was nothing to worry about. "Dad, it's not raining. It's mist."

"What are you talking about? It hit me." I joked, trying to add a little levity to the situation. April laughed but chose to continue climbing higher. She managed to get herself up about twenty feet to a good, solid branch where she stood up and called out in a loud voice, "I am on top of the world!"

Suddenly, she turned her back to me and looked as if she was going to try to reach for a branch about four feet above her and climb even higher. Another branch that was sticking out unexpectedly came dangerously close to her eye, and she backed away and crouched down. But it was too late. The branch scratched her eyes, and she pressed both her hands up to her eyes and face. She was really in pain, and she couldn't open her eyes.

How was I going to get her down now? I wondered.

"April, can you get down from there?" I asked, knowing the answer was going to be no.

"Dad, I can't see. My eyes ache. I'm afraid."

To make matters worse, it started drizzling even harder. Fortunately, she did make her way down a little bit at a time; but she was really stuck at one point, totally afraid to move down any further. At this point, she was only about eight feet off the ground; and I knew that by the time I got out the extension ladder from the garage and worked my way up to her, it would be pouring and it would make everything slippery and even more dangerous.

"April, jump! I am right in front of you, and I will catch you. No problem," I assured her.

"Dad, are you kidding me? I am afraid!"

"Don't worry, you are not that high. I can easily catch you. Jump!"

"Dad, how can I? I can't even see you!" she insisted.

"But I can see *you*, honey. That's all that matters. That's what trust is really all about."

She did jump, and I caught her with no problem. I got her inside the house and washed out her eyes, and after a few minutes, she seemed totally fine. It was certainly a close call, but she was soon in a good mood again and laughing about the whole incident in no time.

At four o'clock, April's cell phone started ringing. First, her friend Alyssa called to see how she was and to tell her the math homework. Next, it was Emma who told her the vocabulary words for which sentences were due Friday. Then Brianne called who doesn't have any classes with April, but she also wanted to see how she was feeling and to find out what she was doing this weekend. Talk about putting the cart before the horse. It was only Tuesday!

While April was on the phone with Brianne, the land line rang, and it was Jessica calling who couldn't get through because April wasn't picking up her cell phone for the past half hour. At one point, April was talking to two girls at once—one on the landline and one on her cell phone. Soon after, April was done with that juggling act, a boy named Andy called. Now that was all I could take! I put an end to all the phone calls for the rest of the night.

"April, that's it," I exclaimed. "No more phone calls. Shut off your phone, and get started on all of your makeup work!"

"But, Dad, I really wanted to talk to him," she whined in a high-pitched voice. I couldn't remember the last time I heard her so exasperated.

"Do you want some cheese with that whine?" I mocked.

April went into her room, and I didn't hear a peep out of her until dinner. Now I knew something was wrong, but at least she completed all her work. I didn't want to see her grades go any lower than they already had recently. I'm sure she was at least partially troubled that I was not spending my usual time with her and her mom because of my preoccupation with work.

Of course, when Sally arrived home and found out about April's stomachache and tree-climbing incident, she was concerned. That was when April came out of her room and calmed her down. "Don't worry, Mom. Daddy took great care of me. We had so much fun today. I wish we could do this more often."

This made me realize that my psychological assessment was probably right on target. April's symptoms were probably psychosomatic, and she would do anything to spend more time with her dad. Who could blame the poor kid? The time we spent together was precious.

I absolutely agree with you, April, I thought to myself. I can't wait for everything to get back to some semblance of normal around here. I tried to look at the overall picture regarding Max and what happened today. I was apprehensive to admit that all of this did seem to indicate that Max was indeed prophetic and capable of doing things beyond what I originally imagined.

THE LAST SHALL BE FIRST

It seemed that whoever sent me to that intersection to gather the traffic data intended to flaunt Max's power. I was convinced more than ever that Max would be able to accomplish anything. Max was a veritable fortune-teller. The prediction of pop tarts, yogurt, juice, and subsequent stomachache was a real eye-opener, but I didn't want to think about the disaster at the highway. Three people dead. Twelve people injured seriously. Predicting the type of breakfast that April wanted was impressive in itself, but using the computer to save lives would be huge. How in the world would we be able to accomplish this? I started thinking deeply about some of the possibilities.

How about preventing global warming? I could easily supply Max with enough data regarding *that* topic. How about uncovering the secrets of learning? How many people who were learning disabled could benefit from knowing the best technique for their own learning style? This was what Sally and I were doing with our Learning Styles Project. If we could use Max, we wouldn't have to wait another year to see how the study would play out. I hoped that we could use Max for all of these types of things, especially if we could find out who was ultimately responsible for creating this masterpiece so we could produce even more of them. I also wondered how the typical person would use this type of power on an everyday basis. Would he only think of his own gain? I am sure that if everyone had access to these computers, the world would change dramatically, but that change wouldn't necessarily be for the better. Even on a small scale, the possibilities were beyond belief. Which college should your child attend? Let's play out all the possible scenarios. Enter each college that he or she was accepted to and then see what would happen in every case. Let Max supply all the details and then simply choose the scenario that seemed most appealing. I was convinced that none of that would be appropriate. Everyone needs some sense of excitement from not knowing too much about his future. More importantly, would we be able to trust the predicted results? How about helping the thousands of people who die from hunger and malnutrition each day throughout the world? Surely, the computer would be able to tell us what crops to grow and where. No, that was child's play. We know this already. Our computers at Langley have been doing that for years. We as a society just don't have the organizational skill and compassion to make these kinds of things happen.

I arbitrarily checked my cell phone and noticed that I had gotten a text message from April. I realized how late it was, and I actually forgot to kiss her good night earlier. The message read, "For through the Spirit we eagerly await by faith the righteousness for which we hope" (Galatians 5:5).

I knew it would be beneficial to reflect on those words, but I also felt compelled to do some serious thinking. Could we as a society handle the truth about Max? I didn't believe so, but perhaps I should ask Max. Then I realized that Max was part of the problem. I found it virtually impossible to be objective when working with Max as it was becoming arrogant and overbearing, or at least that was my perception. How could a machine take on personality traits? Well, if any machine could do it, then Max certainly could.

I needed a diversion, so I decided to again see what my life could have been like, especially now that I had more confidence in the validity of Max's predictions. I discovered what would have happened if I merely changed the topic of a paper that I wrote as a freshman in high school. I actually wrote a report about "The devastation of divorce in the modern family." Now, however, I altered the topic to look as if I selected my theme the power of positive thinking, in which I would have used a series of books by Norman Vincent Peale as my main resource. I found that this one change somehow altered my life entirely. According to the results reported by Max, I would have gone to Seton Hall University in New Jersey. After graduation, I would have joined the Peace Core and spent my life doing mission work in the Philippines. I would have started my own mission, and it would have spread to many different areas of the world. I would have combined positive thinking, prayer, and believing in Jesus Christ as the Savior. Many more people might have been truly saved. I wondered why this didn't happen. If this was actually meant to be, then there should have been a way for it to occur. Perhaps my current life would somehow lead to something even more beneficial, though I really didn't see how that could ever happen, considering the confusion my mind was now experiencing. I woke up with an uncomfortable feeling of regret that I missed a golden opportunity to make a huge difference in the world.

During the night, I received another e-mail from RJM. It had a tone of urgency.

"Tom, you are now ready for the greatest task of all. We will fully utilize Max. Regrettably, we don't have much time left. Stay home for a few days and wait for further instructions."

I pounded the keyboard then rose from the computer. I was furious, but at least I knew that it might be over soon. Besides, I was much too tired to do anything about my anger. I was also confident that I would soon find out who I was dealing with and what they were planning on doing with Max's extraordinary gift. I hoped they had ideas that would lead to great things for mankind that would make the world a better place to live and advance civilization to a whole new level. I was confused because whoever created Max should have been able to use his expertise to develop the necessary programming techniques and shortcuts that I learned and discovered. It was true that I sometimes relied on my vast computer programming knowledge and statistical background, but there must have been others with these skills. To further increase my angst, April stayed home from school with an upset stomach again, and this seemed more serious than the pop tart incident. She also had achy joints and a headache. Since I would be working from the house anyway, I stayed home with her for two days and took care of her. This gave us some quality time to talk. If it wasn't for the fact that she was in some pain on and off and I was now constantly thinking about what would happen next whenever I was contacted again, it would have been a delightful couple of days. We reminisced about last summer and what we would be doing once school let out in June. We talked about doing more surfing, and we tried to guess what Bethany Hamilton was up to.

As April and I continued to bond those couple of days, I brought up the fact that I was so happy and grateful that I was able to enjoy such a wonderful relationship with her. It was the type of rapport that a father and daughter should always have. She was equally delighted, and she had no doubt that it would always be this way. Sometimes I couldn't resist the temptation to bring up the possibility that when she hit the turbulent teen years, our relationship might have to be temporarily "strained" as it was with many teenage girls with their dads. She always took offense to that type of talk, and this time she threw a pillow at me that hit me directly in the face. I distorted my face and pretended that it was going to stay that way until she apologized. I noticed the pillow that she threw at me. It was the one that read, "Any man can be a father, but it takes someone special to be a dad." That about said it all, and I hugged her until she practically couldn't breathe. We had that pillow for a few years. I remember the time when April was six or seven years old. Her best friend was over, and they were ready to play a game, and April's friend Jenny asked her, "Maybe your father wants to play with us?"

April quickly jumped in emphatically, "That is *not* my father. He is my dad, and don't you forget it!"

The turbulent teenage years. I knew there might be some tough times ahead. What kind of father will I be when there is a new baby in the house? Will I be able to share my love with April and another child? I wanted another child, but I was worried as to how it would affect my relationship with April and Sally. I knew that I had enough love for another child, but would I have enough energy? Would my mind and body break down before I ever had the chance to show that I could continue to be a good father to April, husband to Sally, and a father to a new baby? Ever since I began this project with Max, I could feel my own health deteriorating due to stress and fatigue. In four months, I would be a new father. Check that. I would become a new *dad*. I vowed to enjoy every day with April along the way. And when we got to her teenage years, I would relish every disagreement, every fight, and every moment with her. I was getting a little overly dramatic here. What I needed was strength. I finally found what I needed. I remembered the verse, "Do not grieve, for the joy of the LORD is your strength" (Nehemiah 8:10).

On the third day home with April, I was prepared to take her to a doctor. By 10:00 AM, I was tired of waiting around for a contact by someone who I still didn't know I could trust. I checked on April, and she was now in a great deal of discomfort. Her stomach was hurting on and off so much I thought that it might be her appendix, but what did I know? April was resting on the couch and had been pain free for the past twenty minutes, so that bought me a little time. I suddenly had an idea! I had a doctor right here! It was called Dr. Max. I entered as much data as I could get my hands on: medical records, her meals for the past two weeks, her current temperature, and anything else that I could think of or that I had access to, even if I didn't see how it could be relevant. It only took about thirty minutes for April's pains to return with a vengeance. Now I had to take her to the hospital and quickly. The only problem was that I did not have the time to wait for the results that Max could offer. For some reason, Max was taking a long time to process all the information. Normally, Max would have given me something back after only a few minutes. It was already fifteen minutes since I entered all the information. It hardly ever took this long and the few times it did was due to the fact that it had to sort out much more data than this. I came to the conclusion that Max simply couldn't stand to be wrong about anything, and that it took so much "pride" in its track record of accuracy that it simply wanted to be totally sure before it drew any conclusions. I didn't have any more time to waste. I needed to get April down to see her doctor. I called Sally from the car, and she agreed to meet us there. At about 11:00 AM, a new doctor saw April, and Sally quickly filled him in with some of April's most recent medical information. I was anxious to get back to the house and check in with Max. Would it be able to come up with a prognosis with the sketchy information that I quickly supplied? I know it sounds crazy, but I trusted whatever Max had to report especially considering its track record. I somehow felt that Max would be able to tell us more than the doctor. I was reluctant to leave April, but I knew that Sally was there, and I really wasn't going to be of any help. Still, I couldn't think of a good enough excuse to get back home.

Then I thought of something. If April needed to be taken to the hospital to stay overnight, she would need some essentials. No, the doctor was not talking as if she needed to get to the hospital and stay overnight; even though when this happened two years ago, April was required to stay for a couple of days. How about all of her medical records? I brought only a few of them since I didn't have time to look for everything that was tucked away in various folders. Surprisingly, the doctor did not think he needed any other information for now, but he did need to run a few tests of his own.

Then I suddenly cried out, "I left the gas burner on in the kitchen! I was making tea when we had to leave, and I forgot to shut off the burner." They all seemed to buy it. Sally instructed me to get home and wait for her phone call in case they did need me to bring anything back for April.

"And take a rest when you get home. You look stressed out beyond belief!" I pretended that I didn't know what she was talking about, and I rushed home right away. I was sincerely worried about April. I had a feeling that something was disastrous, and I was very eager to see what Max had to report. In fact, I temporarily forgot that I was expecting a message from RJM.

When I got home, I immediately checked the printer since I had Max automatically set to print anything that it came up with regarding April's condition. I wondered if I provided enough information for the results to be valid. I supplied Max with just about everything that I possibly could, considering the fact that I only had about thirty minutes to do so. Just then, my cell phone rang, and I jumped to answer it. At first, I thought that it could be Jack Russell. I hadn't heard from him in almost two weeks. Whoever it was, the warning was clear enough: "They are coming. *Protect Max.* More importantly, please protect yourself."

Then he hung up. This was not much to go on. What was I supposed to do? Who was coming? I was tempted to forget about Max and protect myself by getting out of there as fast as I could. I did own a handgun, but I wondered if there would be enough time for me to unlock it from the safe and load the magazine. Besides, I was such a novice with a gun I quickly double locked the front door. I would have called the police if I had any idea what I would tell them. If I said something like, "I need help, someone is coming to get my computer, it is valuable, and it knows things!" I would sound ludicrous. My mind was running away from me. Lack of sleep…my sick daughter…I should call Jack. Regrettably, however, I did not trust him at all anymore. For all I knew, he could have been in trouble as well, and I hadn't heard from him in such a long time.

I decided to load the gun and have it ready, just in case. After that, I checked Max's printout regarding April's condition. It was a rare bone disorder called fibrous dysplasia. According to Max, it was life-threatening. There was no known cure.

I dropped the gun that I was holding and choked back tears. I couldn't believe this. I wished that I never asked Max to diagnose April in the first place. I desperately hoped that Max was wrong this *one* time. I sat in despair on the couch for what must have been half an hour even though it felt like an eternity. I didn't want to admit it until now, but I realized that my life was spinning totally out of control. I tried to choke back the tears, but it was no use. The stress was beyond my control now. Between the lack of sleep, the pressure of trying to find out what was going on with Max, and now the life-threatening illness that April supposedly had, I simply couldn't take it any longer. To make matters worse, I had a loaded gun next to me, and I was not thinking clearly.

I collapsed on the couch, and I must have passed out or fallen into a deep, deep sleep. For some reason, my mind raced back to last summer. The dream I had was vivid, in color, and in superb detail. Some dreams are premonitions. This dream was about the past, and I could see and feel everything exactly how it happened. I remember thinking to myself in the dream that this can't be a dream. In a dream, does the person dreaming *think* about anything? I could feel myself thinking and remembering exactly the way I felt last summer. It was so unbelievable how all of my senses were involved. I could see the colors, hear the sounds, and sometimes feel the pain.

Last year, Sally, April, and I signed up for a triathlon to be held on August 25 to raise money for a local scholarship fund. It was a series of three events that included three hundred meters of swimming, a ten-mile bike ride, and then a five-kilometer run. For us, it was *supposed* to be for fun. On the other hand, Sally happens to be very competitive. She was not bragging, but she certainly had a lot of confidence in her ability to excel in this type of event. April was only ten years old, and she was quite a natural athlete herself. At the same time, she only played sports for the fun of it as well as the social aspect, and she didn't like to train very much. April was apprehensive, but I managed to convince her that it wouldn't be too difficult for her, and she eventually agreed to participate. I was glad since this would give us all a chance to train together, and I was looking forward to going on long bike rides and swim laps at the town pool. There were still two small problems. Actually, there was one big problem and one bigger problem. April hated to run. I mean, she *really* hated it. The sports she played recently, softball and basketball, did not require much conditioning; but I knew that with a little bit of work, she would be able to become a pretty good runner. After all, three miles is not exactly a marathon.

I remembered the entire memorable summer unfolding in splendid detail. We returned home from surfing at Myrtle Beach where Sally wrecked her knee with a partially torn tendon. She was convinced that she would be able to participate in the triathlon, but from then on, she didn't refer to it as a competition. She was hoping to merely complete the event and finish respectably. For the rest of the summer, Sally went for physical therapy two days per week and still managed to do some jogging on the soft track near our home. She also managed to swim a few times each week. Being a teacher and having the summers off certainly did have its advantages.

Besides spending a good amount of time at the beach last summer, we also had the opportunity to do some serious biking. The triathlon would include ten miles on the bike, and this was one thing we all enjoyed and did well. While biking, the pedaling motion actually helped to strengthen Sally's knee that was compromised in her surfing spill. The problem was that when we all went on a few bike rides together, we found ourselves having too good of a time. We would stop for lunch, sit along the river, and we would often talk to various people whom we knew. We had fun for sure even though it wasn't helping our training, not nearly to the extent that we needed in order to participate in a triathlon. Before too long, April was beginning to have second thoughts. She was very reluctant to do any running at all that summer since it was in fact one of the hottest summers on record. I was afraid this was going to be a problem, and I hated so see April back out of this event, especially since we had already paid an entrance fee of $150 for the three of us. Besides, I knew that April could do this if she only put her mind to it. I ended up resorting to bribery by promising to buy her a brand-new digital camera if she merely completed the triathlon. I also assured her that I would literally be there with her every step of the way.

"Come on, April. You can do it," I encouraged her. "Just breathe naturally."

"Dad, I have to stop. My legs ache," she complained.

"Oh, let's have a pity party for April!" I proclaimed sarcastically.

"Dad, I'm serious. I think that I am going to collapse."

"You can make it! You have that Russo toughness. Be a winner, not a whiner!"

"Forget it, Dad, running is just not my thing. Now my lungs hurt, and I can hardly breathe."

"But, April, we haven't even gone around the track once yet. We haven't even finished a quarter of a mile."

"Okay, I'll try. But I will only do two laps, and then I'll walk another lap or two."

"That won't get you through the triathlon. How are you going to build up to three miles?"

"I'll power walk the rest." April had a new sense of confidence when she realized that she might actually be able to power walk about as fast as someone could jog.

After completing two more laps on the track, we walked another twenty minutes or so. April convinced me that she would eventually be able to power walk at a very respectable pace and either jog, walk, or alternate between the two when it was time for the triathlon. As she power walked a few laps, she actually walked fast enough that I had to jog to keep pace with her. Besides, we still had four weeks before the big day of the triathlon. For the next four weeks, we continued to train, even though our training mostly consisted of family bike rides around the park and some swimming at the town pool two or three times each week.

Now comes the very big problem that I alluded to earlier. I can't swim very well. Ever since I was a child, I didn't really swim. I flapped around in the water like a wounded duck. For some reason, I had the necessary stamina on land, but in the water, I got tired to a point of exhaustion after a mere fifty feet. *Not a problem*, I thought. I would train, I would swim everyday if need be, and I would work on building up my stamina in the water at the town pool.

"Your technique is all wrong!" Mike Patterson yelled out. "You have to keep your face in the water!"

Therein lies the problem. I hated to put my face in the water when I swam.

"That's why you get burned out after only a few minutes," he continued.

More like a few seconds, I thought, but I tried to heed his advice. Mike was a high school history teacher, and he was off for the entire summer. He also happened to be a man of great faith and a really outstanding individual; however, he sometimes had a warped sense of humor. He obviously had nothing else better to do than to watch me swim, or at least flop around and give me pointers. He was quite the accomplished swimmer himself, and he could have completed the triathlon if he wasn't such a lousy runner. Regardless, he seemed more content in breaking my chops, and he proceeded to show me the correct way to swim.

"Stick your face in the water like this, Tom. It's so easy, but you're making it into a problem in multivariable calculus."

I thought to myself, *If it was a problem in calculus, at least I would have a fighting chance.* But it was no use. Just like April had trouble with running, I had trouble with swimming. The only difference was that she would be able to get through the running portion of the triathlon by power walking or even walking normally if need be. It might take a while to complete the event, but at least April was not going to drown. On the other hand, I was *sure* to drown. It would not be while I was training at the town pool since at least there I could control how deep the water was where I swam. At the triathlon itself, the water level of the pool would very likely be at least eight feet deep!

My plan was to build my stamina up as much as I could and then basically swim one lap at a time. After each lap, I could hold on to the side of the pool and rest for fifteen seconds or two minutes, whatever I thought I needed. It might take me forever, but at least I wouldn't die. We reasoned that even if April was way ahead of me after the swimming portion, I surely would be able to catch up to her on the first or second lap in the biking phase. The biking phase would consist of three loops around a section of the town, and they were just about 3.3 miles each for a total of about ten miles. The final phase was a run of five kilometers, about 3.1 miles. By then, I was hoping to be with April, and I could jog while she power walked, and perhaps I would be able to get her to run at least part of that last phase.

In the end, it all turned out to be one of the most memorable summers of my life, and I wanted everything to be firmly etched in my mind forever. It didn't seem to matter that I was at risk of drowning, or at the very least embarrassing myself. Nor did it matter that April was not coming close to pushing herself to get ready for this event. At the time, I was really a little disappointed that April was not giving one hundred percent in all of this. In fact, one night during that summer, I showed April and Sally a little math trick that I thought they would both get a kick out of. It was here that I learned something that convinced me that there are surely more important things in life than giving one hundred percent all the time. My goal was to play out a little activity with letters and numbers to demonstrate the importance of what it means to give one hundred percent to anything. If you take the twenty-six letters of the alphabet and assign each letter a number from one to twenty-six in order:

A = 1, B = 2, C = 3, D = 4, E = 5, all the way up to Z = 26, we would find that if we spelled the word *knowledge*, it would total ninety-six percent. If we spelled *hard work* and again took each letter and added all these values, we would now be up to ninety-eight percent. On the other hand, if we spelled the word *attitude*, it would total one hundred percent. April enjoyed this and tried to come up with some of her own. She did come up with something that I thought was quite impressive.

If we spelled *love of God*, it would total one hundred one percent. Sally and I were lucky to have a kid like April. In my dream, I continued to remember everything in perfect detail, right up to the day of the event. We arrived at the site of the triathlon at six o'clock in the morning. We placed our bikes among two hundred other perfectly aligned, almost brand-new, top-notch racing bikes. Already, I could sense that something was wrong. I noticed all the state-of-the-art racing bicycles on the racks that were each worth thousands of dollars. These people were serious! Sally and I were using bikes that were twenty-five years old, and April was using an old mountain bike that we got at a garage sale. We were understandably in way above our heads.

We found out that we would all be in the third heat like we requested so we could stay together. At least initially. Sally was now totally determined to ignore the remaining pain of her knee and do the best that she could. Throughout the summer, she was able to do just enough training and rehab work that I was confident she would do well and be safe. In fact, her last words to us were, "Stay together, you guys, and I will have a drink ready for you at the finish line." Thanks for that vote of confidence. At least she assumed we would make it to the finish line. I knew that April would be fine as long as she pushed herself, but perhaps I was asking for too much.

I noticed something as we neared the water. The pool that we would be swimming in was four feet deep at each end and only five or six feet at the middle. This was the break that I needed! I wouldn't have to hold on to the edge after every lap! Every time that I needed a rest, I could simply walk in the water, and I knew that I wouldn't drown! April actually noticed the depth of the water first and said, "Dad, look, today is your lucky day. Either that or God is totally with you. Isaiah 43:2 says, 'When you pass through the waters, I will be with you; and when you pass through the rivers, they will not sweep over you.'"

It turns out that I don't even remember much of the swimming phase. I must have walked through the water for most of the three hundred meters. I remembered the transition from the swimming to the bikes. By the time I got to the bikes, Sally had her helmet on and fastened, and she was walking her bike across the path to the road where she would be able to hop on and leave us behind for good. April was finishing up putting on a shirt and tying her sneakers. I walked over to the bike rack and nonchalantly dried off. I guess I didn't consider the fact that we were in a race. I was planning on staying alongside April even though she had a head start on me because she completed the swimming part a few minutes before I did, and I took forever and a day to dry off. I easily caught up to her after one of the three mile loops. When I reached her, April was off of her bike drinking some water and trying desperately to catch her breath.

"Dad, someone yelled at me to get off the road!" She panted, still breathing heavily, trying to suck up as much oxygen as she could.

"What are you talking about? What did they say?" I asked, not believing her.

"They said 'no daydreaming.'"

"That was rude, but you may have been in their way."

"No, I wasn't! Just forget it. But I feel like I am going to pass out! I don't want to continue. You go on ahead and finish." Again she insisted, "I really feel like I am going to faint!"

At this point, I knew that I could give her a little dose of her own medicine.

I replied, "Remember this, April. Isaiah 40:31 says, 'But those who hope in the LORD will renew their strength. They will soar on wings like eagles; they will run and not grow weary, they will walk and not be faint.'"

That refocused her and kept her satisfied, at least for a while. We got back on our bikes and pressed on. We still had two more laps to complete, and parts of each loop had some serious hills. Would we be able to make it? I guess the dozen or so family bike rides that we enjoyed earlier that summer were not enough preparation for this. I actually didn't care about the fact that we were doing so poorly for my own sake, but I could tell that April was getting more and more discouraged each mile that we rode on our bikes. Every minute, at least one or two bikers would pass us as if we were standing still. Sally did manage to pass us by when we were finishing up our second lap, and she was completing her third lap, ending the biking phase for her. She barely acknowledged us as she sped by. Oh, she might have said something cute like, "Are we having fun yet?"

I think I said, "Yes, can't you tell?" I was glad her knee was holding up.

When the next wave of serious-looking athletic racers passed us by, I was afraid that soon everyone would pass us. Again, it wasn't just for me that I cared. I didn't want April's first experience with a significant athletic event to end up in disaster. For some reason, I was not worried that either one of us would fall off the bike and really get hurt. Much worse than that. I was worried about humiliation. All this time, April and I were side by side with each other, keeping the exact same pace unless one of us would temporarily speed on ahead if there was a downhill. Thankfully, we always ended up together. It was actually a nice bike ride if it wasn't for all the people passing us by, the hills, the pressure that I was putting on me and April, and of course, some pain in the legs, neck, and in the butt from sitting for so long. Still, we pressed onward. We were very close to the last mile of the biking portion of the triathlon. Another person passed us by. Then another. Next, it was Michael Patterson. He had entered the triathlon after all. I could see that he started out in heat number twenty. As he sped past us, he shouted out, "Come on, slowpokes! Quit daydreaming."

I was infuriated. He was rubbing it in. "How are you doing, April?" I cautiously asked.

"Not bad. I'm glad it is finally almost over. I could use a rest."

I guess she conveniently forgot that we still had 3.1 miles to run as soon as we finished the biking portion. I knew that if we really hurried, we could at least catch up to Mike and salvage a shred of dignity. I realized that even if we caught up to him and passed him, he must have started at least fifteen minutes after us. His time would be adjusted of course. In spite of that, I knew that we could at least give it a try. In fact, I knew that I could probably not only catch him but beat him by ten, fifteen, and possibly even close to twenty minutes if I was by myself. After all, I had managed to actually see Mike run a few weeks earlier; and believe me, it was not a very pretty sight. If I could pass him running, it would be a very satisfying accomplishment that I wanted to have a shot at. Reality struck, and I submitted to the fact that there was no way that was going to happen. The promise that I made to April about sticking with her no matter what took precedence over my own pride.

As we jumped off the bikes and got ready to begin the running phase, April grabbed my arm and said, "Dad, you go on ahead. You can pass by a lot of these people. You are much faster than any of them."

"Oh, come on, April," I tried to persuade her. "I know that you can keep up with me and run for a while. Just try it."

"No, Dad, sorry, but I can't do it," she protested, almost in tears.

"Just try. After all, that's why they call it a *tri*athlon. Everyone should try their best."

April wasn't buying it. "Sorry, but I want you to go on ahead. You can beat these people. Look at how slow they are running. They are all burned out from the swimming and the biking, just like me." She gasped to catch her breath. "Look at your friend Mr. Patterson. I know you want to beat him."

April certainly realized that I would not be happy knowing that all these people were ahead of us, especially Mike Patterson. We saw Mike about fifty yards in front of us. There was no way he was going to run much of the last three miles. I was hoping that April would join me in catching up to Mike and running right past him. I thought, *When we're even, we're leavin'.* Perhaps not. "No, April, I'm staying with you." I swallowed my pride. "Besides, you can run a little and power walk the rest. You'll be fine."

"No, Dad, I'm just taking it easy. It's my stomach and my head. They really hurt."

That's when reality struck me like never before. Was April sick back then? I felt awful. I was trying to push her to do her best and to be more competitive while my first concern should have been her health. At the time, I didn't have any idea that April had any particular ailment, but the poor kid was only ten years old for Pete's sake!

"That's okay. Take some water, rest a little, and we will both walk real slowly. We'll talk. We'll go as fast or as slow as you want.

"Thanks, Dad!"

That decision was one of the best I ever made. We had a great time walking, talking, and laughing. We found ourselves talking about the past and some funny things that happened over the years. We also talked about her mom and wondered how she was doing. I knew that Sally would be worried when she saw that April and I were not finishing for quite a while after she had. Then I realized that we were actually doing okay considering the fact that we were way out of our league. Suddenly, however, April tripped on a crack in the street and scraped her knee pretty badly. Shockingly, she was determined to press on. She seemed to be enjoying our conversation and playful banter. I quickly wiped the blood from her knee and told her what a trooper she was.

I suddenly jumped up! I woke up with the thought, *How I wish it was last summer again.* I wanted to wipe away the blood on her scraped knee. *That* I could do. Skinned knees are easier to fix than broken dreams. I immediately fell back asleep.

We could see Mike Patterson ahead of us almost the whole time. He was walking too. Then he would jog about twenty feet and then walk again. I could have easily caught him and passed him. A few times, April insisted that I run the remainder of the course. She tried to convince me that she would be all right by herself and wouldn't care if we separated.

I declared, "No way. I promised that if you wanted us to stay together the whole way, I would."

"But I don't want you stay with me anymore. I want you to go on ahead. And more importantly, I don't want you to be mad at me, Dad!"

"How could I ever be mad at you? This is just a stupid race. It's not even a race. It was supposed to be fun. It *was* fun, and we did have a few laughs. I really enjoyed training together throughout the summer, and we never would have done all that if it wasn't for this triathlon. I don't know about you, but I loved it all. And we're together now. Come on, we only have about a mile to go. If we start running now, we still might be able to pass some people. Come on, you can do it.

"Dad, now I *know* that you're mad!"

At this point, I have to admit that Mike Patterson was really getting to me inside my head. Instead, I backed off. "No, I was only kidding. Let's walk the rest of the way, and we'll jog down the hills only if you want to."

We then came to a small farm between two houses. April noticed that they were growing huge watermelons on a good portion of the land.

"Dad, why do you suppose that watermelons grow on a weak tiny vine in the ground while the tiniest acorn grows on the huge oak tree? Shouldn't it be the other way around? Shouldn't the massive watermelons grow on the sturdy oaks while the acorn grows on the tiny vine?"

"I'm not sure why that is, honey. The little amount of biology I studied was many years ago."

"But, Dad, do you suppose that God made a mistake? How could that be when we all know that God is perfect?"

"Well, you're right. God is perfect, so he must have had a reason."

"Someday we might find out why this is."

Just then, a huge wind blew for about five seconds, blowing an acorn down, and it hit me right on top of the head. I was startled for a few seconds, and April showed her concern and asked, "Dad, are you all right?"

"Yes, I'm fine. It was only an acorn."

April replied matter-of-factly, "Thank God that it *wasn't* a watermelon!"

We continued like that for the rest of the way. Talking a little, laughing a little. Then we looked ahead, and we saw the most beautiful deer crossing the road. It must have been only about twenty feet ahead of us. We walked slowly to try not to scare it. As it walked past us, we could see that right behind it were two of the most adorable fawns that either one of us have ever seen. They were so young and tiny. We stood there in admiration when one last runner ran past us. She was clearly in pain and hurting, and she was very slow. Our last chance to avoid coming in last place just limped past us. By the time we stopped admiring the gorgeous deer, that other runner was about forty feet ahead of us, and there was only about one hundred yards to go in the race.

When we came nearer to the finish line, we heard the band playing and people cheering. We saw hundreds of red, white, and blue balloons. There was a great deal of excitement. We might not have been in last place after all since we did notice an older man also hobbling toward the finish line about 20 yards ahead of us and we saw that he was only about fifty yards before the finish line. April must have felt the excitement of the moment, and she started sprinting at top speed toward the finish line. We had a little joke that she called upon someone by the name of "Burstow." As in burst o' speed. She easily passed the older gentleman when I was still walking. It was only then that I realized there were a lot of people there, watching and cheering. I finally started running toward the end, and I ran in through the chute of the finish line. I came in dead last. April came in what appeared to be third from last.

Sally greeted us and told us how well we did even though I knew that was a lie. We were horrible. On the other hand, Sally came in number 89 out of 250 participants, which was commendable considering her training was limited during the summer due to her injured knee. I tried to justify the whole humiliating experience in my own mind since I had fun in training with Sally and April, and I did stay with April the entire time. I actually did consider the whole experience a success. I *really* did. And I was very proud of April for completing the triathlon and not coming in last place like her old man.

"Good job, April. I'm proud of you," I said, trying to sound enthusiastic. "Nice going. You actually finished. Now, let's get out of here," I said in a huff. I desperately tried to hide the fact that I was livid.

"Dad hates me. That's all there is to it," April protested. "I tried my best."

"Dad doesn't hate you. He said that he was proud of you," Sally chirped, trying to sound convincing.

"That's right, but can we just go home?" I asked in a calm, matter-of-fact voice.

We walked over to where the bikes were still stacked and gathered our things. There was a concluding ceremony where they had oranges, snacks, and the distribution of the awards. We wouldn't be staying around for *that*, thank you very much. Unless they had an award for last place, which I would proudly accept and deposit directly into the nearby lake.

Instead of sticking around and facing further humiliation, I quickly and abruptly loaded the bikes into our minivan and looked over toward the finish line where they were already beginning the closing ceremonies. Someone was running toward us. It was Mike Patterson.

"Come quickly, you guys. You got an award," he exclaimed at the top of his lungs, no less. I thought, *Keep it down, Mike. Everyone will hear you. What is this nut talking about?* He's got some nerve rubbing it in, and I was fuming. Was there really an award for coming in last place?

"April, it's for *you*. You have to hurry in order to make it there in time for the photo," Mike insisted.

April always relished a good photo opportunity, so she perked right up. I still wondered why Mike had to be so insensitive. It was simply rude and obnoxious. After all, she came in third from last place. The only other person she came in ahead of besides me was a sixty-seven-year-old man with a prosthetic leg. We were a little shocked, and we were all still wondering what Mike was talking about. I knew that he had a dry, sarcastic sense of humor; but if this was a joke, then it was totally tasteless and out of line.

"I'm not joking around," he said, as if he could read my mind. April came in first place in her age group, and they are taking pictures of all the winners from each age category. April was in the fifteen and under bracket, and she came in first place!"

Well, in my mind, that changed everything. Now I really *was* proud of April. I still couldn't comprehend how she could have beaten anyone besides me and the old guy. It turned out that there were no other participants who were in the fifteen and under category. I couldn't believe that no other young person, girl or boy, had the motivation and capability to attempt the event. It really was quite an accomplishment that April at least had the determination to participate in such a worthy cause. We really did have such a good time along the way.

Also, Sally beat Mike Patterson by a few minutes, and I thought that it was quite a successful achievement for her. This turned out to be one of the happiest and most memorable days of my life. In the overall scheme of life, as much as a triathlon is such a minor thing, I consider that whole time pivotal in showing me that God is absolutely in command of everything. He will help us to find a way when we trust Him. I learned from that whole experience and benefitted from it in a very profound way.

Then reality struck me like a cold splash of water in the face as I realized that this was in the past, and I had some real problems to contend with right now. As my sense of calm disappeared when I awoke, I realized I had slept for nearly three whole hours in a deep, deep sleep; and I felt a cold, somber feeling. For all that time, I had no worries or problems and no knowledge of Max. I had no idea at the time that April might be gravely ill. April was terribly sick according to Max, which had a track record that was simply ridiculous to dispute.

Just then, I heard a jiggle of the door handle at the back of the house. I knew that someone was coming for me and Max. I had to be assertive, and I could not take any chances. I grabbed my Glock handgun and remembered that it was now fully loaded.

I knelt on one knee ready to shoot. I was sweating a little, but I wasn't even shaking like I usually did every time I held a gun in my hand since I was now enraged with adrenaline. If I had not gotten the devastating results from Max regarding April, I would not have been so angry and aggressive. The back door was being unlocked and now opened!

Ready…aim…I would shoot the first chance I would get. I didn't care anymore.

"Hi, Daddy!" It was April and Sally who for some reason decided to come in through the back door.

"Tom, what is wrong with you? My key didn't work to open the front door. It must have been double locked. Why did you even lock the back door? And what are you doing with that gun? Are you going crazy? I *knew* the stress was getting to you." Sally was hysterical, and her voice was louder and higher pitched than I ever remembered. I quickly managed to calm her down.

"Don't worry. The gun isn't even loaded with the clip. I was just checking on it. I'll put it right back in the safe." Sally still had a bewildered, troubled look on her face, so I quickly changed the subject. "What about April?"

"They are running some tests on her blood, but right now she feels a lot better. The doctor thinks that it is the exact same type of bug that has been going around lately, some type of forty-eight-hour thing. He isn't worried at all, but he will get back to us in a couple of days if the blood test shows anything. April even took a lollypop from the doctor's office."

"Look, Daddy, a strawberry lollipop. It's my favorite flavor." April proudly held up a half-eaten strawberry lollipop. She appeared so poised and calm as if nothing happened. "Dad, while we were waiting for the doctor, I was reading something in a medical journal."

I thought to myself, *I guess they didn't keep the Bible at the hospital if April was stuck reading from a medical journal.*

April continued, "It said that when we die, our hair and even our fingernails continue to grow for a few days. Isn't that amazing, Dad?"

I quipped, "Yes, that may be true. But I'm sure that e-mails and text messages taper off."

"Funny, Dad. Don't quit your day job," she joked back. "Can I watch TV?"

"Sure, April. I'm so glad that you are feeling better."

Fortunately, Sally didn't want to make a big issue out of the little gun incident because she didn't want to worry April. Later that night, I reiterated that the gun wasn't even loaded. I was actually surprised that Sally let it go although she did insist that I start seeing Dr. Panthos again, on a regular basis. I had a feeling that sooner or later, I would have to tell Sally more of what was going on with Max, but now was still not the best time.

Deep down, I was delighted that Max was finally proven wrong. I was totally satisfied that the doctor's report seemed so good. It was *better* than good; it was great. Max was clearly fallible, and I had to be careful not to fall into the trap of believing everything that it came up with from now on.

TROUBLE AT HOME

The next day, we thought about who to invite to April's birthday party. She would be turning eleven years old next month. We liked all of April's friends, and most of their parents were also good friends of ours. They were all sincere, genuine people who knew that we are all rich according to what we are, not what we have. Some folks in our neighborhood on the other hand were so obsessed with material possessions, and I was disappointed to see that in many cases, they actually thought their success was totally from their own doing. I often reflected upon the message gleaned from Luke 14:11, "For all those who exalt themselves will be humbled, and those who humble themselves will be exalted."

If it were not for God, none of us would have anything. All that we have, all that we are, and all that we can ever become is from the grace of God. I am all for getting ahead and having a good life with worthwhile accomplishments and the many benefits that life brings, as long as we can give credit where credit is due.

Even though we started out planning April's party, we couldn't help talking to her about being thankful to God for helping her feel better. We told April many times, "Thank God that you are his masterpiece. He will bless you, and he has you in the palm of his hand."

Sally also knew what was important. She became a teacher because she wanted to touch the lives of children and to help children enjoy learning. Sally was an admirable teacher because of her caring nature and encouraging personality. She constantly made learning fun for her students, and she often spent hours at home designing lessons that were intended to open up the minds of the children she taught. They say that in education you don't have to bring in an elephant to teach the color gray. That makes sense on some levels. On the other hand, Sally's philosophy is, "Why not? After all, you will then be sure that the children will remember 'the color gray!" Also, when children have trouble learning a concept, many educators simply throw up their hands in disgust and proclaim, "Well, you can lead a horse to water, but you can't make him drink." Her comeback to that lame excuse is, "That may be true, but I will put salt in their oats before I give up on them."

The next day was Saturday. April went to Elise's house, and Sally was arduously writing lesson plans and grading papers. I had to get out of the house and clear my head. I put on some sweats and grabbed a water bottle and headed out the door ready for a run. I was lucky if I could manage to run a couple of miles in the state that I was in, but I was eager to give it a try.

"Tom, where do you think *you're* going? You look like death warmed over!"

Sally could definitely tell that I looked horrible, but I didn't think it was that noticeable.

"I'm going to run a couple of miles," I casually responded. "I need to get a little exercise in."

"Please pay attention to what you're doing out there. I don't want you to get hit by a car!"

"Okay, I'll make sure that it's a truck or a bus," I said under my breath. I didn't think that Sally heard me as I raced out the door.

I was barely outside when I heard her call back to me, "Not funny!"

After a few minutes of running, I thought to myself, *Who am I kidding?* I really can't do this. I went back to the house, got in the minivan, and went for a drive. I was worried about falling back to a deep sense of hopelessness and dismay. I had a thought, no, more like a feeling that I had to keep busy in spite of how tired I was. *Depression has a hard time hitting a moving target*, I thought.

Now I was sure I was not of sound mind since one of the first things I noticed while driving was a rather large man, quite husky just like Jack Russell, jogging on the street coming toward me. Oh my, that man looked remarkably like Jack. I was tempted to turn around and catch up to him and finally confront him face to face and fill him in on everything. But could I still trust him? I did a three-point turn right there on the busy street. I just *had* to see if that was him. I caught up to him quickly and saw that it wasn't Jack. In fact, I wasn't sure if this rather large man was simply jogging to reduce or perhaps he was a disabled motorist who was reduced to jogging. I convinced myself that my eyes were merely playing tricks on me. I was under so much pressure now that I couldn't even see clearly, and my thoughts were muddled with confusion. I needed to pray. I had to implore God that I would have the fortitude to see this through, and that everything would soon be resolved. I simply couldn't take the pressure any more. I asked God for courage. I kept reminding myself that I can do all things through Christ who strengthens me. I passed a church, and I noticed their bulletin board message. Was there anything that could help me?

Don't tell God how big your storm is. Tell your storm how big your God is.

Well, I had a storm brewing, for sure. I kept driving and came across another sign, which read, *Courage is fear that has prayed.*

And I certainly could use some of that courage about now. I was still looking for an answer to questions when I didn't even understand what the questions were. Then I saw the sign, *Miracles are answered prayers, not coincidences.*

Pathetically, I was too busy thinking about how monumental my problems were. I tried very hard to refocus my thoughts toward how monumental my faith was. It momentarily gave me new hope. I decided that with everything going on, I would have to "give it to God" and let him direct my path. How could I go wrong then? I also decided to give thanks to God. I even remembered Colossians 3:17, "And whatever you do, whether in word or deed, do it all in the name of the Lord Jesus, giving thanks to God the Father through him."

I felt a little better at this point, so I rushed right home. Sally left me a note that April went with Elise, Kevin, and their parents to a movie. Sally went on to say that her own parents needed her for a few hours, and that she made something for dinner for later, reservations at her favorite restaurant. This bought me some time to spend on the computer and I immediately found a series of e-mails waiting for me.

"Tom, any trouble yesterday? I tried to get you by phone, but you haven't been answering. I don't have much time left. Be home at twelve noon today, and I will contact you."

I thought, *Trouble? Do you consider my daughter being mistakenly diagnosed with an incurable disease trouble? Do you consider my being stressed so close to the breaking point that I almost shot my wife and daughter trouble? Who are you, and what do you want from me?*

I also noticed another unusual e-mail that was an offer of sorts. Someone wanted to discuss terms for the sale of my computer. I was tempted to let them make me a fair offer, and I'd take it. Then I remembered that it was not *my* computer in the first place. I could never stoop so low as to steal something that simply didn't belong to me. I also remembered the tremendous power the computer had. It might be wrong sometimes, but it was more right than wrong. In fact, it was hardly ever wrong. Its results might be difficult to accept, even deplorable sometimes, but it tells it like it is. No, I would keep old Max.

Another hour went by. This time, I received a text message. "Trouble at eleven. Protect yourself. And Max." This time, I *did* call the police. They tried to convince me that they would be here if there was any evidence of foul play. They suggested that I lock the doors, stay inside, and call them if something really happened.

Sure enough, at eleven thirty, there was a knock at the door. There were two men who looked serious, intimidating, and ready for a battle. Fear rushed throughout my body. I felt like a coward. I was shaking like a leaf on a breezy day, and my heart was pounding out of my chest. I knew I could quickly slip out the back of the house to safety. I thought, *It's much better to be a coward for a minute than to be dead the rest of my life.* I hesitated, then I got my nerve back. I looked through the window and saw that there was a van parked out in front with bold lettering that said, "Bruno Martini General Contractor." I got out my Glock and double locked the door. A minute later, the two men banged on the door for a full five minutes. I kept quiet and hoped that they would go away. Sure, I had my handgun, but I wasn't extensively trained at the "farm" like some of my pals at Langley. That hardcore, tactical training surely would have come in handy right about now. Instead, I was told in no uncertain terms right from the beginning of my days at the agency that, "Your talents were in other areas." That was okay with me. I was trained to write computer code, and I am a systems analyst. I certainly wasn't trained for "combat." I hated to think about what weapons these men had, right outside my door. The gravity of the current moment struck as I stood there frozen.

They demanded that I let them in so we could talk. They indicated that their boss claimed to know all about my computer, and that he wanted to make me a reasonable offer for it. I insisted that I didn't know what they were talking about. They were quite dogged and would not take no for an answer. "I don't know what you are talking about. I am a sick, feeble old man with a heart condition." I tried to be convincing even though the truth of the matter was I had my pistol aimed squarely at my birch door in case they decided to break it down and enter the house. They were quite obstinate, so I lied and said that the police were on their way.

One of them called out, "You'll be sorry! Our boss always gets what he wants, one way or another."

I realized that others must have known about the arcane powers of Max, and they might do anything to acquire them. The men went back to their van and seemed to be making a phone call. I was worried. *Here we go again*, I thought. On the other hand, experience is a brilliant thing. It enables you to recognize a mistake when you make it again. I called the police a second time and tried to sound more convincing, even hysterical. I swore to them that there were two suspicious men outside my home in a van that were planning to break in. The police dispatcher indicated that there were absolutely no squad cars available, but they would try to send someone in twenty minutes or so. Of course, he also insisted that I should lock all of my doors and stay in the house. I was sure that it was only a matter of time before the men came back to the front door, broke it down, or shot right through it and came after me to get Max. Five minutes later, I decided to call the police back, and I made up the story that the men just broke down my front door and entered my house, so I shot them. I said that it looked like they were dead, and that they should come quickly. Three minutes later, I could hear the sirens of three police cars and an ambulance. The police saw the van parked out in front and caught the men with a load of illegal guns in their van. They also found that the van was stolen. The police came to my door and demanded to know why I lied and told them about shooting the men. In response, I demanded to first know why they originally told me that there were no squad cars available, and the soonest they could have someone here was twenty minutes. We had a good laugh. They made a substantial arrest of two men with a horde of illegal guns, and I was back inside by myself waiting. Now it was up to the police to find out what these men were doing with such firepower and why they were here in the first place. I had my own problems to deal with.

It was now twelve thirty. I got another e-mail, and this time it included an address where I was to go to the very next day. I was to tell no one what was going on. I shot back an e-mail indicating that I would be there at 8 AM. I was hopeful that I would finally have some answers.

That night, I couldn't fall asleep even though I was so tired. I prayed that I would have the courage necessary to maintain my sanity and see this through. It might all be ending soon. On the other hand, this might be the beginning and not the end. I went down to the basement and looked through some old textbooks. I found a letter that was folded up, stuck inside one of the pages. It was a handwritten note from my sister Kate from many years ago.

Dear Tommy,

Congratulations on your second graduation from Georgetown and two master's degrees! I am so proud to have you as my brother. You mean the world to me, and I am glad that we have gotten so close over the years. (Don't you dare tell them this, but I feel that I am closer to you than I am to Johnny or Dave.)

I was glad that I could help you through your sadness when Carla died. Throughout the years, you helped me so much too. I remember the time when I was nine years old and some of the boys at school made fun of me. You told me that one day they would be sorry they were so mean because I would grow up to be the prettiest girl in school. And you were right! Then when I started dating in high school, you helped me sort out the weirdos from the winners. Of course, there is all the math that you always helped me with from middle school through college. I just want to say thank you for everything, especially for all of the love and encouragement you have always given me. Good luck with Sally; she is certainly something special.

I will always remember what you told me about believing in myself, having faith in God, and that it is not over until God says it is. Thanks!

Love,

Katie

Later that night, Sally found me downstairs. I fell asleep with Katie's letter next to me, but I was slumped over the computer with a little bit of drool coming out of my mouth and onto the keyboard. My eyes must have still been red and moist from crying. Sally nudged me and indicated that she wanted to talk. *Here it comes*, I thought.

Sally began compassionately enough, "Tom, are you all right? I'm getting worried about you. You appear so distant lately. You don't seem like yourself."

"Who do I seem like?" I asked sarcastically.

"Don't try to be a wise guy. It's not funny! I know that your work is very important to you, but you usually don't let it get to you emotionally and allow it to drain you physically."

I could have used that as an opportunity to fill her in about Max and at least give her a taste of what was happening. I chose not to.

"I have to do whatever Jack thinks best for now. He is still in charge of this whole thing," I pretended to say with confidence in Jack.

"But can you trust him to look out for *your* best interests?" she asked doubtfully.

"Well, he is insensitive sometimes. But remember, he *was* there for me years ago when I really needed him." I paused for a few seconds, and then I continued, "I *have* been stressed out lately and exhausted. This work project has taken its toll on me."

Sally snapped back, "Oh really, but you hide it so well!"

"So it's okay for you to make a joke about this, but not me?"

"Sorry," she apologized.

"You're really not in tune with all that I'm going through with work and his project and all of the complexities involved."

"Oh, but I am, Tom. Who do you think informed Johnny that things are not right with you? I was so disgusted about your demeanor lately that I asked him to talk to you and try to get to the bottom of this."

"Oh, so *you* were the one! What did you tell him?"

"Just that you got yourself wrapped up in something regarding computers, and I can't begin to comprehend the magnitude of whatever it is or why it is driving you to the brink of…disaster. I also asked him if he knew anything."

"I shouldn't involve Johnny."

"Why not? He's your *brother*!" Just be sure to get your priorities straight. Why don't you just quit…you don't need this nonsense."

"I can't just quit now," I exclaimed emphatically. "I don't want to jeopardize their support of our Learning Styles Project. Besides, this computer assignment is potentially a matter of national security. I really have to see it to fruition."

"But not if it is detrimental to your health…and our marriage!" Sally couldn't catch herself in time. I'm sure that she would have preferred to refrain from that last statement. I had no idea our marriage was ever an issue, and if I had any inkling that it was in jeopardy in any way, I would have found some approach to put an end to all of this. Or better yet, I would never have agreed to get involved with it in the first place. I also should have been more aware of everything that Sally was going through lately. I wished that I was more sensitive to all the pressure she faced at work and the fact that her body was undergoing changes almost daily. Luckily, instead of continuing to argue with Sally, I did what I do best. I shut up my face. I moved closer to her as she was now sitting on the bed. I sat down next to her and held her. It was not an ordinary hug. It was a passionate embrace that said it all; that everything was going to be all right. It indicated that we were always there for each other, that we loved each other unconditionally, and that because of that love, we would get through anything. I was positive that we both were feeling a connection that nothing could ever destroy. Besides, I didn't mention any of this to her, but it was theoretically possible that it could all be over as early as tomorrow morning.

WHO IS THIS MAN?

The next day turned out to be another beautiful sunny day, and the air was crisp and cool. It was about seven forty-five when I arrived at a luxurious home in one of the more affluent sections of McLean. The black iron gate was left wide open, so I drove up the driveway about one hundred feet toward the front lawn of a gorgeous colonial home. The house was beautifully landscaped, and there was a tall flagpole right on the front lawn proudly displaying the American flag. As I curiously walked to the side of the house, just far enough to see in the back, it looked as if there was a three-car detached garage. I also noticed a built in swimming pool that was fenced in further in the back. I could detect tennis courts and a patio with an impressive barbecue grill, all suggesting opulence that I had not seen in quite a long time. Some things began to make sense now. I deduced that the generous weekly checks for my "services" originated from the owner of this luxurious colossal home. When I walked back to the front of the house, I saw that there was a wooden wheelchair ramp leading to the front door. It actually appeared that the ramp was recently built since there were small pieces of wood off to each side of it. I knocked on the door and rang the doorbell for a full five minutes, but nothing happened. No one answered the door.

Finally, the door opened automatically. I walked in and found myself standing in a majestic grand foyer. I could see a beautiful fireplace in a huge living room. Across the room was a man sitting in a wheelchair. He motioned for me to come toward him, and he immediately shook my hand and told me that his name was Robert Jacob Marxman. It was beginning to make some sense at least. He explained how he was the mastermind who designed sophisticated computer programs for the government, which could eventually be used to address any problem imaginable. His computer was configured to allow access to everything ever published. That was his ultimate goal anyway. His physical abilities had deteriorated significantly within the last six months, so he realized he was no longer able to continually manage all of the fine tuning it would take to improve on what it could do. I, in turn, wanted to fill him in on everything that had happened so far including everything that Max was able to accomplish. The problems that I worked on the past few months and what Max was already able to do indicated that Mr. Marxman could indeed have been telling the truth. I wondered why he chose me. Moreover, what did he really want me to do for him? As for why he could not do all of this himself, I had a pretty good idea. He was a genius, perhaps the greatest computer expert and inventor the world has ever known. Sorrowfully, he needed help because he was dying of Altoschrotomis. That was the scientific name of what most people know as "Lou Gehrig's disease" or ALS. He was diagnosed with it about four years ago. He had been using Max to work on finding a cure for the dreaded disease for the past four years. In the beginning, he did the best that he could, trying to hold up and take care of himself. For the past year, he had a nurse stay with him for most of the day. They became friends, and lately, she was a loyal and dependable aid who was with him at all times. However, she was not a doctor; there was no cure right now for ALS, and viable treatment options were extremely limited.

A few years before Mr. Marxman was stricken with ALS, he briefly worked with a team that explored the development of quantum computers, which characterized a completely new model of computer intelligence. These computers will use quantum bits to propel computer technology into totally uncharted territory. Marxman abandoned the project because the types of problems they could solve were extremely limited and would be for the foreseeable future. He then used all of his time to continue the advancement of his own computers. He configured them to absorb every shred of medical information available until it could find a definitive cure, but the computers were not ready yet. During the past few years, his health had been failing, and he was making less progress. He had one hope left. Max was the only special computer still available, and Marxman got his good friend Jack Russell to help him by recruiting the only person that could be trusted for this, someone who was capable of accomplishing the lofty goal of helping Max find a cure for his ailment. In reality, Jack was simply his pawn. Mr. Marxman gambled that Jack could be trusted to keep it all a secret. As a matter of fact, it was Marxman that convinced Jack to have me placed under a type of temporary leave at the agency so I was not even working for the CIA in any official capacity for the past two and a half months. That explained why the only checks I received lately were not from the government, but from Marxman's special account. I was really working for Marxman, and Jack was the only one at Langley who knew about it. Mr. Marxman even told me that the men who originally delivered Max back in January were not from the CIA. They were friends of his, and he found out that they almost inadvertently revealed who sent them. Anyway, Marxman knew that I would be totally loyal to Jack, and that Jack could get away with this, but it wouldn't last forever. What we were doing was bordering on illegal. This explained why Jack's attitude was so capricious. He was truly in a quandary given his lofty position as the assistant director of Science and Technology, and he would have been held accountable. On the other hand, he wanted desperately to help Marxman, knowing that he was going to die.

Anyway, I was the one person that Marxman specifically wanted. I wondered how he knew that I would be able to eventually uncover the secrets and the awesome power of his inimitable computer. Then he told me that about two years ago he came across my name as a prolific computer and statistical mind who was capable of doing great things. It turned out that some of my methods were actually even more advanced than Mr. Marxman's since I was privy to some of the latest advances in computer programming. He and Max came to the conclusion that I would be able to use his special computer to someday expedite the process of finding a cure for ALS. He also knew what I discovered—that Max could actually learn and get better and better at reasoning things out and drawing conclusions if it had a chance to "practice." Marxman knew that Max needed to be pushed in ways similar to how I used it, and this would enable it to improve sufficiently. Unfortunately, it took time, which Marxman probably didn't have. A few months ago, he realized that in order to have a chance to benefit from a potential cure that Max might be able to supply, he needed Max to accelerate its learning. Max and I were his last hope. I now had the knowledge and the creativity necessary to get the most out of Max. Just as importantly, Max now had the "strength" and was at the proper level of sophistication necessary for such a laborious task. Mr. Marxman made it totally clear that he was astonished with what Max and I were able to accomplish. He monitored most of our work and expressed his surprise as to the direction I was taking. I started getting nervous at that point. There was no way I wanted to discuss some of the techniques that I used; they undoubtedly would have piqued his interest.

"What you did so far was superb," he beamed. "I never would have been able to achieve some of the successes that you had with Max. Some of your ideas and programming techniques were enthralling."

"Thanks, but it was all Max," I humbly protested.

"Not really. Don't be so modest. I also liked the way you used Max to play the ponies. You must have cleaned up!"

"Oh yeah, sorry about that."

"No, no, that's okay. I was actually hoping that you'd make so much money at the track that I would never have to pay you a salary. I guess you've been so engrossed in the experiments lately that you've been too busy for that sort of thing."

I quickly realized what a genuine, down to earth man I was dealing with. I wanted to tell him about everything I have been going through lately, including the details about how I used Max to play out various hypothetical scenarios. I also wanted to share the vivid dreams that I have been having and the turmoil that Max put me through when it mistakenly reported that my own daughter was gravely ill. All of that would have to wait.

Marxman surmised that Max was able to access data from every source imaginable including data storage centers, and that it was able to utilize everything necessary to solve the problem or answer the question it was posed. Perfecting this technique was something Marxman was never able to do. I now wondered if there would be sufficient time to help him considering the fact that his health was fading fast. Furthermore, there were people out there who somehow knew about Max and the potential power involved. I asked Marxman about the phone call warning, but he sincerely didn't know anything about it. I mentioned the text message telling me to "watch out." He insisted that he didn't send it either although clearly someone did. If it wasn't for those warnings, I would have let the men in, we wouldn't have Max, and I might have been killed. Not only that, I may have put my own family in serious danger. Marxman then promised that he would hire two of his most trustworthy, qualified men to watch my house without anyone else knowing.

It turned out that Mr. Marxman worked for the CIA for twenty years at one point. He was kept under the radar although he ranked high in the Intelligence Division, and he was allowed the freedom to continually work on the computer technology as he saw fit. He worked on many top secret projects and at one point was on the staff of the director of the entire CIA. Mr. Marxman officially retired three years ago, but he was working with various types of special computers for the past ten years. Ironically, he kept all of his knowledge regarding Max and some of the other unique computers to himself because he didn't know who *he* could trust. When he was stricken with ALS about four years ago, he tried to step up the intensity of research and discovery, but his health faded too quickly, and he was forced to retire. Lately, he realized that he would never be able to do all that was necessary. That's when he contacted Jack Russell who was once his closest friend. Jack did what he could but recently decided to step out of the picture. He saw the potential ramifications and conflict of interest issues, and he wanted no part of it. That's why I haven't even heard from Jack in nearly a month now. Jack did promise Marxman that he would wait before he took any action. But for how long?

Thus, it turned out that Marxman had easy access to many important files and mounds of documents and information of all types due to his high security status. Subsequently, Max was provided with everything, but there was so much more involved with its inconceivable ability. Max was able to tap into so many other highly secured devises as well as storage clouds throughout the world that were once considered impenetrable. My own ingenuity was certainly a factor because I utilized programming techniques that Marxman never realized on his own or even thought possible. He was so impressed with what Max and I accomplished that he let us have more time than he originally planned. I felt that as long as April's health was no longer in question, I would be able to focus on helping

Marxman. In fact, since April's doctor still never got back to us with anything negative, all I was concerned with right now was helping Marxman.

I spent about two more hours with Mr. Marxman while he shared his story. He could speak seven different languages fluently, which explained how Max could do the same if I chose to let it. He told me about his illustrious career with the government, his outstanding accomplishments with computers, and his enthusiasm for life. On the other hand, he also revealed that his life was not always trouble free. He knew he did some things while working on various covert operations that were unethical at best, abominable at worst. He admitted to me that he was deeply ashamed of some of the egregious acts that he committed while gaining intelligence in various foreign countries. He lived with burdensome guilt and anguish for much of his life. I also learned about his sincerity and generosity, and I was so eager to help him. He was a special, inspiring human being who was genuine and likeable; he was someone who simply wanted to live to do more in life.

"Tom, can I fully depend on you?" he asked me, knowing how I would respond.

"Absolutely! You can count on me," I promised him. Robert Marxman was a man with magnificent charisma. I couldn't help liking him, and I desperately wanted to assist him. I felt such a positive connection with him that I hadn't felt with any man other than my own father who passed away five years ago.

Still, I was totally exhausted physically, mentally, and emotionally. I was worried how Sally would take any bad news regarding April's health if someday she *was* seriously ill. I concluded that I was just being paranoid due to the long hours and stress of the past few weeks and months. Luckily, speaking with Mr. Marxman helped my own focus and temporarily renewed my energy.

I realized that I had to get right to work, so I quickly loaded my car with boxes and boxes of information on both ALS and

Mr. Marxman's personal medical history. There were flash drives, which held every bit of known research pertaining to ALS. The medical records of almost everyone ever diagnosed with ALS were also on flash drives. Other flash drives containing various medical reports filled three shoeboxes. Unfortunately, some of the old records that Marxman recently recovered were from years ago, and these were never converted to disk or flash drive. They would have to be scanned in, the old-fashioned way. Max might need this information. We could not take anything for granted; we simply had to include everything. Look at the mistake Max made with diagnosing April after using only a limited amount of information that was accessible. Ironically, Marxman saw firsthand that supercomputers were coming up empty as far as finding definitive cures for many ailments that society is still plagued with. Max, on the other hand, was much more promising than anything that Marxman ever used in the past including the supercomputers at Langly. He told me that months ago, he considered soliciting the advice of the medical field, but he did not trust anyone. Why would they use Max for *his* ailment when the world could benefit from many other aspects of its power? Not only that, but Max had not established a track record of phenomenal accuracy at that point.

I assured Mr. Marxman that I knew what needed to be done. He had no idea how much time he had left. Every day he was feeling more pain, and he was losing his ability to do the simplest of tasks. He had someone come in every day to help him feed himself, and he was now eating only two small meals per day. His weight was reduced to 118 pounds, and he was clinging to his last hope, me. I could not let him down. However, I still had one more thing to do on my way home.

I stopped by the hospital and insisted upon speaking with April's primary doctor, Dr. Baker. I had to wait over an hour, but he finally saw me. He indicated that the news was not good, and that he was just about to call us with information regarding April and her tests. He informed me that April's stomach troubles were only a small part of the problem. It was actually a rare bone disease that was the root cause of all of April's physical problems. It accounted for everything, including her occasional headaches. He told me that this disease was always fatal, and he wrote the name on the back of his card that he handed me. He told me that although the prognosis was not good, he would be in touch with a course of action. He may have said more, and he probably tried to be encouraging, but I didn't hear a single word that he said. I was distraught and overwhelmed, and I choked back tears of despair. I finally looked at Dr. Baker's card and saw that the condition that April had was exactly what Max had earlier forecasted—fibrous dysplasia. Max was indeed right after all!

I sped out of there, devastated. I had some real decisions to make now. How should I tell Sally and April? My mind was racing, and my heart was pounding. My daughter was the most beautiful, adorable, and exceptional child I could have ever imagined. She was smart and kind, determined and compassionate. When she was a toddler, she would sob in sympathy whenever she heard a baby cry. She loved life and God. And of course, she loved her mom and dad who were not supposed to ever let her down. April memorized Bible quotes and seemed to have one for every occasion. Without a doubt, April would now be up against the battle of her life, one that her parents might not be able to help her with, a fight that she might not be able to win.

I suddenly changed my thoughts back to Marxman. How did he know that I was the most capable person to find a cure for ALS? Because I was honest, and I could be trusted? Or because I could see the overall picture, and that it was vital to cure him first since he was the key to going forward. Marxman trusted me much more than I would trust anyone whose daughter was dying from an ailment that had no cure, someone who was desperate. My mind whirled with possibilities, and it was filled with the overwhelming magnitude of the task at hand, as well as my own despair. I now realized that Max should not be used to find the most compatible mate for someone. We did not need Max to predict the test scores for second graders or to predict what would happen if someone took a job in another city twenty years ago. What is past is gone. All we have is now. All we have left is in the future, what remains of it. Yes, I thought I knew exactly what I had to do.

AN IMPOSSIBLE SITUATION

There is no way to describe the intense pressure I was feeling. The next day, we spent most of our time with the doctors at Georgetown University Hospital. If April's doctors had been a little more on top of things years ago, we would have had a much better chance to get her to a treatment and cure. I also hated to admit that Sally and I should have been more proactive when April showed signs years ago, but we simply didn't do enough to get her to the right places for checkups. Could Max find a way to go back in time? Of course not. It could only tell us what might have happened if we detected April's disease earlier. I wasn't going to waste one minute of my time with things that should have been or might have been.

I wrestled with all the possibilities. I knew that I agreed to help Marxman. On the other hand, Mr. Marxman was a wealthy man who already experienced life for sixty-seven years. Unfortunately, he didn't have any children to help take care of him, and he was never married. He was a classic "workaholic" who only recently discovered some of the profound joys that life has to offer. It was mostly due to his sickness these past few years and pending death that he learned to appreciate the real beauty of living. No matter what happened, it would be very difficult, almost impossible for

Mr. Marxman to recapture his youth and enjoy his life once more. On the other hand, April was only ten years old, turning eleven in three weeks. She had her whole life ahead of her. I needed a cure for my precious daughter right now. Yes, I knew that Mr. Marxman was running out of time, but April might be as well. I had already wasted a few days sending Max on the ultimate "search" for an ALS cure. I suddenly changed my focus and asked Max how long it would take to outline a cure for April. Max disclosed that it would take somewhere between two and three weeks. Possibly. Without a cure, how long could April survive? Max reported that there was no way of knowing, but her sickness was probably too far along for it to come up with a definitive cure in time. It was the saddest, most disappointing news I had ever received. The worst part was that I now trusted Max. I knew that it was Max that originally identified April's illness even before the doctors came out with their diagnosis. In some ways this whole thing was like some kind of test that I was not prepared for, unlike anything I have ever faced in my life. I wasn't sure if I should continue with the ALS research. If I dropped everything right now, I still thought I had a slight chance to work on a cure for April. I considered appealing to the real experts in the medical field, figuring I might have a better chance. Then again, I could not risk it and expose what we had with Max and what we were on the verge of doing. I wasn't sure if anyone would even believe me. I needed someone else whom I could trust. But who?

The next day, the doctors at Georgetown University Hospital decided April would need to stay indefinitely for tests and constant monitoring. Sally or I might have to stay with her throughout the entire day. I wanted more than anything to be with her every minute, but I convinced Sally that the project I was working on was in fact top secret, and it was vital to our national security, terms she heard often. We decided to formulate a long term game plan. My sister-in-law Sophie was a registered nurse in the neonatal wing of the hospital, and she immediately agreed to help us out. She had some flexibility with her schedule so she arranged to be with April when needed. On days when Sally went to work, I would be with April until about two thirty in the afternoon when Sally arrived. Otherwise, Sally would be with April during the day, and I would arrive later. Of course, sometimes my work with Max interfered, and I didn't always arrive until late in the evening.

I simply couldn't tell Sally about Marxman and the ALS work. If she suspected for a minute that Max might be able to find a cure for April, she would have insisted that I use Max for that alone. Furthermore, I probably would have agreed since I did not have any compelling argument for continuing with the search for an ALS remedy, especially when my own daughter's life was at stake. Sally knew that April's condition was grave, but she still had no way of knowing about Max's claim that April could die without a quick cure. At this point, the doctors never addressed any time frame at all. They simply had no clue.

In a perfect world, we would be able to do it all and have the resources to solve everything; however, since there was only one Max, there would have to be priorities. The first assignment would be to come up with a cure for ALS. After all, it was Mr. Marxman's machine, his invention. Next, a cure for cancer. There are six hundred thousand people who die each year from this disease. My daughter? Her disease was so rare. Only ten thousand people in the country have this rare disease. Check that. There are exactly 9,876 people according to Max. What right did I have to use Max for April's problem? What we really needed was more computers designed like Max, but as the expression goes, when they made Max, they literally broke the mold.

The demands of the past few months and my complete exhaustion clouded my mind and my judgment. On the days when it was my turn to go to the hospital and be with April, I would stay for only a couple of hours and then leave to go home to work with Max. I desperately wanted to put the ALS research on hold until we could find a cure for April's disease. I might be able to get that done in two weeks. I would hope and pray that she would be able to benefit from whatever Max came up with, and then I would hope that Mr. Marxman was still alive. Then I would work on ALS, but this is not what I promised Marxman I would do. I wanted April to come first. I felt as if I had the burden of the world on my shoulders as I had all these choices to make.

I decided to continue to put all my time and resources into finding a cure for ALS for Marxman and everyone with that ailment. I was committed to Marxman, so I needed to find something else that would help April. I wanted to have some hope, but I didn't see a way.

Sally and I continued to try to explain to April what she was up against. April needed to be told the truth about the disease that she had. It was attacking the bones throughout her body, including her skull. Sally was in some sort of denial and was therefore taking a more positive approach. She was telling April that since the doctors were working nonstop, a cure could come any day. She emphasized the importance of positive thinking. Of course, I knew for certainty that the doctors were clueless about April's case. Not only that, I had a chance to look for April's cure on my own, but Max was busy working on something else instead.

April was as upbeat as ever when I came to the hospital. She immediately put away her iPod, and I could hear she was listening to a classic song by Johnny Cash. "Dad, I missed you yesterday. I memorized seven new Bible verses. Three from the Old Testament and four from the New." "That's great! I found a few new ones for you too. Remember, don't just read the verses from the Bible, say them out loud. Declare them with confidence.

All God has to do is say the word. You are a child of the almighty God!" I then handed her one of the slips of paper that I had. It had the verse, "For God so loved the world that he gave his one and only Son, that whoever believes in him shall not perish but have eternal life" (John 3:16).

God gave his only son to die so that we might live. I was being asked to sacrifice my only child so that Marxman and others might live. April and I began talking, and I tried to reassure her and give her some encouragement. As much as I loved seeing her, I was hoping to get her to fall asleep so I would be able to rush home for a few hours and get back to work and continue dealing with Max. Then Dr. Baker called me out of the room and into the hall.

He was very complementary toward April. "Your daughter has such a splendid attitude! She is always so positive!"

"Thanks. Anything else?"

That's when Dr. Baker's demeanor went back to its usual stoic form. He again explained exactly what we were up against. I took notes. I would need to know precisely what details to supply Max if I ever got the chance. I would also need access to every bit of information that was available regarding her disease. Before he walked away, he left me with one more thing. As much as I didn't appreciate hearing him say what he did, I was not discouraged. I still had one bit of hope.

He told me, "What we have here is an impossible situation. No one should have to face what your daughter is going through."

"But, Dr. Baker," I pleaded, "Is there anyone who can help her? In the world?"

"No, it is *impossible*. No man or woman has adequately studied this disease since it is so rare. It will be *impossible* for anyone to help her now. I'm sorry. It will be like moving a mountain."

Even as he said these words of despair, I was more encouraged than ever before, and I did not give up hope. In fact, what Dr. Baker said *inspired* me. Twice he used the word impossible.

Coincidence? Or miracle? I looked at the papers that I was still holding. I still wanted to give them to April. I went back into her room.

"April, I have to go for a little while. I will be back soon," I promised.

April, who was usually so cheerful, leaned toward me and grabbed my hand. She was now clearly disappointed. "But, Dad, you just got here! Who's staying with me today? Where's Mom? Don't you love me anymore?"

"Of course, I love you. More than you know. I am trying to help!"

"Dad, where is God? I have been asking for his help, but sometimes I feel alone. You are hardly ever here, and when Mom is here, she spends most of her time trying to find the doctors, and she gets mad at them. I thought that God would help me, and I would never be alone even if you and Mom were not here."

"I know how you feel, April. It is really mostly my fault. God entrusted me as your father to always be with you when you needed someone to be there for you. I promise that I will do a better job."

"No, Dad, it's not your fault. I just got a little frustrated. Sorry."

"I will help you to pray and ask God for his help. First, let me tell you a story that might help you to understand."

I told her the beautiful, inspiring story called footprints in the sand.

"April, one night, a man had a dream. He dreamed he was walking along the beach with the Lord. Across the sky flashed scenes from his life. For each scene, he noticed two sets of footprints in the sand: one belonging to him and the other to the Lord. When the last scene of his life flashed before him, he looked back at the footprints in the sand. He noticed that many times along the path of his life, there was only one set of footprints. He also noticed that it happened at the very lowest and saddest times in his life. This really bothered him, and he questioned the Lord about it. 'Lord, you said that once I decided to follow you, You'd walk with me all the way. But I have noticed that during the most troublesome times in my life, there is only one set of footprints. I don't understand why when I needed you most you would leave me.'

The Lord replied, 'My precious child, I love you. I would never leave you. During your times of trial and suffering, when you see only one set of footprints, it was then that I carried you.'"

Do you see how God will always be with you?"

"Yes, Daddy," she whispered. Then she gave *me* something. It was an envelope with a piece of paper folded inside. There was some writing on it, but April explicitly told me not to read it or open it until later. I folded the envelope in half and put it in my pocket.

Before I left her, I finally handed her the papers with the verses, and I said to her, "Baby, try these. Look these up. They will make you feel better."

The papers had some Bible verses that were words of hope and healing. I knew they might be our only chance. "April, ask God for help. Ask him to heal you! But then be sure to *thank* Him for healing you."

"*Okay.* I will, Dad. I love you."

"And remember, God has you in the palm of his hand." I again reassured her. I added, "April, I don't think this illness is going to keep you from your destiny. It is going to help you *fulfill* your destiny." I had no idea why I said that. It just came out randomly for some inexplicable reason.

April took the papers that I gave her. They were all significant, very important verses from the Bible.

"Worship the LORD your God, and his blessing will be on your food and water. I will take away sickness from among you" (Exodus 23:25).

"The righteous person may have many troubles, but the LORD delivers him from them all; he protects all his bones, not one of them will be broken" (Psalm 34:19–20).

The next one, I knew that she liked and appreciated. Bethany Hamilton used it a lot in her own story of faith and healing that April heard and cherished.

"For I know the plans I have for you, declares the LORD, plans to prosper you and not to harm you, plans to give you hope and a future. Then you will call on me and come and pray to me, and I will listen to you. You will seek me and find me when you seek me with all your heart" (Jeremiah 29:11–14).

The last two that I gave April were the ones that gave me the most hope and inspiration even as Dr. Baker was speaking to me about how bleak it looked for April. I thought that it was more than a phenomenal coincidence.

> What is impossible with man is possible with God. (Luke 18:27)

> Because you have so little faith. Truly I tell you, if you have faith as small as a mustard seed, you can say to this mountain, 'Move from here to there,' and it will move. Nothing will be impossible for you. (Matthew 17:20)

As soon as Sally arrived at the hospital, April was taken for some tests. I carried on about my work assignment and how it was a classified, top secret project that was a matter of national security. Sally believed me. Her trust in me was worth so much even though I didn't always feel that I deserved it. I told her that I would meet her at home knowing that she would probably stay at the hospital until about nine when they basically kicked her out. I went home to work on various ways to efficiently enter some data regarding ALS that I got my hands on at the hospital. I was determined to get this done before Mr. Marxman could no longer benefit from the results. This went on for a few more days. The worst part about the whole thing was lying to Sally and sometimes April. I would get to the hospital on days when it was my turn to be with April, talk with her for an hour or so, give her some more verses to look up, and then try to get her to fall asleep. Then I would see who on the hospital staff I could bribe to gain access to more of their files on ALS. Ironically, the money that I hoarded from my racetrack winnings came in handy as I still had a few thousand dollars in cash to work with. It was a continual cycle that went on for days. More data. More lying. More tinkering with Max and more distress as the news pertaining to April's condition was coming in. There was very little hope for April. I knew that I should stay with her. Every time I arrived at the hospital to see April, I knew it might be the last time I ever saw her. My heart was literally aching. I realized that I couldn't go on like this much longer. I was sleeping only two hours per day either at the hospital if I fell asleep with April or while working with Max at night.

Sally knew that something was wrong with me since I was walking around in a daze. In fact, she must have been so upset with me that she chose not to even confront me about my demeanor. My thoughts were so cloudy I felt like I was in a permanent state of confusion and awkward despair. A few times when Sally and I were both at home together or at the hospital's waiting room when April was going for tests, Sally would see that I had been crying. She was probably so disappointed in me for putting our family second, but she didn't say anything. For some reason, I felt that I was doing the right thing, and that everything would work out. I also knew what Sally was going through, but I could not be of any comfort to her. Unfortunately, Sally and I both knew what we were up against regarding April's condition, and she still had no idea what was going on with me and all the work that I was doing with Max and ALS. I shuttered to think about what Sally would say if she knew I was not using the computer to at least try to find a cure for April. If she had any idea as to what Max and I were able to do over the course of these past few months, she would have insisted that we utilize Max for our own good and for April.

I don't remember the exact moment that I decided to turn it all around and to genuinely give it all to God. I realized what was buried deep inside me, something that would help us even though I didn't understand all that was happening. I needed to trust in God. I thought of something fitting that April once showed me from the Bible. It was Proverbs 3:5, "Trust in the Lord with all your heart and lean not on your own understanding."

Not only that, I also remembered that here was one of the connections from the Old and New Testaments that April once proudly showed me and Sally. In Romans 15:13, it is written, "May the God of hope fill you with all joy and peace as you trust him so that you may overflow with hope by the power of the Holy Spirit."

I decided that God would allow something to happen that was unprecedented. I felt that something would occur that would allow us all to feel God's presence. In fact, the next time I was alone with Sally at home, she came up to me. We sat together in each other's arms, and we each knew what we both were thinking. Sally let me know that she trusted me, and she insisted that she was not angry or upset any longer. She also agreed that we had to trust God, just like it seemed April was doing. Even though the medical report didn't look good, that didn't matter. Even though we didn't see a way, we knew that God *had* a way, and that God's way is not always the same as our way. God is still in control. Through all of this, I was so glad that Sally and I still had an inseparable connection. I thought to myself that it *is* true—what God has joined, no man, calamity, or sickness can divide.

I now believed that God would provide a way to help April when it looked like there was no way in sight. I knew that if God was for us, nothing could be against us. Surely, God was pleased with April's faith and would not let anything keep her from the destiny that he had prepared for her. This was enough for me for now, and I realized that there was a time in my life, probably long ago, that I used the line, "Just trust in God. He is faithful and just." I barely remembered it, but that one idea was etched in my mind permanently, albeit very blurred.

Marxman stopped calling. I did stop by to check up on him. His aid answered the door and confirmed that he was not doing well. I told him to hold on because Max was very convincing that a cure would be coming soon, that it would be quite definitive, and that it was sure to work. When I arrived home, I reached into my pocket and realized that I still had the envelope that April gave me the other day. It was a poem and it was something that I would treasure for the rest of my life. She must have been thinking about Father's Day even though that was a long way off.

> Dear Dad,
>
> I'd like to start by saying, "Happy Father's Day!"
> I wrote this poem 'cause I had some things to say.
> You always helped me out writing poems for Mom.
> I know it was always tedious, but you always kept calm.
> But today is your day—my time to entertain.
> I hope you'll enjoy a walk down memory lane.
> It all started when I was just a small tot.
> You held me and fed me and hugged me a lot.
> We used blocks, software, and recorded our voices.
> You taught me so much and presented me with choices.
> You read to me and taught me math and the ABCs.
> We acted out adventures and climbed tall, tall trees.
> You took all my friends to places they've never been
> Your jokes and comments would make them laugh and grin.
> As I got older, I could do many more things.
> You and Mom will always be there, no matter what life brings.
> Life will have challenges, but I know I can handle it all.
> Thanks to you and Mom, I will never fall.

You were there to help me with all my math questions.
I am truly grateful for all your suggestions.
Not only in math do you excel, however.
Sports are your field, no matter the weather.
You guided me in basketball—you had amazing control.
You even taught me to "pump fake and go to the hole."
I had so much fun when you coached our softball team,
You were persistent and dedicated—you went to extremes.
You stayed home when I was sick or I was alone,
Something I feel, I still haven't outgrown.
But the best gift of all is your unconditional love.
A trait that comes only from heaven above.

The next time I saw April, she was as cheerful as ever, and I noticed how she made herself at home. Throughout the hospital room, she had stuffed animals, mostly elephants, on every available space in the room, and she had several articles of clothing strewn throughout as well, just like at home. Her newest pair of sneakers were tucked under an old dinner cart that seemed permanently stationed in a corner of the room.

April greeted me as if I was never gone, "Dad, can you tell me again the story about what heaven is like?"

At first, I didn't know what she was talking about. "What do you mean, hon?" I asked in all sincerity.

"How people will be helping each other and how you can tell the difference between heaven and h-e-double-hockey-stick."

Now I knew what she was referring to. A story describing heaven. I began, "Well, first let me begin by telling you about... the other place."

Her eyes grew wide, and she clearly listened intently.

I continued, "There is so much food, you wouldn't believe it. There is every kind of delicacy. It is like this huge buffet of every food known to man, delicious cuisine, better than anything found in the finest restaurants of the world. Pitifully, the problem is that people who are there cannot partake in it. You see, they have forks and spoons attached to the ends of their hands, and they cannot bend their arms to put the food into their mouths.

"What about heaven?"

"Heaven? Almost the same thing happens there. There are all kinds of gourmet foods available, the most delicious foods imaginable. The only difference is that there, people were able to eat because they were feeding each other. That is the only way, of course. That's how God wants it."

A beautiful subtle smile appeared on April's face, and her eyes were closed. I happened to look down again at her sneakers perched under that old dinner cart and noticed something that I did not see earlier. Her favorite sneakers were muddy with grass stains around the bottom edges. I began to ask her about them, "April, how did you get your new sneakers so dirty?"

As I looked again at her angelic face, I could see that she was already asleep, and I didn't want to disturb her. I would go back to the house and work with Max.

GET HERE IMMEDIATELY!

Two days later, I finally got an answer from Max. I realized why it took so long to come up with an answer, in this case a cure. Max wanted to be absolutely positive before it announced anything. This was always the case with Max and it seemed that it was never wrong. The good news was that Max confirmed there was a way to reverse ALS. Regrettably, the kinds of treatments and therapies required were extremely controversial. No doctor in America would agree to follow such protocol, and it would be impossible to get him out of the country. Our only hope was to find some special holistic doctor who would be willing to risk everything to attempt this. This doctor would need to have experience in alternative medicine and be willing to take a serious risk. I actually knew someone who was an expert in the field of homeotherapy. She was as good as there is; however, I was initially reluctant to think that she would take the chance on delivering a course of action that was unproven, untested, and controversial. She would have to follow a protocol supplied by a computer even though she never witnessed its amazing accuracy firsthand. Yet I was hopeful that if there was anyone who would help us it would be her. Dr. Mei Lee had gone on to become a leading expert in alternative healing including herbal medicine, spinal acupuncture, and other forms of alternative therapies. Her parents lived in China, and Mei studied in Macau for several years as part of her extensive medical education. I actually had to learn about Macau as part of my initial CIA training years ago. Macau is similar to Hong Kong in that it maintains its own legal and monetary systems and has a considerable tourism industry. Mei also lived in India for another year during various research projects involving embryonic stem cell treatment that was initiated about five years ago, and it was instrumental in alleviating various conditions. Since she realized that type of thing was not going to be extensively allowed in the United States, she subsequently abandoned that endeavor to pursue other alternatives including ozone therapy, various forms of chelation, hyperbolic oxygen therapy, and other types of nontraditional holistic remedies that *were* allowed here. Mei lived in Macau, China for a few years, and practiced medicine at the Macau University of Science and Technology Hospital in Cotai, so it was totally plausible that she would be able to use these resources. I wish that I had thought of her earlier! She could have helped me use Max and hasten the entire process. On the other hand, she also might have been obligated to have our entire operation shut down. If she didn't find merit with what I was doing and it's potential for a cure, she could have informed the proper authorities, and that would have been the end of everything. Nevertheless, I desperately needed her help, and this was a chance that I had to take. According to Max, if I wasn't involved with Sally twenty years ago, Mei and I would be married, and we would have moved to California. She would not have gone on to become a doctor, but rather, she would have been a biology teacher for a high school in southern California where we would have raised our three children. In reality, we *can* cure ALS and Mei's expertise in holistic medicine might be the key. Without Mei, we would not be able to help Marxman. The fifteen-page printout that Max supplied included the details of medicine, therapies, herbs, and other curative information that was listed, which I could not begin to comprehend. The combinations seemed so definitive and specific, as if it was geared perfectly to what Marxman required to be made whole. I noticed that mentioned in the prescription were various Chinese herbal medicines as well as qigong, a form of Chinese healing. I was truly elated that Mei was such an expert, and I felt relieved. I also noticed that mixed in each set of instructions supplied by Max were words of advice such as, "It is critical to have a positive attitude. Don't forget to pray. Be sure to read the Bible. Trust in God." Was this coming from Max? How could this be? I simply didn't have the time to sort it out or to analyze the details.

Fortunately, Dr. Lee's office was easy to get to, and I went there immediately. As soon I arrived, I instantly noticed that much of her office was ornately decorated in crimson. As I walked in, there were beautiful red petunias, red wallpaper, and red drapes. In the Chinese culture, the color red is sometimes considered a propitious omen. In fact, back at Georgetown, it was Mei who told me that she thought red brings good luck. We had many good-natured debates about luck. I didn't believe in luck. I still don't. I believe in divine intervention, the omnipotent power of the Most High God, but that type of discussion with Mei was meant for another time and another place. Right now, it was clear that Dr. Mei Lee was eager to see me after all these years, and it was necessary for me to fill her in on everything, at least as much as I possibly could. It just so happened that she relocated back to the Washington, DC area about a year ago, and she actually knew that I married Sally, and that we had a daughter. I filled her in as best I could about Max and Mr. Marxman, and I told her about April and her condition. Mei trusted me wholeheartedly, and I trusted her. In fact, she agreed to begin working with Marxman even though I did not have time to tell her how confident I was that the information Max provided was probably valid because Max had a track record for being right about so many things.

I wondered if Mei even wanted to know that we might have been married and living in sunny California with three children. According to Max, if it wasn't for my lack of interest in her years ago, she would not have become a doctor. What was I thinking? How do I know that would have happened? I was still hoping that somehow, Max was not infallible sometimes—that was the only thing that was keeping me going. We didn't know if Max was right about the treatment for ALS. How could it be right about what would have happened in the past based on a simple decision made twenty years ago?

When Mei first looked over the protocol for ALS treatment, she seemed skeptical at best and defiant at worst. Why would she acquiesce to such a controversial, unproven protocol? Even for her it seemed unusual, and she was a trailblazer in alternative therapies. She was a huge proponent of restoring the natural balance of the individual using whatever methods were necessary. As she read further and further, her facial expressions changed a few times until finally she seemed to agree with what Max advocated. All of a sudden, her dark brown eyes began to shine. She claimed that what Max prescribed actually made total sense once she realized everything that Max was promoting. She was intrigued by some of the combinations put forth by Max, and she agreed to help us. She danced around her office gathering up the ingredients and supplies that she needed. She had almost everything right there in her office, which was a bona fide warehouse of herbs, nutrients, and basically all types of holistic remedies and alternative therapies from all over the world. We also had to get Marxman to her office quickly for ozone therapy as well as a special type of acupuncture, which was all part of the treatment. I called Marxman, and his aid agreed to get him to Dr. Lee's office within the hour. We had some hope, at least for Marxman.

In the meantime, I raced home to get to Max. I wanted to start the entire process all over again. Now I was more hopeful and confident than ever, so I started entering April's information along with everything that we knew about her disease. Talking to Dr. Lee gave me more hope for April. I knew that anything was possible now, and Mei agreed that I should do the same thing for April's condition. Fortunately, over the past few weeks, I learned how to expedite the entire process. It only took about four hours to enter some of the most important information that I had been gathering for Max. I got worried that something was wrong since the preliminary results that Max usually provided regarding the type of information it needed were not coming back. I was realistic, and I knew that a cure would take a great deal of time, even with our improved aptitude. I needed to enter much more data including information about other rare diseases known to man. That is something that Max indicated it needed in order to be more effective. It would analyze trends and utilize facts regarding many other diseases that have been cured such as polio, smallpox, tetanus, and tuberculosis. It would surely take at least four or five days to redirect Max.

A few hours later, the only results that did come back were specifically regarding April. I was afraid to look at first. When I finally read the printout, a feeling of indescribable malaise overtook me. I was suddenly overwhelmed with grief, despair, exhaustion, and guilt. My hands were literally shaking, and I could barely raise my arms or stand up. When I finally stood up, I was so dizzy I sensed the room spinning around me out of control. My heart was beating faster and faster. I felt anger toward Max, a type of intense hatred that I didn't think was possible to feel toward an inanimate object. I tried to move but could not. I read the printout again. Max did not say that April was dying; this time Max said that she had just died! It listed the time of her death, 3:00 p.m. That was five minutes ago!

I forced myself to imagine April singing in her hospital bed, alive and well. I chose not to believe that April was dead, but I again realized that Max had never been wrong about anything so far. Although everything was impossible to completely explain and Max was an enigma, the results had always been substantiated, every single time. Now, I was left with an anguish, a feeling of such overwhelming grief that I cannot describe. I didn't think that I could physically get myself up, but I knew what I had to do. I looked at Max. I looked at the words on the screen. "April died at 3:00 p.m."

Nothing else mattered. I did what I said I was going to do. I completed my "assignment" for Marxman. My final agreement with him over two weeks ago was that if I was successful in finding a cure for *his* disease, I would then be able to use Max any way that I saw fit. I remember what I thought of Max in the beginning. It was an incomparable computer with one hundred times the speed and one hundred times the power as any other device its size. Now I knew the truth. It was more like one hundred times the anguish, one hundred times the poison. The whole scenario was disheartening. On the other hand, there was the hope that we could still use Max as a prototype for other elite computers so that someday we might be able to have more computers like Max. Better than Max. Perhaps it would result in computers that would not get your hopes up and then have them come crashing down. All of the world's problems would be solved one at a time, in order of importance. I considered the question of who would have the unenviable responsibility of determining that priority. Who would be the one person to play god? Even if there were a few more such machines, who would take control? How much would some billionaire pay for such a device? What good would any of this do me now? It would not be able to find a cure for my own daughter. Max announced her death. How was I supposed to come to grips with that? I was afraid that I could never face Sally again. She would be stricken with grief and never speak to me again, and I wouldn't blame her. I decided that I had to try one last thing before I put an end to it all. I had one more question to ask Max before I left for the hospital to see April. I momentarily stopped praying that she was still alive, and I typed in something for Max to consider.

I thought out loud as I typed, "Max, this is the end of the line for you. Based on everything that you have seen, learned, and been exposed to the past few months, what insightful concepts can you leave us with? What are your last words of wisdom that you would like to impart on all of us? Any last thoughts? Any deep, meaningful suggestions?" I typed my question in eager anticipation, but I was truly in a hurry. Fortunately, the response came back almost instantly. I crouched down. I wept. I literally fell to the floor more from exhaustion than from shock even though it could have been both. I couldn't believe the words that Max left for us. After all it has seen and been through, it left us with just one profound idea. Maybe there *was* some hope.

Now I thought about everything that had happened, and I came to the conclusion that no one should ever be subjected to the roller-coaster emotional rides that I went through these past few months. I found my special disc that stored a type of software program that I helped to develop years ago at Langley. It was labeled Russo's Boot and Nuke. The program was designed to fill up the computer's drive with bogus information and format the drive again. In less than three minutes, it fulfilled its purpose, to completely destroy the hard drive and that's exactly what I wanted to do. For some unknown reason, I wasn't even content with that. I suddenly felt a type of rage that I have never experienced in my entire life. I looked over to my baseball bat that was mounted against the wall across the room. I made my way toward it, took it out of its case, and firmly gripped it like I did back in my high school days. This would be more satisfying than what I had just done, and it would remove any chance that Max could be salvaged. I was crazed with an intense anger as I spent at least five minutes smashing Max to oblivion, and I made sure that the drive's platters would never spin again. I knew that this was all a waste of time and energy, but I couldn't control any aspect of my body. I was an enraged maniac, and I was sweating profusely. I then fell to the floor and again felt my arms and legs go numb. The reality of April's death struck me with full force at this point, and I lay stunned and exhausted on the floor with my face buried in my trembling hands.

I fell asleep for hours, but this time I didn't dream. When I woke up, I realized that I didn't see, feel, or remember anything the entire time. I painfully thought that any chance I had to see April might have slipped away. It was nearly 6 PM I had five frantic messages on my cell phone, all from Sally. Each one was more desperate and louder than the one before. They all demanded that I got myself to the hospital right away. The last message specifically mentioned April. "April will never forgive you if you don't get here right away!"

I know, but now she was gone. I would never forgive myself. I took the paper that had the final message from Max and was relieved that it was surely the last thing Max would ever produce. My dealings with Max were finally over. I grew to respect, cherish, and then revere what it could do. Now, however, all I did was abominate the very thought of it. I knew I was thinking irrationally. To fault Max for any of society's ills would be like blaming the rooster for the sunrise, but my thoughts and decisions were clouded from fatigue, stress, and guilt.

I glanced at the printout once again. I knew it couldn't be from Max. I knew that only God provides hope when there is no hope. With God, it's never over until He says it is over. I raced to the hospital with a shred of hope. I didn't want to call and find out bad news over the phone. Sally was there already. I just didn't know if I should go directly to April's room. If she died, they would have taken her from the room, and I don't know if they would even let me see her. When was the last time I saw her? Then I remembered. I left her with a few Bible passages on faith, healing, and trust. If she was still alive, I would have one more message for her. They were the last words that Max would ever produce. *Please be there, April.* I realized that her room number was 302 of the pediatric wing. I was hopeful that something good was going to happen. I went down the hall of the hospital wing where April would have been. Please hang on. Please be alive in your room. I passed by room 309. I was getting closer. I thought I heard Father Jim's booming voice, the beloved pastor of St. Luke's, in the distance near April's room. Why would *he* be here? Was it too late for me to even see April alive again? I looked down the hall to April's room and it appeared that Dr. Baker was standing alone outside of her room reading a medical chart. As I got closer to him, I could see that he might have been crying, but he wiped his eyes quickly. As he saw me, he grabbed me, hugged me, and exclaimed, "I have never seen anything like this in 30 years of practicing medicine. Go inside your daughter's room and see for yourself," he offered.

I took a deep breath. There was a lot of noise coming from her room. Just before I saw April, I noticed that Sally was crying. I immediately thought of Max and glanced at the words it gave me just before it was destroyed. I finally made the connection. April's room was 302. It was prophetic that the last words sent out from Max were, "LORD my God, I called to you for help, and you healed me" (Psalms: 30:2).

Earlier, when Max spit out that verse, I knew there was still hope left. If I would have remembered that April's room was 302, I might have noticed the connection earlier. That is not a coincidence. I think this all played out the way it did for a reason.

The only other message from Max in that final printout was the word *believe*, in huge letters. I remembered the sign in front of the church, "Miracles are not coincidences; they are answered prayers."

I hugged April, Sally, and Father Jim. Aunt Sophie was there and so was Elise. She tried to visit April as often as she could and Sally picked her up on her way over to the hospital. I was glad that April's best friend was there to share in all of our jubilation.

My beloved daughter was alive! I handed April the last words form Max. Everyone filled me in on what happened that day. Sally left school early and arrived at the hospital at one thirty. April was being monitored closely because she had gone through a bit of special testing that day. When she fell into that deep, deep sleep, everyone who was there stepped out for a cup of coffee in a nearby waiting area. They didn't find out until later that April's monitor indicated her heart stopped, and she basically "flatlined" for a minute. By the time the nurses and the doctors got there, everything was completely back to normal, and April woke up on her own about ten minutes past three. By then, everyone was back in the room, and April explained what she thought happened with a profound calmness about her. The first thing she said was, "I need to check something in the Bible." April kept seeing the numbers 302 flashing across the sky in her dream and the same words that Max left us with from Psalm 30:2 appeared continually, repeating over and over again.

April opened the Bible, and it appeared right there in front of her. She had randomly opened the Bible to Psalm 30:2 when she woke up earlier and read the same verse that I had just given her. No one said a word. We all knew what it meant. We had all witnessed a genuine, indisputable miracle.

April told everyone about a beautiful bright light that she saw in her dream. She was sure that it was heaven. As it turned out, she was only able to see a glimpse for a few seconds, maybe a minute at the most. Was this the time of April's "death" that Max revealed to me? The fact remains that April did wake up. She was alive, doing well, and claiming to feel much better.

Everything was finally beginning to make sense for me now. Everything happens for a reason. Some things have to be taken on faith.

Later that night, the other doctors all confirmed what Dr. Baker mentioned to me earlier that day when he met me in the hallway outside April's room. There was no sign of illness in April's body! It was as if she never had the disease in the first place. Take that, Max! Stick that in your pipe and smoke it! On the other hand, thank you, Max. Thank you for being the instrument of real faith. Max made the choice clear between science and faith. Follow the science and have a chance for a cure. On the other hand, have faith in God, trust in God, and be saved for sure. Clearly, the determining factor was ingrained in the fact you had to believe, as April did.

The next day, I drove back to the hospital and saw that April continued to feel better. Sally insisted on sleeping at the hospital, and under the circumstances, the doctors agreed to let her. They really didn't have much choice as far as Sally was concerned. I stopped by Dr. Lee's office, and I saw that Marxman's trusty aid already brought him to her office, and Mei was going over the entire treatment plan with him. Ironically, Mr. Marxman spoke fluent Cantonese since he spent a few years in China when he first hooked up with the CIA. Not surprisingly, Mei took an immediate liking to him as if they were old friends, and it didn't take her long to convince Marxman that he needed to get his essence back into balance. Marxman also told Mei the full story behind Max. Little did they know that Max was gone. Having computers like Max was not a panacea. In fact, I believed they would be detrimental to society. Global conflict would have resulted from everyone seeking to control its power and so would significant heartache and false hope because some things cannot be done on human terms. Max was simply toxic, and I had to do what I did. There was no other rational choice. There was only one thing in the world, in the universe, that we could always count on, and it wasn't Max.

We had gone for a tumultuous ride the past few months. Some of the occurrences were truly mystifying, but these events surely happened for a reason. Unfortunately, we now had no proof that Max even predicted them because it was gone as were all of the records. Nevertheless, I knew that Max did some things that no human being could ever have done. More importantly, we all knew that God ultimately saved April; and that if any cures were going to take place, we did not need Max. What we needed was faith.

DO YOU BELIEVE?

After taking a week off to catch up on some sleep, I was finally able to continue the Learning Styles Project. At this point, I knew the "learning style" that had been missing for some of the children. It was *faith*. I needed to see the concept for myself after being through everything that happened over the past three months. Many people in government and in education respected our original work, but now Sally and I had to convince parent groups, educators, and government leaders that this latest profound concept was another key to reaching even more of our young learners and augmenting their success. Fortunately, the push lately was to provide school vouchers that could be utilized by families who preferred private schools for their children. In particular, I advocated schools that matched the proper learning modality for each child with a further emphasis on having faith in God, trusting in his divine plan, and acknowledging the fact that we are merely instruments of a plan higher than simply our mortal existence. The timing was ideal, and this newest wave of schools was ready to catch on.

We still needed to see if the newest component of faith significantly enhanced the success of the children even more, and if parents would choose this type of school for their children.

The parents involved would have to be totally on board and agree, but no one was forced to do or believe in anything they were not comfortable with. As far as funding? The students who were doing poorly in their current school were going to cost the government huge amounts of money for remediation and special programs anyway, so why not try a new approach? There was still a risk involved. If I didn't have substantial evidence to back up my claims, all my work could be in jeopardy. I was also wondering if I would get the backing of religious leaders who might not want to support my plan for fear that it might *not* be successful.

The other "minor detail" was that Max was no longer around to provide the affirmation that would be needed. *Ironically*, I thought, *Isn't that what faith is in the first place? Believing without concrete evidence?* Well, I may not have Max around any longer, but I did have significant evidence. For example, what about April's cure? The medical community was totally baffled by her miraculous recovery. Her doctors would testify to the fact that April indeed had a rare bone disease, and that she was on the verge of dying. She fell asleep sick but woke up completely healthy, a genuine miracle provided by God. If this was not due to her unwavering faith, then how can anything account for it? The real challenge was in transforming the idea that faith in God is vital in healing to the notion that it is also crucial to learning for enough children that it should be used as a key ingredient in their educational plan.

Second, I would argue, what about Robert Marxman? He was getting better every day. Dr. Mei Lee was a witness that he was improving from near death to the point that he was walking again within two weeks. Mei knew about Max and how it found the cure for ALS. She was a famous doctor who was getting more and more notoriety as she described everything from her point of view. Still, there was so much more to Mr. Marxman's story, and it needed to be told. Once Robert Marxman was completely healed, he might be able to explain how Max worked, how he programmed it, and how we can build more like it.

I had the unenviable task of explaining my role in destroying Max in the first place. At the time, I snapped and eliminated Max. I was stressed and on the verge of a nervous breakdown because I found out that April might be dead. However, the other reason I destroyed Max was because I didn't trust the government to do the right thing.

When I was forced to meet with some of the highest ranking officials in Washington, they were furious with me. I thought that many years back when I had to meet with the superintendent of schools to explain my "inappropriate relationship with a female student," it was the most stressful, taxing day of my life. This time, I had no idea what I was in store for as I had to explain my actions to the director of the CIA whom I finally got to personally meet after all these years. I also finally met the director of the FBI and the US secretary of Homeland Security. Lucky me. I was grilled for three straight days, and they threw everything at me except for the hot lights shining in my face. Years ago, my twenty-minute meeting with Dr. Morgan, the superintendent of schools, seemed like having tea with the freakin' queen compared to that three-day nerve-racking ordeal with these high ranking mucky mucks. On the other hand, with the help of God, I knew precisely what to articulate in order to paint the picture of what I was going through. I didn't commit any crime. If anyone did commit any illegal act, it was Robert Marxman for supplying me with the computer that had access to data not intended for the general public. On some levels, they should have been glad that I destroyed all the "evidence." Ironically, they weren't going to do anything to Marxman for the simple reason that he was now a national hero, a shining light. He was truly blessed and a champion in the eyes of many. (Not to mention the fact that Marxman was once one of their own). I found this to be the epitome of hypocrisy, right up there with the time when I noticed a "Buy American" bumper sticker on the back of a Toyota Corolla.

During that grueling "interrogation" with the government officials, I kept hearing the terms used over and over, "Improper use of government resources, cyber hacking, computer fraud, and the fact that I was liable for destroying Max." They tried to vilify me, impugn the work that I did with Max, and repudiate any of the astonishing claims that Max boldly predicted which came to fruition. None of that mattered because I knew the truth and what we were able to accomplish. It was finally decided by someone at the highest level of government that there would not be any charges brought up against me as long as I agreed to document everything in writing. I could easily comply since April is not the only Russo that meticulously keeps a daily journal. I was able to supply a detailed account of all that occurred since the very first day of the project and my report explained everything to them. Well, *almost* everything.

Needless to say, it all really came down to the fact that I would have been in severe trouble if Marxman was not around to corroborate my account of the story. Marxman admitted that having access to all the information that he supplied Max with still didn't account for everything that we were able to do. Max's performance was a mystery that transcended human imagination and comprehension. No one was able to explain some of the things that I described.

For the Learning Styles Project, another vital consideration was this—would there still be enough interest in having children subscribe to this type of faith-based school? The parents' attitudes were critical, but we insisted that the children be approached without parental involvement, and that we were allowed to ask these youngsters whatever we deemed necessary.

The summer approached, and we knew we would soon see the results of the questionnaire that would determine which learning style school would be best for each child for the following school year. It was all monumental because this time, almost two hundred fifty thousand children were surveyed compared to the seven thousand who originally led to the mere twenty pilot schools. The questions that determined what learning modalities were most advantageous for each child were all carefully organized and correlated by learning style categories. The questionnaire had exactly fifty questions, which served its purpose, and the children were fittingly placed in the best school for them. When we initially formulated the survey, we didn't know what we did now about faith and God. I also had to check with Mei because at that point, she still had the original printout, which had instructions for ALS treatment that included: "Have faith," "Believe in God," "Be positive," and "Be sure to pray." Could those same principles apply to learning?

When the same committee that I originally formed met again, we were all prepared to redo the entire questionnaire. Everyone wrestled with the possibilities, but in the end, we decided to keep all fifty questions exactly the way they were initially posed. We decided to add only one more question to the survey. It would tell us exactly what we needed to know for sure.

Question no. 51: Do you believe?

WORDS TO LIVE BY

A little more than a year later, I stopped by Sally's new school in early September on what seemed like the biggest day of the year. Everyone was looking forward to an assembly in which they all got to see one of the reasons why they were able to attend this brand-new state-of-the-art school. At the end of this year, many more schools in the state of Virginia, Maryland, and Delaware will have to be reorganized based on the most recent survey. Over a year ago, when the new questionnaire was collected and the results were analyzed, we found that thousands upon thousands said yes to question number 51. And the following year, even more chose yes. What a challenge it has been to accommodate all the children who decided to include learning styles and faith into their educational plan. At first, new schools had to be built. As more and more children wanted to be shifted from the school they were already in, an entirely new configuration had to take place, utilizing many preexisting school buildings. This time, I had an actual team to help take on the immense task of organizing everything. Right now, however, I was totally caught up in the moment. Even though I had heard Mr. Marxman speak on numerous occasions, this day was more special than any of the others for the simple reason that I was also able to see both April and Sally.

The children were so excited to see the famous Robert Marxman that it took the principal, Sally Russo, a few minutes to quiet them down. "Children, it is an honor to have Mr. Marxman here with us. I know that all of you have heard *of* his story. Now you will hear the rest of the story directly from him."

How could the government agree to the controversial notion that a publically funded school could promote the worship of God and virtually endorse Christianity? Partly because Marxman wanted it that way. His munificent donation of twenty million dollars that resulted in the construction of this school where so many students were thriving was only the tip of the iceberg. Funding would undoubtedly continue while individuals and organizations poured dollar after dollar into this type of format, trying to get on the good side of Marxman. Some of the most important, profitable companies in the world were understandably trying to ingratiate themselves to him. The outpouring of money coming in from some of these corporations was colossal, downright immeasurable. After all, they wanted to be there for Marxman so that when more computers like Max were finally produced, their company would be among the first in line to reap the benefits. "Follow the money," Dave always said. He was right. Government officials were not going to look the proverbial gift horse in the mouth. Furthermore, the school choice vouchers that the politicians were all now supporting and trying to take credit for would conveniently supply more of the money necessary to continually fuel these types of schools. Children were flourishing because of the proper learning modality enhanced by a faith-based approach. Indeed the test scores and overall results were sensational, and these schools were facilitating the success of many children. We actually started with the many parochial schools in the area since they were so easy to adapt. All we had to do was reconfigure by learning styles, determine which students did actually believe or want to believe, and let the momentum build. Before we knew it, we needed to accommodate huge amounts of students who knew they would benefit from what we had to offer. Mr. Marxman emphasized that he openly promoted Christianity, but he also supported universal ideas such as believing in God, trusting in God, and working and living for God.

In fact, the mission statement that Sally helped to write for this school said it all, and it appeared right outside her office:

> Our goal is to nurture and sustain the God given gifts of all children and empower them to reach their fullest potential both intellectually and spiritually. Student learning is fostered through collaboration of their optimum learning styles including faith in God, compassion for others, and following Christ's teachings. We create life-learners and practice positive thinking as well as trust in God. At the same time, the children are encouraged to act according to their own conscience and beliefs.

Fortunately, everyone was winning, especially the children who had learning difficulties in the past. Some who had severe problems in comprehension and aptitude in the past were now able to overcome their deficiencies and demonstrate marvelous success. In addition, the government leaders were in awe of the money that was coming into these programs. Marxman made it abundantly clear through press conferences and lectures that donations from companies were accepted, but there must be "no strings attached." He often said, "Donate because you feel it is in your heart to help children use learning styles and faith to enhance their success, not because you or your company will receive special considerations whenever computers like Max are produced."

Mr. Marxman began by telling the children a little about his own childhood and his love for computers when the technology they all took for granted was in its infancy. It was a very entertaining story of computers, supercomputers, and Max. More importantly, Mr. Marxman shed light on his journey of healing and faith. After the very first day of treatment, Dr. Mei

Lee left Mr. Marxman and assured him that she would be with him every step of the way. He was feeling so confident that if the therapy put together was implemented, it would be successful. In fact, he had time that first night to carefully read through the entire report. He noticed that along with all the meticulously documented medical advice from Max were other words that at first did not really make sense. Words such as "Believe," "Have faith" "Be Positive," and "God Loves You." Did this actually come from Max? Mr. Marxman didn't think so. He was amazed that included with a scientific formula uniquely formulated to address his own terrible affliction that he was suffering from were words of faith and hope. Not only that, later on when he heard about the story of April and her healing, he was totally in awe. He reflected on the book of Psalms and especially the healing verse 30:2. He went to the Bible and read all the verses on healing and faith that he could find. Each time he found a verse on faith and reflected on it, he felt better. He also thought about what it means to repent. He noticed that in Mark 1:15, it says, "The time has come," he said. "The kingdom of God has come near. Repent and believe the good news!" He remembered his Greek, and he thought about the actual meaning of the word *repent,* which basically means to change over the mind, to alter one's thinking. So he did. He changed his thoughts from guilt to forgiveness. He moved his focus to hope, healing, and health. He meditated on love, life, faith, and favor. He began to truly believe. It was at that point that Mr. Marxman realized that through penance and grace, his mind would be clear enough to see the absolute truth, not only about his seemingly hopeless, desperate physical condition, but about life itself.

Suddenly, Mr. Marxman flashed a few of his favorite verses on the enormous screen in the auditorium. He read each one out loud:

> 'If you can?' said Jesus. 'Everything is possible for one who believes.' (Mark 9:23).

Immediately the boy's father exclaimed, 'I do believe; help me overcome my unbelief!' (Mark 9:24)

Hearing this, Jesus said to Jairus, 'Don't be afraid; just believe, and she will be healed.' (Luke 8:50)

Jesus said: 'I am the resurrection and the life. The one who believes in me will live, even though they die; and whoever lives by believing in me will never die. Do you believe this?' (John 11:25–26)

Then Jesus told him, 'Because you have seen me, you have believed; blessed are those who have not seen and yet have believed.' (John 20:29)

"Children," he beckoned. "Look at what is in common!" He took out his red laser pointer and directed it to the word *believe* in each passage.

Mr. Marxman continued to talk about how he memorized each one of these verses. Not only that, for the next few days and weeks, he made the words a part of himself. He realized that these verses were also about saving his soul, not necessarily saving his life. Furthermore, he realized that it was far more important to save his soul *than* his life. Perhaps he could do both. Or more accurately, he thought, *Perhaps God would do both*. In fact, after only a few days, he began to feel better. Much better. Before long, he felt better than he ever did his entire life, including the days before he had ALS. Marxman knew that he had access to a cure for ALS that Max provided, and that gave him hope. He was determined to get better. He reflected, he prayed, and then he ultimately had an epiphany. He was grateful that his passion for life was reignited, and his soul was completely restored. He decided that he would recuperate completely and tell his story to the world.

The most dramatic part of the story was when Mr. Marxman told everyone exactly what happened the night that he turned fear into faith. He stayed up all night thinking, reflecting, and praying. He ultimately decided to discontinue the prescription for ALS therapy that Max had provided. Then how did Marxman get healed? It was faith in God that cured him since he stopped following Max's protocol after that very first week. Initially, there was some skepticism that the remedy supplied by Max would work. On the other hand, there was absolutely no doubt at all that he would be healed by believing and following…no, living the words on faith and healing that he read and felt that night. Mr. Marxman realized that with our own words, we prophesize our future. From then on, he decided to proclaim only words of hope and healing.

He finally understood the words of Romans 4:17. If we are going to live as children of God, we have to agree to call those things that are not as though they were.

This was the compelling story the world never got tired of hearing, which inspired millions of people throughout the world. Marxman mentioned that through his faith in God, the sickness that was sure to lead to his demise would instead be used for an instrument of faith for himself and many others. Mr. Marxman was always sure to mention that what he did would not work for everyone. He insisted that most people who were afflicted with ALS or some other grave illness should consider the options. Holistic doctors such as Mei Lee were using the treatment outlined by Max and having success reversing the symptoms of ALS. Many were going on and finding themselves completely cured of ALS after less than one year. On the other hand, many more people who had ALS, cancer, cystic fibrosis, and other diseases were able to find relief and augment a cure for their ailments through faith and prayer. Marxman made it clear that if one did not truly believe and give glory to God, it would not work. It would be "done to them according to their belief." He continued, "And more important is the fact that my soul is in the right place. That was the easy part since it occurred as soon as I decided to accept Jesus Christ as my personal Savior." Marxman knew that he had more to accomplish and offer the world and, most importantly, he had an abundance of God's favor to accept and enjoy.

Marxman was almost finished, "Everyone has to decide for himself what to do, how he can best learn, what he should believe in, and how to let God work through him. God *will* work through you if you let him. Just look at me!"

I also recognized something new that flashed on the screen, which was clearly intended for the adults in the audience. "Now choose life, so that you and your children may live" (Deuteronomy 30:19).

At first I wondered why he added that verse, but then I remembered that it was aligned with an antiabortion campaign, and Marxman recently joined that cause.

"And remember one more thing. You might be the only gospel that your neighbor hears."

Now if all this wasn't preaching, I don't know what is. Marxman now did everything for the glory of God, and he was in no hurry to divulge what he knew about the formation of a special computer of any kind. He surely knew that the time would soon be here, but for now, he was enjoying his chance to talk to the children, especially since he never had any children of his own.

Sometimes I had the privilege of accompanying Marxman when he gave this inspiring talk. I was delighted to be invited, especially on the occasions when April joined him. I was so proud of her. Clearly, God has something remarkable designed for April's life, and I was so grateful to God that he used her in this way.

April told her own story about how she was in the hospital for almost two weeks, often alone. She actually saw the medical report, and she was able to eavesdrop when the doctors spoke about how grave her condition was. She simply refused to believe a word they said. Instead she chose to embrace the faith that she always had. After all, the doctors didn't know her. They didn't know about her special relationship with God, about the promises God put in her heart, or how she was going to honor God by making a difference in the world.

For I know the plans I have for you, she often thought.

April told how every day when she was in the children's wing of the hospital, she would go to the recreation area and meet other children who were sick, some with terminal illnesses such as cancer. April would play with them and talk to them freely about her relationship with God and the glory of God. Some of these children never heard the things that April spoke to them about. Some didn't have parents who believed in God, and many of these children *never* heard the "Good News" about Jesus Christ. They were children of all ages. Some were merely five or six years old, some were April's age, and still others were teenagers. April gave many of them hope and a new perspective. To April, being a good Christian was shining her light for people to see. April was truly making a difference without even realizing it at the time.

Thankfully, this entire ordeal touched April in many profound ways. It allowed her to trust in God more completely and to believe more confidently. Her faith in God rose up higher and higher every day and her relationship with him blossomed more deeply than she ever could have imagined.

April also told how she sometimes told the nurses that she was going back down to the children's area, but she would instead sneak out of the hospital to go to a nature park right around the corner of the hospital grounds. A few times, she even made her way all the way to Volta Park, which was at least a ten- or fifteen-minute walk away where she had a secret hiding spot. Yes, sometimes the park was muddy, hence April's muddy sneakers. This is where she felt healing take place as she prayed, read the Bible, and wrote prayers of thanks in her journal. She also spoke to God out loud. She would say, "God, thank you for healing me. Thank you for the life you have given me, but I believe that you have much more waiting for me."

April finished by proclaiming, "Yes, science is good, and the doctors do have some of the answers. But in the end, even if science works, God must lend his gracious hand in the process."

So let's try that question one more time, and this is for you. Do *you* believe? Do you want to believe?

Testament of Faith

I thought about going back into the world of education as a teacher, but I first wanted to complete the first wave of the Learning Styles Project and assist in the formation of a national game plan. Mr. Marxman wanted me to work for him, but I kept thinking about the words, "If you love what you do for a living, then you will never have to work a day in your life." Marxman was assembling an entire team of creative programmers who were among the best and the brightest in the world. I was content to let them sort everything out and then persuade the government and the rest of the public to really make a *difference* with all of that power. I did agree to help out on a limited basis, but I could see some of the pitfalls that were bound to arise. Data mining in the past would be considered passé compared to what was on the horizon. Big data mining combined with some of the trailblazing techniques that I used with Max could render our mindreading tricks blasé since any thoughts put into an electronic device were there for the taking. Phone calls, e-mails, and postings of any kind could be scooped up with ease by "Big Brother." No thanks, I didn't want any part of that, but I was hopeful that Marxman and his crew would be able to do some amazing things for everyone's benefit.

How about this for the icing on the cake? Something happened when Marxman spoke in public, which proved once again that God is still in charge, the ultimate "director." He is on the throne, and he is a faithful God. I was in the audience, and someone came over to me and introduced herself. I should say, she reintroduced herself. It was Heather Thompson who was also an invited guest of Mr. Marxman. Heather had gone on to become a teacher and was teaching English Literature for the past fifteen years. With the help of Marxman, she would be working at a high school nearby that joined the Learning Styles Project in a faith-based school that was also geared toward matching learning styles.

"Mr. Russo," she beamed. "I *hoped* that you would be here. Do you remember who I am?"

"How could I *not* remember who you are?" I couldn't hide the fact that I was so happy to see her. It seemed that she hardly changed at all even after all this time. She still had gorgeous light brown hair, the brightest green eyes, and a smile that showed the most pronounced dimples. No, it was impossible not to recognize Heather. She was tall, lean, and she looked fantastic, just as I remembered her from years ago. "Look at you after all of these years!" I exclaimed.

She filled me in on her life in about five minutes. She told me how she graduated from a high school in Maryland and then went on to Loyola University. She earned her teaching degree and then later earned a master's degree in English literature.

"I am so proud of you! I always hoped that everything would turn out well for you. You are really a special, gifted person." I didn't know what else to say. I was delighted for her while I simultaneously felt miserable about how it ended over twenty years ago. I thought of the baby for a fleeting second before she interrupted my thoughts as if she could read my mind.

"I want to introduce someone to you. This is my son, Adam!"

"What?" I exclaimed. I couldn't hide the fact that I was astonished.

Heather again knew what I was thinking. This indeed was her son with whom she was pregnant twenty years ago. She never did have the abortion. She carried that baby to full term, delivered a beautiful son, and could not let him go. She raised him with the help of her family, and she finished high school the following year. Heather then put herself through college and while she was teaching, attended graduate school at night.

"Mr. Russo—"

Now I interrupted her. "Call me Tom."

"Okay," she agreed. "Adam is a computer science major, and he is on pace to graduate from Virginia Tech in only three years. He will go to graduate school next year for master's degrees in statistics and computer science. Sounds familiar, doesn't it?"

"Wow, that is outstanding, Adam. How did you get invited to this event?" I was truly impressed.

"Mr. Marxman invited us," Adam chimed in.

Heather continued, "Mr. Marxman is sort of sponsoring Adam and paying for all of his schooling. Adam was recruited by Mr. Marxman to join the team he is putting together that will develop the next wave of Max clones."

"They'll be even better than Max," Adam confidently jumped in again.

I was perfectly relieved. I guess you could say it was another miracle. It was a pleasure to get re-acquainted with Heather after all these years. I often wondered what became of her, and now I finally found out. I could see that Adam was a talented, intelligent young man who was able to live and make a contribution because of Heather's prudent, faithful decision twenty years ago. Heather did the right thing after all, and God rewarded her with a wonderful son.

"Adam, I really like your plan. Get as much education as you possibly can. You could wake up one day and find that everything is gone: your youth, your health, your possessions. But that is one thing that no one can ever take away from you. Your education."

"Or your faith," Adam almost interrupted me when I was all primed to go on my own sermon on the mount. I could easily see that he grew up to be a genuine testament of faith, and Heather went on to tell me that my encouragement and words of inspiration were what ultimately made her decide to change her mind about having the abortion.

Adam turned away for a few minutes to focus on Mr. Marxman's speech. "I love this part," Adam beamed as he walked a few steps away from Heather and me.

Heather leaned toward me and came closer, confiding, "Adam knows everything!"

"What do you mean?" For some reason, I was surprised.

"I had to tell him. He has a right to know."

"What are you talking about?" I earnestly questioned. For a brief moment, I sincerely had no idea what Heather was referring to.

"For one thing, he knows that if it were not for the grace of God, he would not be here today. He would never have been born, and if it were not for you and your encouragement and your final words to me, I would not have had the courage to do what I did and keep my baby."

"What exactly did I say?" For some inexplicable reason, I couldn't remember. I guess I somehow repressed a great deal of what happened regarding my entire relationship with Heather.

"Tom, you used to say, 'Just trust in God. He is faithful and just.' And I did. So I gave birth to Adam and lived for God's glory from then on. I trusted in God, and he brought Adam and me to where we are now. You could say that he *delivered* us!"

"Nice pun, Heather." I tried to change the focus. I was beginning to feel very uncomfortable. I had a lump in my throat, and it was only a matter of time before I bawled my eyes out.

"I also got *that* from you, Tom," Heather responded, sensing my discomfort. "You were quite the punster yourself back in our day."

"Oh, you remembered."

"Of course. I remember everything about what happened between us back in high school. Maybe you can't remember or choose not to." Heather didn't seem angry or upset. In fact, she was smiling, and her eyes sparkled just as I remembered twenty years ago. "Tom, you told me more than once, 'Don't feel the pain, but miss the message.' I did feel the pain, but I also learned the lesson that God is all forgiving and all powerful. He is a faithful God, and I refused to let him down. And that is the best decision I ever made in my life. I would never have forgiven myself. You were right."

This was one of the happiest days of my life, knowing that Heather was thriving, and that Adam was alive and well after all. Throughout my entire life, I was living with guilt, thinking that I wasn't able to help Heather and convince her to do the right thing. Just then, Adam walked back toward us, actually back peddling as he couldn't take his eyes off Marxman and his concluding remarks. Adam was repeating everything Marxman said under his breath. I could see that he was a superior young man with all of the potential in the world. And as he would later say, "All the faith in the world too."

"It's all over except for the shoutin'," Adam exclaimed, referring to Marxman's speech that was nearing its conclusion.

"Nice cliché, son," Heather proudly responded. "That's another thing that Adam got from you, Tom."

"What do you mean?" I played dumb, something I apparently do very well.

"Adam and I were permitted to read many of your old government reports. Mr. Marxman was able to procure some of the nonclassified reports for us to peruse, and he thought that we would get a kick out of seeing some of them. They obviously made quite an impression on Adam here."

This was another clear example of God's favor and mercy, and I was extremely grateful.

A TRUE HERO

A few months after I reconnected with Heather, I was in Dr. Panthos's office for what was hopefully my last therapy session for a long while. He turned on his computer while I plopped myself on his couch. He was quite the modern psychiatrist. Instead of taking notes on the traditional notepad, he always typed into his computer, banging away at the keyboard while I spilled my guts. Thankfully, he was able to help me sort out everything that transpired the past two years. He even helped me remember some additional experiences from my younger days as a teacher. Another reason why I was well liked by many of my students was because I was a fair grader. I would teach my lessons and then give the test. That's exactly how it should be. Of course, I saw first hand how the realities of the real world are so much different from school. In school, you get the *lesson* first, and then take the test. On the other hand, in life, you get put to the test first. Then the lesson always *follows*. Sometimes that message is loud and clear; sometimes, it can be subtle and obscure, totally up to us to figure out. This is what makes life difficult. Whether or not we gain from these lessons is completely up to us. In my case, I feel that I have unequivocally benefitted greatly from everything that happened even though I learned the lesson *after* the test. It was ironic that I finally learned the lesson that faith in God is *always* rewarded. I needed to be tested to realize that I could rely on my faith in God to see me through an ordeal that was too much for me to handle on my own. I needed that faith to guide me through everything, including my relationships with my family and in my appreciation of life itself.

I spoke with Dr. Panthos and conveyed to him how fascinating it is how some people cross our paths in life for a specific reason. Heather Thompson was one example, but so was Hank Davis. He was undoubtedly part of my test in life. I told Hank on many occasions that God is all powerful, and he will always give us another chance. I wanted to take advantage of my own second chance when I dealt with Hank. I often reflected on the entire story of Hank, which was truly inspiring. It was awesome how Hank rose from disappointment and failure to unexpected success as he finally got his act together. I told him many times that he was due for a comeback, a turnaround of monumental proportions. Hank was certainly no fool, and he took all the money that I helped him to earn on that beautiful spring night at the racetrack and used it to finally get himself completely out of debt. Not only that, he had enough money left over to start a little business. Hank started a shuttle company that transported clients to and from some of the airports in the Washington, DC area. Hank owned two minivans, and a few times during the summer, he and his helper hooked up with Marxman's group who travelled to various cities along the east coast, usually the Philadelphia, New York, and Boston areas.

It was early September, and Hank was transporting Marxman's crew to several top universities up the east coast. Marxman brought with him a few of his software engineers and his best computer programmers. They were doing a combination of publicity work (as if Marxman needed any more of *that*) as well as a series of lectures. Marxman enjoyed giving speeches from time to time, and we occasionally allowed April to travel with his entourage to see the sights and to speak for a few minutes. Usually, Sally or I accompanied them when April was involved; but on this trip, Sally had a principal's conference to attend, and she was presenting as one of the speakers. I ended up staying home with our son who was almost a year old at that point. I knew that April would be safe with Marxman's little entourage. Adam was always with them as were a few female engineers whom we had all gotten to know very well. Truth be told, they all liked to accompany Marxman in part for the social aspect; not surprising since Adam was a bona fide stud (metaphorically speaking, of course).

After speaking at Messiah College, Eastern University, and Villanova University near Philadelphia, Marxman's group found themselves on the New Jersey Turnpike, one of the most heavily travelled highways in the country heading to New York City and Fordham University, their next destination. They also had speaking engagements planned for Providence College, Fairfield University, and Boston College, then they would return home by plane.

It was on the turnpike that tragedy unexpectedly struck. The van that Hank was driving, the one that April was in, had a tire blowout as they travelled about seventy miles per hour on the highway. The van began to spin out of control, but Hank remarkably regained control of the vehicle and due to his quick action, avoided a terrible accident. He managed to reposition the van out of harm's way and onto a service road that was at least thirty feet away from the main traffic. Of course, the first thing that Hank did was to move everyone out of the van and still further away. He directed them to the top of a small grassy hill, which was at least fifty feet away from where he was working to change the tire. After only a few minutes, a massive tractor trailer came barreling down the highway and onto the service road, speeding totally out of control. The truck rammed into Hank's van and scattered debris in every direction, culminating in a thunderous roar and a fiery flame. Hank was tragically killed instantly. By the grace of God, no one else was injured or killed. They might have been if Hank wasn't so cautious. Fortunately, Hank made them all move far enough away from the van so he could change the tire by himself. Hank ended up going from homeless to hero after all, and it was not the hypothetical fantasyland story that Max reported would have happened if I would have befriended him back when I first met him years ago. In my mind, and in the eyes of many other people, Hank died a real hero.

I also learned a lesson on loyalty but not the kind of loyalty that I thought I had. It was the loyalty of someone like Hank Davis. He was the one who warned me about people coming for Max. I found out that the shady characters that Hank knew from the racetrack were somehow able to find out that I was privy to some device that could pick winners at the horse races. Even though I hardly told Hank anything, the men whom he almost got drawn into working with overheard some of my conversations with Jack when I spoke to him on my cell phone at the track. What further piqued the interest of the loan shark and his crew was the night in March when Hank and the boys stumbled upon winner after winner. The guys didn't exactly play it cool that night. They apparently didn't try to hide their jubilant emotions as they openly enjoyed their winning streak that defied all odds. I would love to get them in a poker game some day.

Anyway, as soon as Hank found out that the men and their boss were up to no good and would do anything to get their hands on my computer, Hank was determined to get the word to me. And he did, once by text and once by phone.

EPILOGUE

I decided to take a job teaching calculus as well as remedial math. The two extremes will be quite a challenge, but I feel empowered since the school is totally geared toward students whose learning styles matched my teaching style. I can be funny and tell jokes! Not really. I will be entrusted to guide the students on the path of learning even though we all knew where their strength and energy would have to come from.

It is interesting and satisfying that Heather Thompson will be teaching English Literature, and she was eager to be a part of a faith-based school system. She credited me with much of her success, not only in her college work and career, but with many aspects of her life. She expressed gratitude for my genuine concern and encouragement. She also appreciated the fact that I showed compassion for her situation in high school, and she knew I was sincere back then because I always gave her my undivided attention. Heather truly made the moral decision back then to do the faithful, honorable thing and keep her baby.

I know where my heart lies. I know we can make a difference if we continue pinpointing the best learning styles for each individual. We are beginning to see that more and more families want a school that is faith-based. More importantly, due to this story, so many people realize that through prayer, faith, and trusting in God, He will provide the right path for them.

I know all this happened for a reason. I also know that God will use you if you let Him. He used me, he used Mr. Marksman, he used my daughter, April, and He even used Max. Thankfully, it all comes down to this as far as I'm concerned—the Lord, Jesus Christ, is my personal Savior. As well as April's and Mr. Marxman's. This is far more important to all of us than how they were cured. For that matter, that is far more important than what learning style is the best fit for someone. Clearly, the most important thing is to trust in the Lord and to know that if we have faith, then anything is possible, and everything will work out for the best. If we have faith, we will truly be blessed and saved. We must let our faith be bigger than our fear.

I find it daunting that as a society, we can grasp the complexities of the Internet, global communication, surveillance devices, supercomputers, big data mining, and whatever will come next. Unfortunately, we sometimes fail to comprehend things that are relatively simple. Like the power of prayer and the fact that we are not given the honor of dancing with the company of angels unless we are willing to accept the pain of the cross. Not to mention one of the most important things that we all need to know—the fact that all things will be done to us according to our faith.

Our son is now eighteen months old, and he is hitting the "terrible twos" a little early. I used to have a few theories on raising kids, but no kids of my own. Now that I have two kids, I no longer have any theories. But that's okay. Sally and I have April to help us out. I have heard many times that parents cannot be a friend to their children. They have to remain authority figures. I am fortunate that I have been able to be a friend to April, and I am determined to always be one if that is what she needs. I might also have to be there to kick her in the pants when need be. I thank God every day that those times are so few and far between. I know that I am truly blessed.

By the way, our son's name is not Ryan after all. Max was not only wrong about April dying at three o'clock back on that day in March. Max was also wrong about our son's name. You just cannot trust computers (for some things). We actually decided to name our son Eli. We did this because we realized that you can't spell the word *believe* without the letters *E, L, I.*

A bird sitting on a tree is never afraid of the branch breaking, because her trust is not on the branch but on its own wings. If we cultivate our faith and starve fear, we allow faith to win the battle with fear. Then, anything is possible. The idea that one needs to see it to believe it is backward. We must believe first, then we can see miracles come to fruition. Stir up your faith. Take the limits off God. He will do things that will utterly amaze you.

CPSIA information can be obtained at www.ICGtesting.com
Printed in the USA
BVOC01*0608060815

412097BV00009B/10/P